Courage in the Face of Evil

Courage in the Face of Evil

BASED ON A TRUE STORY

Mark Shaw

CrossLink Publishing

CrossLink Publishing
558 E. Castle Pines Pkwy, Ste B4117
Castle Rock, CO 80108
www.crosslinkpublishing.com

Ordering Information:
Quantity sales. Special discounts are available on quantity purchases by corporations, associations, and others. For details, contact the "Special Sales Department" at the address above.

Courage in the Face of Evil/Shaw —1st ed.

ISBN 978-1-63357-119-8

Library of Congress Control Number: 2017950758

First edition: 10 9 8 7 6 5 4 3 2 1

Praise for Mark Shaw Books

Beneath the Mask of Holiness: Thomas Merton and the Forbidden Love Affair that Set Him Free

"[Mark's book] can only deepen and add weight to our respect for this scrupulous, devoted and tormented man." —Ron Carlson, author of *Five Skies*

Stations Along the Way: The Spiritual Transformation of Former Hitler Youth Leader Ursula Martens

"Well-written account taken from detailed accounts that gives twenty-first century readers an immersion into life, love, and survival spanning two continents and four decades at the turning point of the twentieth century." —Gene Policinski, COO of the Newseum Institute's First Amendment Center

The Reporter Who Knew Too Much

"Expertly written, Mark Shaw's biography of Dorothy Kilgallen is a riveting true-life murder mystery, thoroughly accessible to readers of all backgrounds ... Highly recommended!" —Midwest Book Review

Road to a Miracle

"What an eclectic life Mark has experienced! This is a fun read." Squire Rushnell, best-selling author of *When God Winks*.

To Cecilia Rexin

An angel of mercy whose diary
is the basis for this story

Good and evil both need deception to surviv.
It has always been this way.

Vera Konig

Contents

Introduction

Located 55 miles south of Berlin near the Fürstenberg railroad station, Ravensbrück housed more than 130,000 women and children from twenty-three different nations between 1939 and 1945. They included Jews, political prisoners, prisoners-of-war, Jehovah's Witnesses, criminals, "asocials," Gypsies, lesbians, prostitutes, and a German Christian nurse named Vera Konig.

It is estimated that between 110,000 and 115,000 of the inmates did not survive.

Prologue

Even though I have spent years in the camps, this is the worst night of my life. I keep wondering what will happen. When will the Ravensbrück SS come and arrest me and find little Andrea, my Russian orphan? Surely this will happen. Why was I so stupid?

It is May 1943 and the prison is quiet. I hear screams now and then, but I don't know if they are real or if they have become so common they seem real. Every time there is a small sound of some kind, I think it is the clomping of German boots. And the SS will drag little Andrea and me to where they will shoot us dead.

As I stare at the planks on the wooden ceiling, the stench of death fills my nostrils. It is like I am having a nightmare, but I am awake and imagining the worst: Jakob's trick has worked—he has exposed Andrea and me, and I feel like such a fool to have trusted a Nazi prison guard who showed me indications of love. I keep crying and praying, but I wonder if God is hearing me, and why he will want to help me when so many others need his help.

Oh, how my faith is tested tonight. Where are you God? Prayer is all I have, and I want to believe a miracle will occur. But maybe all the miracles have been used up and there are none left.

Book I

Chapter One

My name is Vera Konig, and the first memory I have at Ravensbrück is sitting on the lid of the toilet as a roach stared at me. Today is gloomy. Dark clouds everywhere. Sirens wail in the distance as dusk approaches. It is January 1940, a month not easily forgotten.

Currently I am housed in the women's camp: sixty-four wooden huts set in five rows. To the west are the men's camps with the children kept in thirteen huts farther away. The gas chamber and crematorium are close by, permitting us to smell the stench of human flesh.

Before arriving here, I survived nearly three years in Königsberg, set on high ground alongside the Pregel River, rotting in a jail awaiting trial. How absurd to call it a trial! Five minutes. No one spoke on my behalf; no one was there for me. "A filthy political prisoner," the prosecutor said. And where was my family? Were they punished for my work in the underground? I tried to get word to them, but nobody answered.

When I was arrested in Berlin in March of 1937, I was twenty. It is difficult to imagine where I would be and what I would be doing if I had not been caught. Some felt they had a choice when the Nazis began to seize power. They just turned their heads. But many of us could not.

Unlike many persecuted, I am not a Jew, but a Christian: a believer in God, Jesus, and the Holy Spirit. But my Jewish friends were disappearing—entire families gone, their homes looted, their businesses and synagogues burned. Heir Schwab, a leader in the underground, offered some of us a chance to help the Jews, hide them, forge passports, and pass out anti-Fascist flyers. We were students with hopes and dreams. I was studying to become a physician. If I wanted to be a doctor, how could I be unconscious to physical suffering?

Adolph Hitler became chancellor when I was sixteen. It was the same year Roosevelt was elected president of the United States. At first I was caught up in the Nazi propaganda— most of us were. The economy seemed better for those less fortunate. This made my brothers and me happy, less guilty, because we were very wealthy. My father, a banker, owned much land and was a member of the Crown Prince of Prussia's Honor Guard. My mother Elena died when I was very young, but my godmother was the Crown Prince's wife. We had a wonderful home, land, orchards, a plentiful garden, and beautiful Arabian horses. My father, Gerdt, loved the horses, treating them with kindness and reverence. I watched for hours as he brushed their fine coats and admired their beauty. When I rode, I felt the wind at my back and freedom to do whatever God had in mind. I was so blessed.

My father was a mild-mannered man, but he was quite upset when my brother Rolf told him I was working for the underground. He said: "Vera Konig, you could be arrested, and then we will all be punished; we will lose everything." Maybe I should have listened. But when all the freedoms—speech, assembly, press—were terminated, I decided to do something else my father had asked me not to do. That was to read Adolf Hitler's book *Mein Kampf*. It was shocking, an experience that caused me to weep for days. It was a blueprint for change, complete with the ideaology that Jews needed to be eliminated. Hitler said the swastika on the Nazi flag represented the mission of the struggle for the victory of the Aryan man. The book caused me to work harder for the underground. One evening I spent hours in the pouring rain handing out leaflets for a secret meeting to college students. We ran from the Nazis but were nearly caught when one of my friends, Anna, fell near our hiding place.

Finally, we were caught, and weeks after my rotten trial, I am here at Ravensbrück, near Mecklenburg, north of Berlin. On the cattle car that transported us from Königsberg, I heard rumors Hitler is winning, and all the Jews of the world will soon be exterminated. For twelve days in that cattle car, I prayed it would not be true.

I will begin my story three days ago, before we arrived. The day I wondered whether God had truly forsaken me.

* * *

On our way here, we were cramped in one cattle car—seventy-five women with one bucket for a toilet and without a roof or heat. We were fed only twice. When the train moaned to a stop in the early morning of the thirteenth day, some of us tried to stand on frostbitten limbs, brittle and cold. With the help of others, I made it to my feet and looked out a window designed for a cow. It was early morning, January 18, 1940, and light was just beginning to peek out toward the east. I remember a single snowflake falling from the sky. It glided down, softly landing along the tracks, disappearing with all the others. It caused me to wonder if my journey would end in the same way, disappearing too. Suddenly the door rattled opened. Uniforms, guns and sharp icy winds shouted at us. We had arrived at Fürstenberg, the train station for the concentration camp Ravensbrück.

Most of us fell out of the cattle car, our legs not able to support us. Even after stumbling to my feet, I felt I could faint at any second. Some did. I was wearing a light suit, the suit I had been arrested in—the suit I had worn to my trial. With one hand I pressed my freezing face, and with the other I tried to steady Elisabeth Dombrowski. She and I were both from Prussia. We were both tried in the same court for the same crimes, both proclaimed enemies of Hitler's German Reich, both sentenced to

Ravensbrück for six months, a school, according to the Germans, where we would be changed into productive members of society.

Elisabeth and I fell in a heap, holding onto each other against the cold. Several SS guards circled in their gray uniforms with skulls on the collars. They glared at all of us women, comrades against Hitler—Germans, Christians, Jews, Poles, Jehovah's Witnesses, (some are called bible students) Gypsies, and God knows who else, all stumbling, falling, fainting. One of the SS men shouted, "Get up, damn you! You will have plenty of time to sleep in the camp." We all struggled, our legs refusing to cooperate. More SS came, these with growling dogs. It was the first time I had ever seen a bloodhound. It was easy to imagine what they were trained for. Gentle dogs turned into killers.

Large gray trucks pulled up. A young SS with fiery eyes yelled at me, "Get in there." And then quite suddenly, he hit me on the arm with the butt of his rifle. Just as suddenly, I wasn't cold anymore, too scared. I grabbed Elisabeth and we marched toward the truck.

Between the pushing, wailing and sobbing, there was a terrible scream. One of the dogs attacked a woman who was not fast enough. Her name was Liesel, and her legs were covered with blood. At this sight, some women screamed, but somehow we all made it into the trucks, subdued to whimpering, feeling safer, at least from the wind.

In a few minutes the truck stopped and an SS soldier yelled, "Get out, you filthy rats!" I had to swallow hard not to be sick from the language, the treatment, the cold, the hunger. What kind of Germans were these monsters? Until now I had contact only with the Gestapo. They interrogated me each evening, but they had never beaten me. They didn't use foul language. I looked at Elisabeth, her blue eyes tearing, her blonde curly hair in snarled nests. "Six months at this "school," and no end in sight," I said. "I am determined we will survive." She sighed and put her head in her hands.

Four days passed. When we entered the camp, women prisoners stared at us with dark eyes and blank faces, dirty, their ragged striped clothes hanging from bony bodies. Off a hundred yards or so a group of Jews, maybe thirty, were walking with shovels, the David star sewn on their left sleeve. Most were bald with skeletal frames.

One woman among them, tall and forbidding, wore warm clothes, a sweater, and a wool hat to cover her ears. On the front of her sweater was sewn a green triangle, and she wore a red bandage on her arm. She did not wear a David star, and she did not carry a shovel, but the Jews began to shovel snow, working without sweaters, hats, or gloves, some with stockings sagging around their ankles and torn sandals. Out of curiosity, a few looked our way. I wish they had not, because suddenly the woman with the green triangle started hitting one and hollering, "You damned pig Jew!"

I started running toward the guard, to get to her, to stop her, but Elisabeth grabbed me. "You cannot help her," she said, "and you will die trying." I knew she was right.

One of the Gypsy prisoners near us said, "She is their leader. Every day she acts like this. If one of the women stretches her back just once, she beats her."

"What does the red bandage mean?" I asked.

"All prison leaders wear them," she answered. "But the green triangle means professional criminal. That awful woman is like many prisoners who get caught in the devil's circle and then act just like the SS. Some do it to save their lives, but some do it because they are mean and hateful."

A shout from an SS guard caused me to jump. We were ordered into the bathhouse. The warmth hit like a shock, making us realize just how cold it was outside.

Upon command, we all took showers. The water was lukewarm. There was soap, but no shampoo. It felt so good to scrub the grime of the horrid cattle car out of my pores.

When we walked out of the showers, our personal clothes and possessions were gone, with the exception of hairpins. Standing wrapped in towels, we were issued uniforms, underwear, and a nightgown. Prisoners behind a counter handed them out, not asking our size. Of course, some were too large, some too small, too long, or too wide. We traded, mixed, and matched. It was demeaning, all of us in frayed striped prison dresses, flimsy ragged underwear, and brown scratchy stockings. Instead of garters, we were given two strings each, but the stockings still slid down. It was difficult to walk in the wooden sandals. The upper part was ragged and made from fabric like a house slipper.

Next to the woman in charge of the bathhouse stood a younger prisoner with a green bandage on her arm and a black triangle on her chest. We were all confused with the different markings and curious to find out what stood for what. The bath guard introduced the younger woman as Gerda and told us she was our Block-eldest for the Newcomer Barracks. We were told that each barrack had one person in charge, the inmate who had been there the longest. This meant Gerda was in charge of Block 9, our Block. She told us to form groups of five. We did so quickly and marched to our new home. We must have made quite a sight, scared, cold, our stockings slipping, stumbling along in those awful ragged shoes that provide no protection from the snow. Yet as we passed the Jews, I was thankful we had received light jackets. Off to the side, SS guards glared at us, ready to attack anyone who misbehaved.

Block 9 was divided into two large day rooms—the A and B wing, with a utility room, then toilets, and a washroom at the back. Each wing contained a large ward with bunk beds. Two smaller rooms along the sidewall were for the SS guard and the Block-eldest. As we entered our wing as newcomers, the other prisoners gave us curious but friendly and sympathetic looks.

I was told to sit next to Gerda at a table. She told us her black triangle stood for "anti-social," or "bum." She added, "bum" with a crooked smile. It was difficult to know what to believe. She told us she had been at the camp over a year. Before that she was in another camp, Lichtenberg. She seemed cautious with her explanation and her conversation—subdued for a redhead. Like most of the women, her hair was pulled back tight, knotted and pinned. Her eyes were large and round and a watery green, and she had a few freckles on her pert nose. With some weight, she could be pretty. I guessed her age to be about thirty-five, much younger looking than many, but some of the women looked older than they were.

This was the first time in weeks I had had a roof, dry clothes, and free time. We sat around, anxious, looking about, nervously talking. A few of the women broke down and sobbed. Others comforted. I tried to pray silently for calm within me, but it was difficult. All the women look strained and haggard, myself included. Everyone was in various stages of starvation. There were no mirrors around, and it was just as well. I had never been a real beauty, but my boyfriend thought I was pretty with high cheekbones, deep brown eyes, a small nose, and a good smile. Now I was surely not so. My hair was my best feature, long, thick and chestnut colored. At least I still had my hair. God, let me keep my hair.

Chapter Two

Finally, it was noon and time for lunch. A small group put on their jackets and went to retrieve the food. Gerda assigned help to pass out the tin dishes and a dishtowel for each of us.

When the food arrived, we learned why it took only a small group to fetch it. Even though 150 are assigned to Block 9, there were only pots of thin, dehydrated turnip soup with small slices of potato. Too hungry to give it consideration, we drank the soup. Counting the two times we had food on our long ride here, this was only our third meal in thirteen days.

A half hour later, a siren broke the silence. "Work formation!" a guard yelled. All of us, even the new arrivals, had to go even though work assignments would not be made until we received our markings. Soon we were back in our barracks and happy to be out of the freezing snow.

Gerda assigned us bunks. Straw sacks were used in place of mattresses. They were stacked three high. Elisabeth took the bottom, I was given the middle, and the top went to Ilka, a very tall Jewish woman with hair so blonde it was nearly white. Then Gerda handed out blue and white checkered bed linen. She told us to make the beds so a certain number of checks could be counted on each side. If the number was wrong, it was an offense against camp regulations.

When the beds were made, Gerda stood at the end of the room and said, "Ladies, all I can tell you is to do exactly as I show you. If anything is wrong at inspection, all hell will break loose. It could mean a whipping, or kitchen duty for four weeks, or"—she shrugged—"whatever they are in the mood to do to you. Try to obey everything you are told and things will be all right."

After Gerda answered a question or two, we headed back for the day room. Someone with a red triangle and blue bandage introduced herself as Betty, the camp-eldest. She was very tall, very lean, and very loud, wanting to be heard. "Welcome to Ravensbrück," she said in a clear voice. "Please open your ears and listen. The best thing to do around here is forget your homes and families. Thinking of them will only make you sick."

Betty's nose was too long and her mouth too small to be pretty, but her size and presence said she was in charge for our own good. "Concentrate," she yelled, "only on what you are told to do. Soon you will be assigned jobs. Do them right and you will have no problems. If not, you will have more trouble than you can dream of. Work together, obey, and never, ever mouth back or you will have to take the consequences. You have probably already seen a sample of what can happen to you, but you cannot yet imagine how much worse it can be."

"Be smart!" she continued. "Do not give the SS any reason to use their disciplinary action on you. I really dislike scaring you, but you are better off knowing what could happen to you. Think twice before you do or say anything." She turned to leave and then said, "One more important piece of information. You are not allowed to cut your own hair. If you want your hair cut, contact Gerda and she will arrange for it. But you may be ordered to have it cut if it interferes with your work. If you want to keep your hair, find a way to pull it away from your face."

"Are there any political prisoners among you?" she said as she stepped toward the door. Elisabeth, a few others, and I slowly raised our hands. "Okay," she said, "I will deal with you later." Then I asked, "Could you please tell us what the red triangle on your chest means? Do different colors mean different prisoners?"

"Yes, something like that," she said. "The green ones are for professional criminals; red ones are for political prisoners." Then she pointed to her chest and said, "Purple is for religious prisoners, and black is for those who are anti-social." She tossed a half-grin at Gerda and walked out.

After she was gone, Gerda directed us into a short tunnel that led from our Block to the long hallway of the dispensary. Women with yellow arm bandages were everywhere. These women were called "Armbands." Betty had not told us about bandage colors, but I assumed they were medics. They wore white aprons over their regular prison clothes and white coverings over their hair. Most importantly, they smiled at us, the first smile I had seen in a while. Then a medic with only one arm came along telling us all to get undressed.

"Here?" one woman asked. "Here in the hallway?"

"Yes, yes!" she answered. "Everything off, and please hurry, girls!"

Within minutes we had all stripped down, trembling with cold and fear, wrapping our arms and clothes around ourselves, waiting quietly. Finally a door was flung open and a man in a white coat came out. He smiled at everyone and told us his name was Doctor Sonntag. "You will come in the door for treatment one at a time without clothes," he said before disappearing through the door.

A line was formed, and we waited. Elisabeth was in front of me; her body quivering as she stood there afraid of what was going to happen. The one-armed medic waited too, and when there was a knock from the door, she motioned for the first in line. That was Liesel, the woman with severe frostbite and gaping wounds from the dog bites on her legs. Dropping her clothes, her bare bottom disappeared through the door.

After a few minutes, another knock came, and the medic opened the door for the next tearful woman. By the time it was Elisabeth's turn, she was frozen, unable to move. I nudged her from behind as the one-armed medic grabbed her by the arm and she disappeared. The next knock was for me. I swallowed hard, put my chin up, dropped my clothes, said a small prayer and told myself, "I will not cry; I will not."

It was a huge room, gray and cold, and the women who had gone before me were standing off to the side in three separate groups, some of them whimpering. There were a number of white-coated doctors in a row, both male and female, and I was told sternly to step before them. They all stared and took notes. My mouth was forced open, my ears jabbed. I was turned around, prodded and poked, told to bend and stoop. I gritted my teeth. Then one of the female doctors pointed to a scale where she weighed me. "Ninety-five pounds," she announced, meaning I had lost twenty-five pounds. Then, pointing to one of the groups of huddled women, she told me to join them. "That's the healthy group," she said. It was easy to guess how we were being divided: healthy, sick, and old. Liesel was in the healthy group, crying. Her legs had been bathed in iodine but not stitched.

Finally the humiliation was over, and we scrambled out of the room, picking clothes up from the pile at the door, passing them back and forth, and pulling them on quickly. When I was dressed, I began giving the women who were sobbing a pat on the back and a smile, including Elisabeth. But I did not reach all of them before a spindly blondish woman in white came rushing into the hall waving her arms, yelling, "What! You are still here? We saw enough of your asses. Get the hell out!" She was waving her arms, shooing us toward another room, where we walked timidly.

Betty was there, directing us toward some tables. Quietly, I asked her who the blondish woman was and why she was yelling so angrily. In a low voice, Betty answered, "Her name is Margaret Marschall. She is the SS head nurse. Do not ask more."

At the tables, political prisoners in red triangles registered us. Then we were moved to another barrack where we received our own triangles, mine red. I was also given numbers to sew on my dress in sequence: 2985. It stood for transport #29, 85th person.

Betty told us Gerda would supply the needles and thread. Looking at the numbers let people know how long someone had been in camp, a kind of seniority system.

We finally returned to our barrack, reduced to labels and shivering from the cold. Gerda brought in eight coal briquettes, our nightly allotment. It was not enough to warm the huge room. Many of us slipped on our jackets.

Gerda announced, apologetically, "You are not allowed to wear your jackets in the barracks." Many women in their bunks were crying. I stomped around, angry, but then decided it was time to pray in earnest. I fell to my knees closed my eyes, and reached out to my God. When I opened them, I noticed three other women, including Elisabeth, had joined me in prayer. We hugged each other knowing God was our only hope.

Our labels and numbers were sewn on before supper. I felt banned and branded. Elisabeth and I looked at each other's red triangles sorrowfully and shook our heads. Remembering that praying made me smile, I did, and then she did, and then we laughed, which was the first laugh in longer than I could remember. "We are partners in crime," Elisabeth said. "We will get out of this school alive," I told her. "God will see to it."

Supper that first night was better than lunch had been. There was a pint of turnip soup each, and two small potatoes. One loaf of bread was divided into five parts, but had to last until the next night. We ate hungrily, quietly. Gerda told us that after supper and dish cleanup, we were allowed one free hour.

Most of the women walked outside. Gerda offered to show Elisabeth and me around. She said it would be good to know where not to go. It was cold and dark, and I was so tired, but my curiosity made me go. We put on our jackets and pushed our hands into the pockets to keep them warm.

"This is where the Jews live, Block 11," Gerda said as we turned a corner and caught our breath. About fifty were standing in the freezing cold in nothing but their shabby thin dresses and ragged shoes. Most were crying! Gerda rushed to inquire why, learning that someone from the snow shoveling detail had collapsed and could not continue. For punishment, the whole Block did not receive any supper and had to stand in formation for two hours, in addition to the head count. It often took two hours alone.

Hearing this, I fell to my knees, my head in my hands. Elisabeth and Gerda pulled me up, and I pleaded, "Can we not do something? Take them food? Give them our jackets? God, where are you? Why have you forsaken us?"

Just as I turned around, a prison guard with a rifle strapped to his back stared at me in the face. He had sad eyes and a stern look. He talked to Gerda, and then moved on. "Stay away from him," she warned.

The camp siren sounded. "We must return now," Gerda said. "The siren means we must be in our barrack." I could not move—I did not see how we could just walk away as others suffered. Now the searchlight began making a sweep, and Gerda and Elisabeth put their arms around my waist and pulled me back to the barrack.

Inside, Gerda took me aside and by both shoulders. "You must get a hold on your emotions, Vera. You will not last long wearing your feelings on your sleeve. Everyone here suffers. Be thankful you are not a Jew." I was sobbing miserably, a knife in my stomach. Gerda shook me. "Stop, Vera, stop! Look at me. I feel just as you feel, but I have learned to hide it within me. You must learn to do the same."

I looked closer at her, those green eyes swimming, her lips pinched tight. I took a long breath and shivered. "Oh, Gerda. I am lost. I cannot go on."

Gerda held me closer. "You must stop asking why. We will never know why the evil exists. We have to accept the fact that it does, and we must stay alive for the day when it is conquered." She reached in her pocket and pulled out some toilet paper, dabbing at my face.

Elisabeth was waiting, and when Gerda was out of sight, she rushed over and took both of my hands in hers, closing her blue eyes. Tears flooded her face. "Oh, Vera," she said, biting on her lip. "How will we ever be strong enough to make it?" Arm in arm we walked to our bunks.

Feeling like a zombie, I undressed and placed my things in a square bundle—camp regulation—then headed to the washroom in my underwear. There we found women crowded like sheep in a small pen. There were sixteen sinks for three hundred women. There were even fewer toilets, but they were in a different room. While I was waiting, being pushed and shoved, Gerda grabbed my arm. Without speaking, she reached between bodies and tapped the arm of a light-skinned woman so short she was nearly hidden. The woman, squeezed between the others, looked at Gerda and then at me, nodding her head slightly as if to say, "Help me." She had black hair and was not nearly as skinny as most. Somehow, I don't know why, but my heart stopped beating so fast. Elisabeth and I cleared a path for her so she could return to her bunk.

At last we were all in bed as the lights were turned out. I felt exhaustion, a throbbing in my bones. Surely everyone did. Women continued to talk, and there was intermittent sobbing for a long time. I turned on my belly to pray, but first I reached down and found Elisabeth's hand and gave it a squeeze. The first thing I would thank God for was Elisabeth, and then Gerda. Since God says we must pray for our enemies, I decided to say a prayer for that wicked, evil woman who was beating the Jews, the same woman, I suppose, who made them stand in the freezing cold for hours. Nothing made sense to me that first night, nothing at all, but finally nature called me to sleep. And I wondered why Gerda said to stay away from the sad-eyed prison guard.

Chapter Three

Elisabeth and I talk a great deal, mostly of our lives before Hitler, our early teens. She is one year younger than me and, as a little girl, lived in a cramped flat with her mother in a small town about twenty-five kilometers northeast of Berlin. She was an art student at the university and studied bronze sculpturing. Her father was killed in World War I. She loved a man named Alfred, but he ran away with her best friend.

I sometimes talk about my brothers, my father, and whether I was going to be a writer or a doctor. We compare our lives—hers poor, mine wealthy, both with only one parent. She cries occasionally, but I have not been able to cry for several days.

The days are long, and I feel lost. Most of the women knitting are older, and some of them sick, some Jew, some Christian. I have not figured out why a few of the Jews live with us in Block 9, and the rest in next Block 11. The little woman from the shower is Ruth and a Jew, as is Ilka, our top bunkmate. Hilde, Miriam, Hanna, and a few others, whom I do not know well yet, are also Jewish. They are wonderful women, but more timid and fearful; always worrying about being moved to Block 11. I have so many questions. No logic.

Elisabeth and I feel fortunate not to be outside all day. It is bad enough in the mornings and evenings, when we have a two-hour head count. And in the morning there is also work formation. It takes two hours. It is so very cold, and we are not allowed to move. Our face and feet feel like they will freeze and break off, our ears the worst, as our hair is pulled back so tight. I gave Elisabeth my hairpins, as my hair is long enough to tie in a knot.

We learned that some women work outside the camp in factories making bullets and guns. How horrible to make the weapons that kill and kill. The rumors continue that Hitler is winning. The rumors continue that he is killing all the Jews in all of Europe.

I ripped off the bottom of my nightgown to put over my hands and fingers to keep warm. It is January 28, 1940. SS guards hover around us like mother hens. Most are nasty, making lewd comments as they watch us. I learned from Gerda the one with the sad eyes is Jakob Gottfried, another is Ernst Reinhardt. Jakob has a pasty white face, big shoulders, and a large head. He has a constant scowl on his face. Reinhardt is taller with a dark mustache and walks with a limp. They tell us they are working on the wiring, but neither one seems to do much work. They are the enemy, looking for any way to hurt us. I hate them most when they stand by and watch people being clubbed to death and do nothing to stop it. This morning, my eyes met Jakob's as a young Jewish girl was being dragged across the ground by her hair. I quickly looked away, but I hope he felt the disgust I had for him. Do I hate him? Should I hate? Jesus said never to hate anyone, but I feel hate. Is this a sin?

During the morning, after head count, the Jewish work crew leader, that horrible woman I prayed for, came into our work formation and picked thirty women, including Elisabeth and me, and all the Jewish women in our Block. "Get into my work formation!" she shouted. "Hurry! Hurry!" Gerda nodded.

We followed the horrid woman to the utility room. We were given shovels and picks. She never stopped barking at us to hurry. Two of the female SS guards and their dogs showed up. Poor Liesel, still not healed from the dog attack, began to whimper. That caused one of the guards to crack her whip. Elisabeth and I grabbed Liesel by her arms and led her along. At a place about seventy-five meters from the front gate, we had to shiver and wait for thirty minutes while the guards smoked, talked, and the dogs growled. The guards called the evil woman Strecker; a name I will loathe forever.

Their cigarettes out, the guards told us, "Dig out the stones under the snow. Then carry them to that building over there." We began to work, but the stones were heavy, thirty pounds or more. We did not have gloves and my fingers were frozen and scaly.

Our backs ached, women groaned, some wailed. My hands started bleeding. We dropped stones, sometimes on our feet. Gerda tried to stop me but I walked up to Strecker and asked, "We could do more if we had gloves or bandages." Grinning and snarling, she stood there with her gloved hands in her pockets. "Shut up and get to work," she yelled. The guards with the dogs laughed. I noticed Jakob was not.

So it went, hour after hour, until women began to drop. Little Ruth fell first. When I tried to help her up, Strecker yelled at me, "Get back to work," and then others began to fall. The guards brought their dogs closer, and Strecker stomped around yelling, at first at one of us, then another. We all held up our bleeding hands. Finally, Strecker decided there was nothing to do except take us to the dispensary. "You are weaklings!" she shouted. "Weakling pigs."

The blondish SS head nurse named Marschall took us in. She told Strecker, "I will take care of them quickly." My eyes widened, and the whimpering grew louder as she went to the medicine cabinet and took out a big bottle of iodine. She looked at Liesel first, and said, "Put your hands over that bowl."

Poor Liesel, already subjected to iodine on open wounds, began to cry. I spoke up again, saying, "Please, none of us can stand that. Please! Look at our hands."

Marschall said, "You will stand it! And you will be first." With that, she grabbed my hands and yanked them over the bowl, pouring on the liquid fire. I wanted so to scream. I needed badly to scream, but I stubbornly gritted my teeth.

"Well!" Marschall laughed. "That was easy." She knew better, and I saw the look of hate in her eyes for the way I took it. Longing to spit in her face, it was the first time in my life I thought of murder. It also made me realize that my spirit was not yet broken, but I knew it could be, and soon.

Little Ruth was next, screaming her head off, falling to her knees in pain. Elisabeth screamed too, intentionally as loud as she could. It was deafening. Everyone else did the same. This angered Marschall, who kept putting down the bottle to cover her ears.

Not one of us received any bandages. After the ordeal, we were returned to work. And we worked the remainder of the day, with no strength left. We limped around, dropping rocks, blowing on our hands, listening to the guards curse at us and crack their whips over the sound of our crying. Finally, our first day outside was over.

I am still not sure I will be able to pray again for Strecker. I know I must try as God teaches.

* * *

We have been working at the same place now for the last four weeks. Everyone is sick with colds, bleeding hands, and frostbite—some of us more than others. Morale is as low as it can be, or at least I think it is. A laundry is being built on the site where we slave. Our blood is laying the cornerstone.

I am knitting socks with twenty-nine of my comrades. We do not know what happened to Liesel. She collapsed yesterday and was carried away. I pray hard for her. She is only eighteen and was to be married the day she was arrested.

Betty told us this morning that all the political prisoners must stay in the barracks. We must attend head count, but not work formation. Then she left without an explanation. We all stared at each other. What could it mean? Gerda answered, "I do not have any idea, except they must have another job for you. Enjoy the rest while you can."

It is February 25, 1940 and I cannot sleep, but toss and turn, wondering what is in our future. Liesel still has not returned. Gerda explained that she was thought to be a Jew and taken to the Jewish Block. But she is not Jew, and when she got in a fight with the Block-eldest there, they took her to the dungeon-like cells. When someone is there, no one knows what will happen.

What job are they saving us for? Gerda still does not know. Whatever it is, I pray it is an inside job. We sit, wait, and worry. My right hand shakes. Some of the women wet their beds because of the worry. The smell is awful, but no one gripes. Next to the Jews and some others, we are truly blessed.

Mostly, I worry about the Jewish women working in the snow. It is ten degrees below zero and they wear summer clothes. I have frostbite, but they will lose their feet. I wonder if the SS guards sleep well. I wonder what they will tell God on Judgment Day. Again this morning at head count, Strecker kicked women with her boots. And there are always the whips and the dogs. I cannot blame the dogs. They are trained that way. But human beings? Are they really human? No, these are sick and sadistic. Anytime someone screams or breaks down, the SS guards' eyes light up. They often say, "They are just Jew-pigs anyway. Who needs them?" I wonder how they would act if their wives, sisters, or daughters were here to witness their actions.

Someone is screaming in the Jewish Block, again. I feel electricity shoot down my spine. More and more the screaming of Jews penetrates the camp. Constantly I have to fight the urge to run to them, help them. But how? Many times Gerda and Elisabeth have to hold me back, calm me. Gerda's voice is soothing, but her words are strong. Today she said, "This is just the beginning. You will not give up already?" I asked her how she could be so cool. She just looked at me for a few seconds, a strange kind of look. Those eyes of hers have a way of making me listen.

She said, "Oh honey, I am not made of stone, but I have seen so much, so much worse. You, too, will become numb, hopefully. We are like soldiers in the war, horrified at first, and then we see so many casualties we must harden to survive. And look around you, Vera. People will do most anything to survive."

She had made a point I know will haunt me. Why do we have such a will to survive? The skeletal faces of the Jews, the hallow black eyes desperate to survive. I am desperate to survive. Why? Certainly many of us already have earned our way to heaven. God must have a reason for us to survive.

I must stop thinking about the Jews or I will go crazy. I must trust God to be in control of our destiny. There are many religious prisoners in Ravensbrück who are praying—the purple triangles, the Jehovah's Witnesses, and whoever else is among them. It seems ironic that the SS use only religious prisoners for janitorial work—they must trust them more. But if they trust them, why are they imprisoned in the first place? And why am I not a religious prisoner? I am a Christian, and it is the Christ in me that most opposes Hitler and his SS. Nothing makes sense here.

I am called a political criminal because I want justice and freedom for all. I will lose my will to survive if we must live the way the SS dictate. Constantly I pray Hitler will be defeated and we can be free again. But the rumors persist. He is winning; spreading his cruel hatred.

* * *

Three days have passed. Betty took Elisabeth, me, and a few others to the SS head guard, a vicious-looking woman named Binz. I smelled a perfume on her, something cheap. How does she get such things, trying to smell sweet when the stench of death is everywhere around us?

Binz is the second of what we call Head Overseers, the women leaders who report to the commandant. We are supposed to address them as Frau Aufseherin, or Madame Overseer, but I hate that term. They are SS technically, more members of the women's auxiliary. Binz is mean and nasty to the women, power hungry, and so intent on punishing.

Binz asked many questions. She said she will study our files and make work assignments in three days. All we can do is sit, wait, and knit stockings. I hate this waiting. I heard there were openings in the dispensary and clinic. I hope I will be assigned there since I was a medical student. Perhaps helping others would make me feel better.

During our free hour today, I met Anna Hirsch from Block 6. She works as a medic in the clinic. She noticed my shoes, a black pair I was given that are two sizes too big but still so much better than the wooden sandals. She laughed at how hard I tried to hold on to them with my toes. It wasn't funny, but I had to laugh too. She promised to get some cotton for me to stuff in the toes. Anna says the reason she can still laugh is because she works in the clinic helping the sick. I wonder if that is true. Her words sound happy, but grief lines her face, and her hair is dull and thinning. She looks much older than her thirty years. She has been in the camp since its inception after the SS came to her house and arrested her. I admire Anna—she can laugh, and it makes me feel shame for the way I have been acting. It would be wonderful to have such a person for a coworker, as a fellow medic. They tell me I will know in one more day. One more day of waiting to hear the news.

* * *

My hand is twitching, but with joy. My wish through prayer came true. I was assigned to Revier 2—one of the two clinics—along with Elisabeth and a woman named Katja, who is from our

Block. Erna, the clinic-eldest, a very small woman with dark hair, a very thin face, and huge bulging dark eyes, received us in a very friendly manner. She said, "Boy, are we glad to get you. There is too much work to do. Anna will take you to Revier 1 for a tub bath and to get your new clothes, and be sure and get some shoes that fit." Anna was listening and grinning. I have a feeling she had something to do with it all. She is God's angel, for sure.

Wow, a tub bath! What an indulgence! It has been three years since I last had one. And some warm water too. Wow again. After the bath we were given a new summer dress, a light wool jacket, underwear, and brand-new shoes. We also wear a yellow arm bandage that says "Revier 2" on it.

Next to the clinic ward is a nursing office, a lounge where the nurses and medics make up their reports and take breaks. There is a stove with a big pot of water on it, and in the corner is a cot for the medic on CQ (night patrol). Anna, the others, and I stood by the stove for a few minutes to talk. I feel so clean, so happy not to have been assigned an outside job. We conversed like normal people about the things we had left behind. Elisabeth, her blue eyes sparkling under her curly blonde hair, spoke of her artwork in sculpture. Katja, who is covered with freckles and wears her very red hair in a long braid, was a flautist in the Berlin Orchestra. Anna had been a grade school teacher. She said that children had given her a good sense of humor. I told them about being a medical student, and my dream to become a pediatrician. All of us were political prisoners who aided the Jews.

Erna told us to take our time and look around so it would be easier to see what needed to be done. She said, "I want you to work with little supervision. I hate to give orders. We all get too many, and can do with less." It was not difficult to see how very much help was needed at every level.

We began by walking from bed to bed. Anna introduced us to the patients, and we shook their hands and inquired about their problems. They all looked terrible—skinny, their lives worn out, the horrors of the camp in their faces and their blood-red eyes. Two-thirds had severe frostbite—many of them had already lost their toes. Some had lost one-half or a whole foot. Their wounds were discharging fluids—the smell was horrible. I had never seen anything like this. I prayed silently, asking God, "When will we all be rescued from this hell?"

We were determined to do our best. Everyone there was in pain. Soothing was desperately needed. Elisabeth and Katja were immediately loving, caring nurses, their hearts into helping. I went in search of medication and dressings, finally asking Erna where to find them. Because of her bulging eyes, Erna mostly looks terrified, like when she said, "I am so sorry, but we have hardly anything. We have to get by on the little they give us from time to time. We have only a few paper dressings and some ointment left." I could not believe what she was saying. "But where do the supplies come from?" I asked.

"From Revier 1, the head nurse, Marschall, but forget it," she said. I remembered Marschall too well. Erna was shaking her head. She said, "You will never get anything from her in a million years, especially if you ask." Just then, a young nurse came along with a different uniform. Erna whispered, "That is Nurse Agnes, the head nurse of NSO (National-Socialist Organization). She is kind of okay. She came from Krefeld and has already had a few arguments with Marschall."

This sounded like encouragement to me. I approached her in a friendly manner and shook her hand. She did not smile, but somehow her hazel colored eyes said soft things. Pretty, with auburn hair and pink cheeks. I guessed she could not be more than twenty-five or six. We chatted briefly, and I finally mentioned the subject. "Nurse Erna tells us you are very kind to the patients. Could I make a request for them?"

She closed her eyes and her voice was sad. "What would you like?"

"Nurse, please," I pleaded, "the medicine cabinets are practically empty. We need so many things. There is no way these people can get any better with the lack of supplies here."

She made a kind of groaning noise and then said, "I know, but it is not easy. Mrs. Marschall, the head nurse from Revier 1, barely gives us any supplies anymore. You surely know how she feels? If a patient dies, she will not lose any sleep. And I have already argued with her."

"But nurse, you are not a prisoner. Why would you have a hard time? You are one of them, well, so to speak." I thought I had gone too far, and how did I know? Maybe she was not one of them.

She gave a sigh as loud as her groan. "Oh well, I may as well try."

Within a half hour, she returned with a large basket filled with medicine and dressings. "Oh, bless you," I said.

"It was not easy," she said, releasing another one of those strange groans. "Now hurry. Get the water going and use that stuff before Marschall comes to take it all back."

My friends and I felt like heroes. Elisabeth, Katja, and I had tears in our eyes. Anna told a very silly joke about horses, which made us laugh. We worked until we collapsed. I will now pray to God, and thank him for giving me the job I wanted.

Chapter Four

Today is March 17 and a warm wind drifted through the camp. Spring is not here, but it is teasing.

First thing, I washed the feet of Hermine, a little Jewish girl with big brown eyes and the face of a cherub. But she cried and cried. When I asked if I was hurting her, she said, "It always hurts. Everyday more. Every time you change my bandage you put on less and less ointment."

Then she pulled out a blood-soaked rag from under her blanket. I felt sick. She was still crying. "Please do not be mad at me! I used my towel." Mad at her! Dear God, please! Fighting tears, I took the rag and threw it in the oven. Then I wrapped her feet and did not skimp with the ointment. She smiled and said, "You are my mother."

Those of us who work in the clinic get up at 4:30 in the morning. The other workers get up at 5:00. They work until 6:00 at night. We work until 10:00. It is hard work being on my feet all day, but I am helping others and it is worth it. And my frostbite does not compare to the patients I see.

I always spend my hour off in the camp street. Usually Elisabeth joins me, sometimes Katja, and occasionally Anna comes over from Block 6 to cheer us up. The fresh air does our lungs good after breathing the foul clinic air all day. It is smothering, a combination of disinfectant and urine, and of waste from prisoners who cannot help themselves. Reinhardt was holding his nose today as he watched us while repairing a broken pipe. Where is Jakob? Why do I care?

I was so tired I fell asleep in the toilet and when the door opened, I thought my life was over. But it was just Gerda wondering where I was. How lucky it was not an SS woman who would have had me whipped.

Tonight at supper, Betty came in, and she and Gerda made the announcement. The Jewish comrades from our Block 9 were to be transferred to Block 11: Little Ruth, Ilka, our tall top bunkmate with snowy hair, Hilde, Miriam, Hanna, and the others. We all fought tears and tried to make it as light as possible—it was better that way. After supper, during our free hour, we helped them gather their bundles. They are like sisters to us, and they were moved like bad cattle contaminating the herd. I must pray extra hard for them. God only knows how much worse it is in Block 11.

* * *

It is two days later. The Jewish women who were moved from our Block met Elisabeth, Katja, and me in the street tonight during free hour. We were shocked. They were bald, their heads shaved. "Why?" we asked. They did not answer, and tears rolled down their cheeks as they ran their hands over their skulls.

We asked again, and they explained the reason we are not allowed to cut our own hair. The SS uses it to make blankets for the soldiers. When they need more blankets, they shave heads. Elisabeth and I comforted them, told them they looked beautiful anyway, but they did not look beautiful. They were shamed. Women need their hair.

Ilka and little Ruth told us, "The Block-eldest of the Jewish Block is Paula. Everyone hates her, and no one can understand how or why she is so evil. She is a Jew, like the others, but apparently she had a difficult life before Hitler." Later, Ruth said, "They say she was a prostitute from Munich. She is known as a camp spy, and turns her comrades in for every reason she can find. Women constantly plot to get even with her. They also told us there are many children aged four to twelve in Block 11, and most are sick. They beg Paula to take them to the dispensary, but she will not. She answers them with statements like, "What good are children, anyway?" If anyone objects, she takes it out on the children." For me, it is difficult to imagine how she turned into such a monster. What did that Gypsy say about Strecker? Caught in the devil's circle?

We asked them if they had learned anything of Liesel. They nodded no. I should not have, but without thinking I ask Jakob, who was working on the wiring, to check. He looked at me like I was crazy and walked away without a word.

Tonight I pray for Liesel's soul, and I pray for my own. Hating is wrong, and I hate Hitler and the SS more than I dare admit, even to God.

* * *

Today is 23 March 1940 and Elisabeth came rushing to me, her blue eyes floating in tears. She did not say anything but made the crossed-fingers sign of the cell, a warning we give each other when something is dangerous. She had already heard the announcement about to be made by Nurse Agnes, who was motioning us all to her. Her face was flushed, and a piece of auburn hair had fallen in her hazel eyes. In a quiet voice she told us that the SS had instructed medical personnel to no longer treat Jews. We all gasped and stared at one another. Agnes continued, "Not male, not female, not children, not anyone! The SS has ordered—if they die, it is good. They are not fit to live anyway." Before any of us could say a word, Agnes hurried away.

How could we ignore the Jews? We just could not. I asked Anna and Elisabeth and Katja to take a break with me, outside, where no one could hear us. Erna, clinic-eldest, joined us, her bulging eyes needing to see what we were up to. Katja pulled her long red braid around and chewed on it, a nervous mannerism she has. Anna laughed sarcastically and said, "Are we going to make a prison break?" I took a deep breath and said, "We must treat all of the sick. We are nurses."

In seconds we had all whispered our allegiance, shook hands, and returned to our patients. We will, somehow, treat everyone the same. More and more praying will be required.

* * *

My coworkers continued to ask me what was wrong. Why I am so quiet? Could they not see what was wrong? Maybe they chose not to look at our empty supply cabinet with nothing even for the very worst patients. But I had an idea I could not confide to the others, not even Elisabeth, Katja, or Anna. It was terribly risky. For days I had wanted to ask Nurse Agnes for more supplies, but I held off. She had gotten in so much trouble with Marschall the last time she stood up to her. Agnes is kind to us and the patients. It would be awful if she were transferred somewhere else or punished.

It was late afternoon, and I could not face my patients another minute. Their dressings were oozing and painful, and there was nothing I could do except think about all those supplies locked up in Revier 1 by SS Head Nurse Marschall. I had to try to get them no matter what happened to me.

In the toilet, I prayed for God to protect me, but when I walked into Revier 1, my heart began to flutter. I found Marschall in her chair dozing—her blondish head face down on her desk. She woke, bellowing at me, "What in the hell do you want? Get out of here!" I wondered how such a spindly woman could yell so loud. I did not dare speak and slumped to the door. She made hissing noises and said, "I am taking the break I deserve after working all day for you no-good people."

I waited, sweat beading up under my armpits. I started to leave, but she said, "What do you need over at your stink box?"

"Everything," I said.

She gasped. "You must be out of your skull. It is a waste of supplies. They are all going to die anyway. You must know that."

I wanted to jump over her desk and grab her throat, so I put my hands behind my back. She said, "Damn fool," and then took a small package out and threw it at me, hitting me in the face. I grabbed my cheek as she said, "Well? Now what? Is that not enough?"

"No, Head Nurse. We have six new German patients and we are out of everything." I hoped saying German patients would help.

Her eyes flashed at me, but she ripped several fistfuls of supplies out of the cabinet and threw it in a basket. "Now, get your ass out and never come back!"

I could not move, but stood looking toward the cabinet at two green bottles of cod liver oil. I forced myself to plead once more. "Head nurse, two really nice Germans are at the clinic from our Block. Could I have some of that?" My skinny arm was pointing. "You know, to help them get on their feet faster?"

She angrily grabbed the two bottles and tossed them on top of the other supplies. "Now, get out of here and fast," she yelled.

I ran back to the clinic, praying gratefully the whole way. Before I walked in the bed area, I slipped the two bottles of cod-liver oil behind a cabinet. When my co-workers saw the big basket full of supplies their eyes lit up in disbelief. Elisabeth, Anna and Katja danced around clapping their hands. Erna gave me a big pat on my back. I was really proud of myself—oh boy, so proud. But then I sat down, my knees trembling, as though I had just survived a nearly fatal accident. I guess I had. Over in the corner, I saw Jakob. Was that a little smile on his face?

Despite my fright, I know tomorrow I will risk disaster again. I saved those two bottles of cod-liver oil for the Jews in Block 11.

They are in the straw of my bed. Gerda saw me bring them in. For the bottles, she gave me a real lecture, but I knew she was proud of me. I told her that our German patients now have a cabinet full of medicine and dressings, and they could also use the cod liver oil as well. But those poor Jewish women on the shoveling crew have nothing. I must pray harder for the women in Block 11.

* * *

After lights were out and everyone was in bed, I dressed again and took the two bottles from the hiding place. Gerda, in her nightgown, her red hair around her shoulders, held the door for me. It was pitch-black outside, except for the searchlights making their rounds. I was breathing heavy I was so scared. The bottles were cold and felt like they weighed two tons. And in my pockets, I had the bread rations of Elisabeth, Katja, Gerda, and me.

Little Ruth and Ilka met me, as promised, but with tears, so hungry and so grateful. Paula, their evil Block-eldest, had found a reason to punish again—no supper. I did not have time to comfort them and returned quickly, dodging the searchlights, shaking with cold and fear. Gerda gave me a hug. I am still trembling. I could have been arrested, whipped, or transferred to the Arrest Block.

* * *

Today is 2 July 1940. It was a very long day. I cannot sleep. This morning Nurse Agnes came in looking more sad than usual. She had an announcement. "Girls, I have orders from Revier 1. Every patient halfway on her feet and without a temperature is to be transferred out of Ravensbrück. We must supply their names, original Block, race, everything." We all began talking at once, asking why. She closed her eyes to groan and say, "They are to be transferred to a better camp—to Auschwitz."

We all slumped in a chair or onto a bed. Some fell to their knees. *Auschwitz*! Even cut off from the world, we know about Auschwitz, and the stories just keep getting louder. We heard of their gas chambers, where people were told to take showers, and instead of water, deadly gasses came out. No one knew how many had been killed, but the guess was many thousands. The SS guards here often threatened, "If you do not do as told, we will send you to Auschwitz!"

Some of the patients heard Agnes and began to cry. I knew I should go to them, but I could not. I was in shock myself. Agnes continued to explain that all of the Gypsies were to go to Lublin, even the young ones, as most of their mothers were already there. We had also heard the stories of Lublin, nearly as bad as Auschwitz.

Sick to my stomach, I dashed outside for some air, something to shake off the shock. Crying, talking to myself, I paced around in a circle. "What have these Jews done to Hitler and his friends to deserve this treatment?" I wondered. Then I recalled being told that Nazis believe a Jew can have a nickel, and when he turns it over, it is a dollar. Hitler must be jealous of them! With them gone, he will have their businesses and belongings. He has no conscience. All he cares for are special Germans, and he is not one himself. Out loud I shouted, "One day he will pay! If not here, in another world!" I collapsed to my hands and knees and threw up.

"Vera, oh Vera!" It was Elisabeth. She pulled me to my feet and held me in her arms. Then came Katja. The three of us just stood there staring at nothing, tears flooding our faces. Then Anna came out. She looked at me and asked why I was shaking in the heat and why my teeth were chattering. I could not tell her, but cold sweat ran down my back.

The next thing I knew, I was in the lounge on the cot with a hot water bottle, covered like a baby, nauseated, and scratching my itching legs. And they itch oh so terribly. After all these months, my frostbite wounds still have not healed, many still discharging. Before I drifted off, I was aware of the smell of the place, that horrid smell that had been made worse by the summer heat.

When I woke, Katja was sitting on the cot, chewing on her braid. She said, "You look better, hon. A bit of pink in your cheeks."

"Oh Katja," I wailed. "I am so ashamed, acting weak and stupid, but Auschwitz." Elisabeth nodded her head. "We must be strong for them," she said. "For them."

The clinic was whirling, nurses hurrying from one bed to another, calming the patients doing the most crying. How terrified they all were. Elisabeth was supporting a woman who had gotten out of bed, but could not stand up. I went to help. We got her back in bed, and then another was up and on the floor. Everyone wanted to escape, somewhere, anywhere but Auschwitz or Lublin!

As I helped, suddenly the idea to sing came into me. I began humming a song I knew growing up. It was called, "The Flowers of Spring." Some of the Germans knew the song, and they began to sing with me. We just walked around from bed to bed, singing and fussing with the patients. They seemed to calm down, and after we had sung the same song several times, we found another one we all knew. Reinhardt was standing in the corner, watching. I saw him leave and then talk to Jakob. He was bending some barbed wire by the fence.

When nurse Agnes came in, she looked around at all of us singing and smiled, her hazel eyes brimming. She looked so haggard, so tired, as though she had aged twenty years. I asked her if she knew where Erna was, as we had not seen her for hours. Agnes said they had both been meeting with the head nurses about the transfers.

We stayed at the clinic until every last patient was sleeping. When we walked back to our Block in the dark, dodging the searchlights, Elisabeth mentioned how terrible Agnes looked.

Anna reminded us how pretty she used to be. We agreed that she had the weight of all this on her shoulders, and if any of it did not go as the SS wanted, it would be her neck. We could imagine the anguish she must feel.

Chapter Five

It is July 14, 1940, and sleeping last night was difficult. Dreams float in and out of my mind, sometimes pleasant ones with my family, sometimes nightmares where I wake up in a cold sweat.

This was the day the first load of patients was traveling to Auschwitz and Lublin. I jumped into my clothes and ran to the clinic to check on the little Jewish girl, Hermine, the last one I spent time with last night. She had cried so long and hard, and I had cried with her. This morning her eyes were still puffy. I asked her if she slept well. She shook her head and then asked me, "Did you sleep, Nurse Vera? You need your rest more than I. You have so much work to do."

Poor child. She is headed to her death sentence, but she is concerned about me. "Yes, darling," I said, "I had to rest for my favorite little patient." She is just twelve, but her body, because it has not been nourished, is that of a much younger child. She is a poor little Gypsy child with half her foot missing.

"I am supposed to leave today," she said, "but how will I walk?"

I turned away to fiddle with her blanket and fight back my tears. "Don't worry, little one, you are not going anywhere."

"How?" she blurted out. "Dr. Sonntag said I was. How are you going to make it not happen?"

"I do not know yet, little one, but I will think of something, okay?" She looked astonished and confused, but in her eyes I could see such trust. I swallowed hard and hoped to God I could make good on my promise. Her eyes had lit up and her smile sparkled. The siren sounded for head count.

Erna was holding a long list at head count. Before she began, she posted Anna at the door. As I crossed my fingers in my pocket, Erna said, "Now listen, girls. This is a list of comrades slated for the transport to Auschwitz and Lublin today." She slapped the list, her bulging dark eyes fierce. Again she slapped the list. "All those who can walk will go back to their Blocks. Someone from each of their respective Blocks will be here any minute to help them. Their Block-eldests are expecting them. To Dr. Sonntag this will mean they are fully capable of work. They are a long way from being able to work, but we need to get them out of here quick. Better sick than dead."

She gave a long sigh then went on. "Only Germans and Jews who are too sick for work or the transport will remain. The SS policy is that the camp cannot use anyone who is not fully capable of work, but on the other hand, they do not want anyone on the transport who looks too bad or has a fever. The outside world might see some of the prisoners on this trip. We are supposed to be some kind of a school for them, so I suppose they will be pretty careful whom they send. So what can we do for our patients who do not have a fever but are too sick to work?" We all looked at each other and understood. "Good," she said. "Get started. We need this done before Dr. Sonntag and Nurse Agnes show up."

We all worked as though the very devil was standing next to us, and I guess he was. Katja and I took all of the temperatures of those not going back to their Blocks. We simply told the patients their fevers were up, but we did not let them see how very much we elevated them on their charts. We had to pray that Sonntag would follow precedent and not actually check temperatures. We did not give any baths or change any dressings. The patients needed to look terrible. We supposed most knew what was going on because they seemed to be doing their best to look as sick as possible.

When I told little Hermine she had a fever, she asked if it meant more of her foot would come off. I told her that it was a serious thing, but if she remained very still all day, and slept a great deal, it could get better. "Am I leaving today?" she asked, her eyes filled with tears. I told her if she were sleeping, she could not leave. She smiled faintly, looked at me with trust, and lay down quietly.

We were ready for Nurse Agnes when she arrived. She went over the entire ward with Erna. Jakob was with her but he did not look at me. I held my breath and prayed. What if she was wise to what we had done? She commented on how terrible everyone looked and on the elevated fevers. Erna told her some of the fever could be caused from the excitement, or fear, of going to a better camp. Agnes made one of her groaning sounds. Because she is not in charge of admitting and discharging, she did not keep up with anyone individually. She trusted us to do our best to keep the clinic running smoothly.

Dr. Sonntag did not show up after he received Nurse Agnes's report. We had saved our people another day. Just how many days could we save them? It will probably take a little while before they make up another transport to Auschwitz or Lublin. At least we hope so. We were thrilled with the little time we might have bought for them.

Agnes returned later in the day to tell us that we will soon get a huge transport into Ravensbrück—foreign women and children. I am unsure what this means.

I will go to bed now and pray for those on their way to us. I remember the horror of the ride in the cattle car. At least it is summer and they will not be frostbitten when they arrive.

* * *

It is mid-August now, and our work gets harder from day to day, week to week. In both clinics there is a constant stream of people coming and going. Very sick people are admitted, and a few days later, released to work or for transport.

Despite our efforts, little Hermine is gone, shipped to Auschwitz with half a foot missing. It seems we have lost control. Still, we try daily to save lives, and many times risk our own lives to do so. If the Nazis had any idea how hard we work against them, Hitler probably would slaughter us all. Good and evil both need deception to survive. It has always been that way. This life we are living cannot be God's will.

I have lost more weight. When I look at my body and see the sharp edges of my bones, it makes me angry. Anger is something that becomes increasingly difficult to manage. It is mostly exhaustion, my feet and legs hurting. I am often too tired to eat, and give my food to someone who is hungrier. If I am to stay sane, I must be real. So many here just drift away into imagination.

* * *

Now September comes, and we had a substitute medic. Her name is Claere from Dresden. She works in Revier 1 with the head nurse. She pulled strings in order to come over here, thinking it would be easier. We did not have Marschall on our back today, and Claere was surprised we worked as hard as we do.

* * *

Four months have passed. It is December. Katja, Elisabeth, and I were transferred out of Block 9 to Block 6—a political Block, Anna's Block. It has been arranged that all the same nationalities be Blocked together. We miss Gerda so very much. Life is different without her; without her motherly ways.

Our first Block-eldest in Block 6 was a political prisoner, Maria from Karlsbad-Sudetenland She was relatively new at the position and without a good sense of organization. She tried hard to do everything right and keep things going. A nice woman, but she did not do well and had to give up the job.

Another political prisoner, Mina, is now the Block-eldest. She can be hard. Often it is difficult to deal with her. She overdoes things at times and is too bossy. But we see very little of her. We work long hours in the clinic, and the barracks are no longer a refuge, as when we returned each day to Gerda. Block 6 is much more crowded with bunks so close together we have to turn sideways. Elisabeth, Katja, and I were assigned the triple bunk nearest the door, and next to Anna, so as not to disturb others when we come in during the night, as we often do. Poor Katja, the tallest and youngest, took the top bunk.

In the clinic there are new admissions daily. More people mean more patients, more work but not always more help. I often work sixteen hours a day and many Sundays. The kitchen people work these same long hours, as well as some other crews. Despite being so tired all day, when we finally hit the bed, we cannot sleep. I am so deprived of fresh air and too tired to go out. I often take my breaks in a chair, dozing. We all do.

Winter is around again, and that means more frostbite. It smells so bad all the time. Puss oozes from hands and feet that are virtually rotting. Because our heating materials are dangerously low, we can only open the windows momentarily.

The worst development is that Jews are not admitted to the clinic at all now, and we are strictly forbidden to help them in any way. It is so hard to ignore them, and it plays on my conscience, particularly at night when I try to sleep. They are so ill, working outside again this winter. Little Ruth and Ilka are on Strecker's crew carrying coal. They tell us she kicks them constantly. They have lost so much weight, and their hands and feet are a mess. Elisabeth and I try to smuggle ointment to them—terribly risky, but to see them is to weep. Paula is still in charge of their Block so they often go without supper.

I go regularly to the kitchen to beg food, but it is difficult and very risky. The kitchen help knows I want it for the Jews and they do not want to be involved. Spies are everywhere, and they like their jobs. Working in the kitchen means they can always get food for themselves and their friends. But Erika, the kitchen-eldest, will give me food when she sees me. She is a wonderful woman, respected by all, and her assistant, Friedel, is also helpful and compassionate. When I do get food, it is a terrifying ordeal to get it to the Jewish Block. It is farther away from Block 6 than it was from Block 9. I live in constant fear of being caught. Each night I pray and pray, "Oh, God, do not let me get caught. Save me so I may help others."

Today I thought I was caught for sure. On the way back to the barracks, Jakob saw me with my apron full. He knew what I was doing, but so far he has not reported me. I do not know what to make of him. Sometimes he tries to be friendly; other times he looks like the hateful SS guard that he must be to work for Hitler. "Do I hate him?" I ask myself again and then say, "Yes, no, I do not know anymore." Someone said today he is from Meissen, near Dresden. I had a cousin who worked in the porcelain factory there.

* * *

The new year is here, 1941. Transports now come daily to Ravensbrück and the camp grows bigger and bigger. This means more patients for us. And it means more and more Jews are dying because we are not able to treat them. We do not always save the other patients either. We have few supplies and many times not the right ones. Plenty of women have limbs that need amputation, which is not always done. Too many times blood poisoning results and slow, painful death follows. And we have no painkillers. I see less and less of that strong will to survive I used to see and wonder about. The screams, the crying and pleas for a fast death are overwhelming. We can do nothing beyond change their dressings and give them some ointment, when we have the supplies.

We do have some shred of hope. One of the regular Blocks has been turned into an extra clinic. Erika has been moved from the kitchen to run it. If anyone can make things better, it is Erika. She has a special talent for remaining calm and in charge. I pray for her because if it does not get easier. We will be lying here ourselves before long. My prayer was a simple one—"Dear God, protect us all. Be with us. Prevent suffering and comfort those who suffer. Protect especially the children for they may not protect themselves."

* * *

We are pretty much on our own and do not get hassled like the rest of the prisoners, and so far no shakedowns. It is mid-January, and the first snow has fallen and the heating supply is low all over camp, except at the SS quarters. We asked once if we could get a little more coal for the clinic, but we were told, "They are in bed with covers. What for?" The Jews working outside still have no gloves and many have open wounds from last winter. My legs will never be the same either, but at least I am entitled to treatment because I am a German.

Recently we have received several new prisoners who were doctors in civilian life. Naturally they were put to work in the clinics. They know a lot more than we do, but at times, they are helpless too. Despite all their knowledge, they do not have the right instruments or medicine. Erika makes it possible for them to sneak treatment for Jews here and there, at great risk to herself and the doctors. One of the doctors treated little Ruth and Ilka for frostbite. He said they were not in good shape, and there was little he could do.

Erika is rather introverted, and very plain to look at, her features ordinary. But she is an amazing woman everyone seems to know and respect. She has the greatest concern for all the prisoners. Always calm herself, she has that effect on others, and she always knows what to do when the rest of us do not. She runs the extra clinic and helps with ours as well. We say, "We are the hands and she is the head." This does not mean she does not labor. Even Erna, our clinic-eldest does what Erika says. Erika has the rare ability to help, stay out of the way, and also stay out of trouble with the SS.

Today started like a tornado with a constant flow of people suffering from severe frostbite and some with pneumonia. We needed four hands each and more hours. And then we could not believe our eyes. Jews began coming in. An SS guard escorted them all, so we figured there had been a change in rules. We soon learned the guard was new and did not know Jews are not to be treated. Of course, we did not say a word. They had third-degree frostbite, and their crying and screaming tore at our hearts.

In the middle of the day, Erika came over with some extra helpers for our clinic and asked me to go over to the emergency room of the Revier 1. She said there were some brand-new medics there and a lot of confusion—maybe I could help them.

I could not believe what I saw. Sick people were squirming all over the floor, crying out in pain. SS Nurse Marschall and Dr. Sonntag were giving them cardiacol shots—heart stimulants. Soon after the shot, they pushed them out the door. I felt sick and stood in the hallway unable to move. Jakob was standing against the wall. I gave him my hardest look, but his eyes turned away.

Then, to further my shock, I saw little Ruth and Ilka. That same new SS guard had ushered them in. Ilka, so tall and with so little flesh, could have been a skeleton. They were both sick and looked like death. Their heads had been shaved again, and under the thin stubble, their scalps were bright red with fever, their eyes glassy, their arms stained with coal. I stayed hidden in the hallway, holding my breath, hoping I was the only one who knew they were Jews.

They waited, and soon it was their turn with Dr. Sonntag. The first thing he asked was where they worked. Ilka whispered, "We carry coal." Then he asked which Block they lived in. Ilka's filmy eyes filled with tears when she told him Block 11. She started to back up but he pushed her down on the floor and kicked her. She fell against Ruth and they lay there in a heap. Jakob's and my eyes met and he started to move toward the women but stopped.

Little Ruth had blood on her mouth but finally managed to crawl out the door. Ilka just lay there without moving. Somehow she had hit her head on the cement floor and was knocked out. So Marschall got involved. She yelled, "You dirty pig, you cannot block the doorway." Then she kicked her and pulled on her long arms, dragging her. Several women called out to Marschall in order to distract her, and she finally walked away. Two other nurses and I tried to move Ilka, revive her, but she was dead and had escaped to another world. A tear popped out of my left eye. I glared at Marschall and stood up ready to attack her, but a huge hand grabbed my shoulder and pulled me back. It was Jakob. "No," he yelled at me. I yanked his hand away and walked out.

Later, Katja, Elisabeth, and I rounded up as much food as possible, snitched vitamins from the clinic, and smuggled them over to little Ruth. It may help her physically, but her heart will not heal. Those two have been like sisters. Ilka, and part of Ruth, died today.

When I was on my knees praying, I had to put my hands over my mouth to keep from screaming out loud, "Oh God, have you forgotten us? You said a great misery would come to the Jews, but please, they have suffered too long. If they must suffer so, please take them now." I felt bad questioning God, but where is the rest of the world? Where is help that cares? What kind of doctors and nurses could do what is being done to the Jews? Did they not take an oath to help and heal all patients? I feel like my heart is breaking into little pieces.

* * *

It is past mid-February, and I sit alone, late at night, my heart aching. My prayer is that someone far away is listening and will come to our rescue. The situation here is completely mad. Jews are no longer sufficient targets for Hitler's evil.

I did everything not to believe the executions were a reality, but finally I saw it happen. I watched Lehmann and a woman with a hideous reputation—SS guard Bergmann. They were escorting three women from the jail. The women were barefoot in the snow, their clothes hanging on their skeletal frames, their heads shaved. They all looked insane, mumbling, crying. One of them lagged behind, and Bergmann stopped long enough to throw her against a wall.

I was paralyzed, wanting to move but unable to do so. Suddenly Lehmann yelled, "What are you staring at?" He was looking straight at me. "Maybe you would like to join them on their journey to hell?" I walked away fast. About twenty minutes later, I heard shots from the nearby woods.

One execution follows another. A terrible deadly fear permeates the camp. Making it worse, the names of those to be executed are called out after head count each morning. No one could know how it feels to have their name read, until it happens. And every day it happens to some.

Prisoners are shot not only in the woods, but also in the Death Walk, as it is called—a small pass between two gray walls. The walls have thin slits for the rifles to poke through. Prisoners walk through in a line and are shot in the neck. Johann Braeuning, the most feared man in camp, is in charge of this Death Walk. SS head guard Binz, his live-in girlfriend, often helps him. A woman executing women; it is really true? Dear God, are you watching?

This Death Walk is between the jail and the camp gate, behind the kitchen. The shots echo through the camp, each one a knife in our spines. I am certain the executioners are not human but some kind of robots built by Hitler's doctors.

Chapter Six

March is here and we have a new camp commander. His name is Suhren, a tall, blonde, blue-eyed man of sporty stature—just the type to impress Hitler. Within two days of his arrival in camp, he was killing people at the Death Walk.

Chaos and general hysteria have enveloped the camp. People are picked daily for the transport now, one selection after another. Some go to Auschwitz, some to Lublin, some to Bergen Belsen, and some to Bernburg. The old, the sick, and the Jews are brought before Suhren, naked, and he decides where they are to be sent. When I saw Jakob today, I wanted to kill him and all his comrades for what is being done. He tried to talk to me, but I walked away. He is two-faced.

Rumors abound about Bernberg, and the mention of it rings fear to Block 11 as many healthy Jews are sent there. It is supposed to be a mental clinic and convalescent center, but we are told that Dr. Irmfried Eberle runs it as an experimental hospital—a nice doctor helping the devil mutilate before gassing.

If I live through this, I can never forget the scenes of tragedy when the prisoners are picked and ready to leave. There are always some going from the clinic and we nurses accompany them. No one wants to be the first one to climb up in the truck. They look like livestock ready to be slaughtered. Again and again the whips, the screams, the dogs barking, all of it is unforgettable. Many times a mother is ripped away from her daughter, or sisters are torn apart. Tears flow down my cheeks as they embrace for the last time. When they are loaded, we go back into the clinic and throw up, or collapse, or just hold onto one another.

The trucks go to the train station where the cattle-cars are waiting. Two to three hundred bodies are squeezed into one car. Most are sick people. We wonder how many make it to where they are going alive.

We are helpless to do anything except try to calm those who are leaving, and this has little effect. They are ghostly white and wide-eyed with terror. When they cry out, they are punished. Often a young prisoner will step between an older woman and the guards to take the brunt of the whip or a kick.

Each morning, Elisabeth, Katja, Anna, and I dress quietly and walk to the clinic holding hands. We are silent. There is nothing to say. But holding onto each other seems necessary when walking into the smell of death, gore and the torturing question, "Is it my turn today?" I pray and pray and pray for God to see, and hear, and help.

* * *

It is late in first part of April, and still I cry. I cried with Elisabeth and Katja, and others, and now I sit here and cry and pray and pray and cry alone in the lounge. One of our best friends, little Ruth, was loaded on a transport today for Bernburg. I bet she will be mutilated by experiments and then gassed. I remember when she bravely carried the heavy ice pick and shovel in the snow; the work much too hard for her. I remember when she and Ilka had their heads shaved. I remember seeing their hands so horrible from working for Strecker. And I remember the beating they took in the clinic, when Ilka was killed. Little Ruth suffered so losing Ilka. Today when she was waiting to climb into the truck, on her way to Bernburg, she was smiling. She said, "Death is closer now, and death is better."

* * *

It is July and rumors are circulating the camp that Hitler has invaded Russia. A huge country; they were our ally, and will surely fight hard against Hitler. We know Warsaw, Copenhagen, Oslo, the Hague, Brussels, Paris, Belgrade, and Athens belong to Hitler. Where is America? They could not possibly side with Hitler. Are they helping us? Always we listen for news, but it rarely comes.

* * *

It is December 1941. I will remember Erna, our clinic-eldest. Today she was transported to Auschwitz. Before she left, we all gathered around her on our hands and knees. Elisabeth said a beautiful prayer, her blue eyes glistening like an angel. Erna was told she was needed as a medic at Auschwitz, but no one knows the truth. I think she tried to believe it was true. While she was waiting for the transport, she was still giving us all instructions with that terrified look she always wore. We will miss her so much.

I am consumed with work and depression and ready to give up. In my off hours, I collapse exhausted. It is eighteen days before Christmas, a time for celebration of peace and joy, a time to sing and be merry, to bake, to decorate, and to shop for presents. I try not to think of my family when I am working because it makes me want to scream and bang my head against the wall like so many of my comrades do. But each night they are in my prayers. Where are they? What are they doing? Were my brothers forced to fight for Hitler? Have they been killed in the war, or do they sleep in a blanket made of Jewish hair? Before I fall asleep, I think of our happy times together—my brother Rolf fishing and my brother Manfried with Hanna, his girlfriend the schoolteacher.

And my dad would lift me onto my pony—Champ. He was brown with big eyes and a swishing tail. Where is my pony?

There must be thousands of German soldiers ignoring their consciences in order to stay alive. I cannot imagine my brothers ignoring theirs. It is more likely they refused Hitler and are housed in a concentration camp. Maybe they have been gassed for their disobedience. And my father? What is he doing? Was he punished for my work? How will this all end, God? How did it begin? Why? Why? Why?

Katja tells me, "I cannot stand to think about Christmas." She comes from a large, happy family of high-spirited redheads, nearly all of them musicians. She tells us they always celebrated Christmas and New Years for an entire month. In her mind, she plays the music. Imagination is a good friend.

When Katja has the energy, we hear stories about big celebrations and much music. And then she cries, flooding her freckles with tears and hiding her eyes with her braid. The transports still leave daily, but many more arrive. Barracks after barracks have been built, and many barracks have been converted to isolation clinics for the victims of typhus, TB, and scabies. The Germans believe there is no point in vaccinations for those who will die anyway. In fact, it makes life for the SS easier. They can report these people died of "natural causes." Today a prison guard laughed when someone told him that 100 people die a day. Food is so scarce that prisoners watch and wait for another to die and then immediately search the body for food.

People are turning into vultures because they are starving, while the SS look well fed. What could possibly be going through the minds of the SS? More and more I believe they cannot be human. If I had a knife, I would kill some of them—those who thrill in the despair of others. Even Jakob—even though sometimes he seems different than the rest. Today, he asked me where I was from and without thinking I told him Berlin. He said his father lived there. And then before I could leave, he said, "And my mother painted bright-colored flowers on little porcelain vases. I am from Meissen." Then he smiled, but I did not smile back."

Charlotte, a girl from France, has taken Erna's place as Revier 2 clinic-eldest. She speaks good German. She made us laugh when she arrived and got her first smell of our clinic. She said, "I will not stay in this place. This place is not good for my nose." Then she looked at us and realized she had no choice, so she stomped her foot and declared, "I will stay. I will show the SS that the French are not weaklings." She made more angry remarks about the SS in French and when we ask her what she said, she rolled her eyes and answered, "No comment!" Then she walked into the ward and began shaking hands with the patients, introducing herself just like Katja, Elisabeth, and I did so long ago. Perhaps she is another of God's angels, helping to make things better when they seem so much worse.

* * *

It is after midnight in mid-December, and only a few of us remain in the clinic. Charlotte, Anna, and Greta Grosse, a new medic, sit with two patients near death, waiting for the inevitable. Katja is changing the straw in the last bed. Elisabeth and I sit in the lounge with our feet up and not enough strength to talk. I will try to stay sane. I constantly look for purpose. Maybe God is letting me through this because he counts on me for help.

We try so hard to help the prisoners escape the transports that leave each day. We hold little meetings to connive and plot, hoping to avoid spies who are worse than the SS because they are invisible. Thankfully, Erika knows who they are and whom we can trust. But still, we stand with one leg in jail or the grave. The object is to get people on their feet to work. The sick and weak go on the transports first. We alter charts to buy time, we move patients from one clinic to the other to avoid doctors' inspections.

We work hard for women who have relatives with them. We are much more unlucky than lucky, but still, we try to save lives.

We live on two to three hours sleep a night. I have to believe it is God who keeps us going. Some people in the world are preparing to celebrate the birth of Christ, the Son of God, a Jew. I wonder how many Jews will be slaughtered before Christ's birthday.

* * *

Someone, we do not know who it may be, is helping us prepare for Christmas. Bows of ivy were left by the back door. Gerda thinks it might be Jakob, but I do not think so. He still has not turned me in for what he saw me do but maybe he was not sure I had food in the apron when he saw me return to the barracks. No matter, I do not trust him and never will despite his trying to be kind to me. He is the enemy, I must remember.

Regardless, I have a smile on my face. However horrible, we have hope. Gerda and Betty met Elisabeth, Katja, Anna, Greta, and me in the street with the news. Hitler has declared war on the United States. So now there are three powerful countries fighting Hitler—the United States, Britain, and Russia. Three against one; maybe victory will be near.

All of us huddled together after the news, and I noticed how awful we all look, as though we should be patients ourselves. Gerda and Elisabeth, the prettiest of us, even look ghostly. Katja and I look like mops, her with her long red braid, and me with my long knots. Betty, so tall, and becoming leaner, looks like she could be blown away. Greta, a shy girl who has not been in the camp as long, looks healthiest, and her dark hair is neater as it has not grown so long it has to be pinned tight or tied back.

I wonder if we get through this if we will every regain our weight and health. I have been at Ravensbrück so long it is difficult to remember what it is like to be normal, to be free. And I have completely forgotten the taste of my favorite foods like sauerbraten, bratwurst, spargel, baked flounder or sole, and my great aunt's Apfelstrudel. But any thought of a short sentence and my release are absurd. I am doomed to live here until I die or am rescued by Hitler's enemies.

* * *

Time has passed so quickly. Spring is coming. Elisabeth, Katja and I are still begging food for Block 11, sneaking medicine when we can. It is even more difficult than it used to be. There are more and more prisoners in the camp, and rations are skimpy. What we can get together for Block 11, we give to their new Block-eldest, Olga. Paula has gone. Sadly, no one wept when she climbed on the transport.

Olga is a famous political prisoner. She married a labor leader from Brazil, but was tracked down and brought back to Germany. Pregnant, she gave birth in jail. She does not know what happened to the child when she was sent to Ravensbrück. When we give her something for the Block, she smiles with her big brown eyes, so grateful. She always worries that we will be caught. Many times we nearly are, and if she were aware of our close encounters, she would be horrified and probably not take our offerings. She has enough worries with her Block, constantly hiding and nurturing the sick and wounded not allowed to be treated. She works hard to save her women, and they try hard to keep her out of trouble for doing so—so different from the evil Paula's days. Occasionally we can create a happy moment when someone is saved, but it does not last long. Olga likes to say, "If I can save just one life, my life will be worthwhile." She is right.

Tonight I must remember what we learned from Betty and Gerda. Elisabeth, Greta, and I saw them in the street at free hour. They told us of events going on so we could be ready for them at the clinic. Elisabeth and I were both sickened by what we heard and came back to give the news to Katja and Anna, and to comfort each other.

Apparently, the headquarters in the Prinz-Albrecht-Strasse in Berlin has thought of another devilish coup and has sent us a doctor named Rosenthal. He is a former Hitler youth leader and is excited by Hitler's latest command. All pregnant women first entering Ravensbrück are to be immediately sent off to Auschwitz to the gas chambers. A special clinic has been set up for pregnant women already here. They are having their pregnancies ended at six months.

Rosenthal has help for this mission the SS is trying to keep secret. He has taken a lover, a prisoner named Gerda Brandt, who is also mad, and sometimes uses poison on the pregnant women. Our Gerda hates it that they share the same first name. "She is a monster," Gerda tells us. Erika is plotting to run her against the electric wire.

Betty and Gerda also told us that the SS is digging mass graves. Dirt is poured over bodies still stirring. No one cares whether these people are alive or dead. Dear God, is this hell? Have we been sent to hell? I pray and pray and pray, and life, if this is life, continues to get worse when I think worse is impossible.

Today I could handle it no more. When Jakob showed his face in the barracks, he tried to tell a funny story as I was caring for a Gypsy woman name Korina who had just had her left foot amputated. I glared at Jakob and then purposely spilled a bedpan full of urine on his shiny boots as he passed by. It was stupid to do that, and I thought he was going to hit me. But he walked away and never said a word. Now he has two things to report me on, but I do not care anymore.

* * *

It is mid-April 1942, and Elisabeth, Katja, Anna, Greta, and I have been moved to Block 1. Block 6 had an outbreak of staph infection, and the SS did not want any medics contaminated. Our Block-eldest is Rosel from Vienna. She is a very kind and quiet woman. Our camp of hell is so full it seems to be ready to burst, to explode. A Block that originally held 300, now holds 600 to 900. Many have to share their bunks with someone else, and the bunks are too small in the first place. For all who are transported out, twice and triple the number arrive every day.

Chapter Seven

Hitler's birthday was two days ago. We had visits from some of his state people, like last year on the twentieth of April. Himmler was here this time. Blocks 1 and 2 were instructed to "shine and sparkle" for this visit, and Himmler was shown only those Blocks, and our clinic—orders of Suhren, Hitler's puppet.

To me, Himmler looked like the devil himself. His face shined like his boots but his smile was false. He walked like a proud rooster, clicking the boots and using his hands to make points when he spoke. It was Heil Hitler this, and Heil Hitler that. I wanted to throw up on him.

One good thing did result—new linen and cleaning materials were passed out. Our patients had new dressings and were washed, combed, and smiling, or else. The SS did not want Himmler to see the grime and gore of reality. Our Block even got meat that day. The meals since have been skimpier than usual. Rosel, Block-eldest, made sure everything looked perfect for Himmler, keeping Suhren and the SS in a good mood. Otherwise, the whole camp would have taken the punishment.

The Germans are so smart when propaganda is involved. Himmler even released some of the prisoners, making it a great occasion for Hitler's birthday. This is just phony stuff to show the German citizens what a good heart the Fuhrer has. But I am happy that some were released. They will not have to suffer anymore.

* * *

July has come and I pray tonight because if I do not, I will surely go mad, as so many here do. I made a hideous event even worse, and I have been praying to God for my error, for my helplessness. How can I be better? How can I keep from going insane?

Part of the clinic has been converted into a lab, where they are using prisoners instead of animals for experiments, just as they are doing at Bernburg. All nationalities are chosen, but mainly Polish women. A few days ago, I went to the kitchen Block to beg food for the Jews, but before I could step foot in the door, I heard screams and looked down the street. That horrible woman, SS guard Belling Bergmann, was dragging a young Polish girl into the lab. I knew the girl and recognized her immediately. She, too, recognized me and saw me watching. It was Irena, a very sweet girl of sixteen. Desperately she began waving and screaming at me, "Help, please help!" She was white as a ghost and her body was shaking violently. Again she screamed, "Oh my Lord, mercy, help. I need to go see my sick mother in Lodz. I just want to see her one more time."

God forgive me, but I could not go help Irena. She screamed again, "Oh God, Mama, Mama, please! Someone help!" I could not watch anymore and slumped onto my knees and wrung my hands. Bergmann turned around to see whom Irena was pleading to and saw me at the door to the kitchen. I got off my knees, and Bergmann yelled, "Get out of the damned kitchen door or I will kick your ass."

Without thinking, I said, "Sorry ma'am, I cannot do that. I have orders to report to the kitchen. But if you like, I can go back and say that you refused to allow me to obey them."

My stupidity caused Bergmann to march over to me and kick at my abdomen. I dodged her, but then she cracked my shin with her boot, hard enough to cause me to yelp. Then she marched back to poor Irena and really worked her over. Mercifully Irena passed out just before they got her into the lab.

I heard that the lab thought it was good she was not conscious, as it was easier to experiment on her. I was told they threw her on the table, strapped her down, and used no sanitary precaution, no disinfectant, nothing. She woke up during the operation, looked around and passed out again.

Irene, bless her, lived on for several days in terrible pain with a high temperature. Once in awhile, she came out of semi-consciousness and pleaded for her Mama. Today, they repeated the same operation over her screams of agony. This time when she lapsed into unconsciousness, she did not wake up.

Dear God, were you with Irena today? Please make sure Irena sees her Mama in heaven?

The next day, I saw Jakob as he walked by the barracks. He didn't look at me, but said, "Too bad about Irena." I started to yell at him but then I looked at his face and realized that he meant what he said; he did feel bad. Who is this man I hate so much? Have I been wrong about him? As he walked away, I heard him say in a soft voice, "I do not want to be here either." I said, "What do you mean?" He twirled around and said, "Like many others, they threatened my family. They threatened to kill my mother, and my aunt, and everyone if I did not join up. Do you think I am here of free will? We German men have no free will."

* * *

Later than night, I pray again for sanity and for hope. There are no mirrors, but I know lack of hope is in my eyes, as I see it in Elisabeth's eyes, Katja's, Anna's and Greta's. Even Gerda, who I see regularly in the street, looks as though she could break at any minute. Anna never tells a joke anymore. We all keep shriveling in size, which causes exhaustion, which causes inner panic. And we have heard nothing of the war in months and months, except that Russia is fighting for its life, not giving up.

Here the hell goes on day after day. We have more doctors now for experimentations in the lab adjacent to Revier 2. Dr. Rosenthal, his Gerda, and Dr. Herta Oberhaeuser, another she-devil, all are there. Hysteria is a daily routine in the clinic as we hear the constant screams of the victims. I do not know what we would do without Erika. She comes to us regularly to calm the frenzy. She has a way of making people feel secure that the rest of us do not possess. She tells us it is her gift, as everyone cannot go crazy. Nurse Agnes is always helpful, too, but she has become more and more dreary and groans constantly. I remember when she was young and so pretty with her auburn hair and hazel eyes.

The she-devil doctor, Oberhaeuser, makes lists of the people she wants to experiment with—the Torture List, different than the Death List only in the time it takes to die. We are told these experiments are done "to study the healing process" of our injured soldiers.

Hitler must know about all of this. The SS follow his orders to perfection. Hitler is the one who had the idea for the brass engraved skulls on the SS uniforms. How appropriate!

Doctors of all nationalities work in the clinics. They are prisoners and are treated by the SS as inferior doctors—dumb. They are, of course, better than the SS doctors, as they are compassionate and dislike Dr. Oberhaeuser and how she has stooped to the bidding of the SS. We are able to use the foreign doctors to save some of the patients who would otherwise die, and to treat a few of the Jews in Block 11, which they risk their lives to do. We see these doctors as part of God's children, and there is very little racial squabbling among the prisoners.

* * *

It is September, and several weeks ago we were asked to donate blood. They announced we would get extra food rations for the donation. We are told how honorable it is to help a wounded soldier. Most everyone is so hungry and so plenty volunteer. Once the SS found out that more and more people were donating blood, they cut down on the extra rations. Finally they were eating nothing but a little extra milksop. Now the women have been ordered to give blood and are whipped if they refuse. It is apparent in the camp that the women grow weaker and weaker because of the blood loss. Many are dying because of it.

I have been praying hard for a miracle, something that will keep us going, something to give us some cheer. Winter is here and we have received Soviet women and children. They were told they were being "rescued" from their destroyed cities and villages and would be brought to their "new home," Ravensbrück. They are in shock, many in constant hysterics. Most have no idea where their fathers or husbands are. Most only speak Russian. The children cry and cry and beg to go home. Mothers rock them and try to console them through their own tears. The few who speak German tell us that many villagers did not even know the Germans were at war with them. Many did not own radios or receive newspapers. They said that the German army appeared out of nowhere, and then weeks later, the SS, in their black uniforms, turned everything upside down. In the middle of the chaos, families were torn apart. Most mothers and children were separated. Of course, many German families are also torn apart, but this does not comfort anyone here in Ravensbrück.

The Russians wonder why Germans are prisoners in their own country's camps. We try to explain to them that being a German does not necessarily mean you agree with Hitler and his regime. I heard Elisabeth whispering to a Russian woman, "All Germans are not Nazis. I would rather be here than be part of the SS." Elisabeth, with her pretty blue eyes and beautiful blonde hair, her soft voice and soothing manner, is like an angel to so many.

Tonight I pray for the Russians. They are so terribly pathetic, and to make matters even worse, they do not have good immune systems for measles, TB, hepatitis, and contagious diseases. Many of them also have VD. Everyone who comes in sick goes straight to Auschwitz and the gas chambers.

* * *

Today is 25 November. Marschall brought over two Soviet women and three children from Revier 1. She said, "They are ready for the chamber. If it were left up to me, I would send them to the idiot Block, but Nurse Agnes said you have space for them. They have cooties and probably the plague. I do not care." After her rant, she spat on the floor and left. The Russians stared at her with disgust and distrust. They do not realize that Nurse Agnes probably saved their lives by sending them to us, even though we really do not have the space.

Jakob is one of the SS who led the Russians to us. He looked tired, and his uniform is grimy. He is a sad man. I want to speak to him, to ask him questions, but dare not risk it.

Although their clothes hung on the Russian's bodies like sacks, and they were hungry and weary from hours of work, the women showed a certain pride. The children were between ten and twelve years of age and really scared. All of their faces were broken out with what appeared to be scabies. Not too many children had been brought to us but now we hear more will be coming.

I motioned to one of the kids to come, and she did. I took her hand, and she returned my smile. "What is your name?" I asked her. She shook her head. "Is your name sweetheart?"

Shrugging her shoulders, her words were barely understandable when she said, "I do not speak German." Somehow, we managed to communicate enough to understand a few things. I could never pronounce her name, so I renamed her Andrea. I called her that because she reminds me so much of a little girl I used to know who would always ask me for chocolate. She understands and accepts the name. She is blonde and blue-eyed. She could be Elisabeth's child. We are made to understand by one of the women that she is an orphan. Her mother was shot in one of the camps, and her father is missing.

After a few days, I took to this little girl like she was the daughter I always wanted to have. Her face was not broken out like the others, but her body was. She had big, ugly, watery bumps, especially on her legs. I managed to get a little extra ointment for her. I should be ashamed. Everyone should be entitled to the same care, but with Andrea, I could not help myself.

Adults in the camp, with little to share, often take on some poor creature when they reach out their needy hand. A little motherly warmth helps them. Tonight, after I kissed Andrea goodnight, I prayed to God and thanked him. He has answered my prayer for a miracle, something to bring me cheer. After a break and some fresh air today, I sat on Andrea's bed for a while. It appears as though I am working on charts, but there are no spies here.

I am pleased that I delighted Elisabeth and Katja and all of our coworkers, especially Charlotte, our clinic-eldest since I managed to get some supplies for our empty cabinets that were down to a half a tube of ointment. It takes a lot of luck to get supplies out of "Ol' Carrot Face," the name we have given Marschall. This is because each time she throws a fit she turns fire-red. I seem to be luckier than most with sneaking, stealing, and begging supplies.

"Where in the world do you get that stuff?" Greta asked me.

"She has quick hands, like a magician," Anna laughed.

It always makes me proud when they appreciate it. I tell them "I am a lucky magician."

Andrea's skin problem cannot be identified. I know it is contagious because I have found some of the same spots on my own legs. We wish for vaccinations, rubber gloves, showers, and separate beds. These would stop a great deal of the diseases that are going around. Women who are in direct contact with the SS have these privileges so that the SS do not catch anything. Those women also get more food, probably so the SS do not have to look at ugly, bony bodies.

Andrea also has a lump that has reached the size of coin. All I can do is wrap it. Sometimes I use the liver oil ointment. We use it for everything. I try my best to take care of this little girl like a precious gift. She now knows two German words—Mutter, Mama and Schutzstaffel, SS. She shakes her head when she hears the latter.

* * *

Oh God. I have just checked Andrea over again and find that she has developed kidney bleeding. How many problems can one little orphan have? But all the children here are pathetic, most are sick, and do not have shoes or underwear. It hurts all of us to see the SS children with their warm winter clothes while our children have to stand outside with us for head count and formation wearing only thin summer rags. Because of this, many develop kidney/bladder infections, TB, and pneumonia. Many of them die.

* * *

Andrea just woke and called me Mama. It is so cute with her Russian accent. Thank you, dear God. Andrea is a gift I promise to cherish. I have been so worried the last week that I did not have time to think of Christmas. I spent every extra minute with Andrea, dreading what was announced today. All the non-German children are to be prepared for transport. That probably means the gas chamber for them. This included the three Russian children in our clinic, including Andrea. There is no love lost on the children around here. They have to work the same jobs as the adults, ten to twelve hours each day and often without food. Is it any wonder they die quicker than the grownups?

I was frantic. In the street, just at dark, I met a woman I barely knew and poured my heart out to her. Her name is Maria, and she works in the tailor shop. She is Russian but speaks German. She told me that she would love to take the children to her Block. It would be a lot easier for them because they speak the same language. I was so excited, I almost hugged her, but then she told me it was impossible. She reminded me that all of their children were being prepared for transport, and three children left behind would be highly suspicious. "We are trying to find some place to hide our own," she said.

"Oh, God," I said, "What can we do?" We both stood there studying each other's faces and thinking, trying to think of something clever to do.

Finally Maria said, "Have a little patience. I have an idea. I will be back in a half hour." With a faint bit of hope, I ran back to check on Andrea and then hurried back to the street. Maria returned on time. It was very dark by then, and I could barely see the little smile on her face.

"What have you found out?" I ask.

"We must take the kids out of the clinic now. I am a friend of some Slavic women, one from Rumania and two from Yugoslavia. They think they can hide the kids in their Block, the Gypsy Block, for a while."

I was so happy and still terrified. I asked her if the women could be trusted. She snapped at me, "These kids are my little country comrades. And I am a doctor, a pediatrician. Do you think I would hand them over to a traitor?"

I apologized and explained about the camp being full of spies, people one would never suspect. She understood and told me to hurry and get the children. No one was in the clinic except Charlotte and Katja. I told them quickly what was happening, and they helped me. In ten minutes we had the kids dressed, hurrying down the street. Luckily no one was paying any attention.

Medics are always on the run. It is customary to see us hurrying with children.

Near the Block where we were going, Maria whispered something to the children, and then told me to return to the clinic. Andrea began to cry and carry on. Maria did her best and became really stern, but it was no use. Andrea just hung onto me crying "Mama, Mama." I could have pulled my hair out. People were beginning to notice us. I could not risk everything. I told Maria to go on, and I grabbed Andrea and carried her away.

Instinctively I headed for my old Block, Block 9, and Gerda. Thankfully I caught her by herself. She was happy to see me and asked who the little angel was in my arms. I began, "Oh Gerda, I have such a problem. I do not know what to do, and I cannot think how to tell you this."

She grabbed my shoulder and said, "Well, I know you came here for a reason, and you know I always try to help, do I not?"

"Oh, Gerda. Thank goodness for you!" I told her everything. She listened and she watched me as though she was afraid I might explode. Several times she interrupted to tell me to settle down.

At last she grinned and said, "You sure have a way of getting on people's backs. You cannot help the whole camp, you know!" Then she said she would take Andrea and even talk to her using the little Russian she knew. I was so happy I could have burst and had to fight the tears so Andrea would not cry again.

Gerda said the Block now had mixed nationalities, and there are some German children there who will not be transported. Hopefully Andrea will fit in. She suggested we get rid of the "R" for Russian on her patch right away, just in case. I agreed and ripped it off. Andrea was calm then, too cold and tired to object. Still, when I told her I would see her the next day and started to leave, she grabbed me and hugged me as if it were for the last time. Gerda took her quickly into the next room. My heart was heavy but I knew it was the only way to save her, at least temporarily.

I pray tonight for Maria and Gerda, women who are compassionate and kind. And I pray for my little Andrea. Lord, please take care of my precious child, my gift of hope from you.

* * *

It is very late on December 28 and the cold wind and snow are a daily nuisance. But two good things happened today.

The first—I kept my promise and visited Andrea. I had no problems getting away for a visit—my co-workers understand. Andrea is very happy. She has settled down now and must realize that I was not getting rid of her. I promised to come to see her as often as possible. Gerda has already taught her a little English. In a sweet accent, she said, "Thank you, Mama. I love you." I had to run out before I burst into tears.

The second was something very different. Coming back from seeing Andrea, I saw an SS guard beating a prisoner on the camp road about one hundred feet away. I barely looked up since there was another SS guard, tall and heavy in weight, very close to me, watching the incident. Suddenly I heard her exclaim, "That guard is crazy, out of her mind!"

I could hardly believe my ears and thought to myself, "What's the matter with her? These things happen here constantly." When she said something bad about the guard doing the beating again, I whispered, "Then stop it!"

She turned around to look at me and said, "I mean it. I am embarrassed to be one of them." I looked at her suspiciously, wondering if she was testing me. But I had to remember that the SS place big promotional ads for these pure Aryans. They are promised the moon if they do their jobs well. Some give up their positions for jail when they realize what is involved. Others love it—the opportunity to exert control over the most educated women prisoners.

I asked her name, and she told me it was Elfriede Petzold. She had just arrived, and already she wanted to quit. I could see in her face that she meant it. Poor soul, I thought. No one quits here. I decided to take a risk and confide in her, tell her all the things that are going on. She looked surprised, and said she would help where she could. I wonder if she will, or whether she will be hardened and become mean like the other guards.

It is the last day of 1942. Elfriede barely had an opportunity to be helpful. Spies were onto her quickly because of her being critical. She traded her SS uniform for a prisoner's uniform. She was beaten and spent today here in the clinic before being transferred to the jail. Through her tears she told me, "I don't want to wear an SS uniform, and I am not clever enough to hide how much they repulse me."

I thanked God when I met Elfriede. I thought it was a good thing. Now I asked God to forgive me for encouraging her to help. I am told there are other SS here disgusted with the horror, but they do not make a fuss. They just wait to be transferred away. If compassion is shown us by any of the guards, the others make it that much worse for us.

Chapter Eight

Gerda visited me at noon on the fourth day of the new year, 1943. She was very upset. Two camp doctors were expected at her Block in the afternoon. I had to get Andrea out of there fast. But where can I hide her? I assured Gerda that I would think of something quick.

Nearly hysterical, I want to the Russian, Maria. She said, "You Germans are always in a panic. But of course I will hide her." And she did, bless her.

* * *

It is now mid-January and Jakob and his friend Reinhardt have been hanging around here the past few days. They are doing more electrical wiring, but we wonder if they are really here for that reason. Jakob has not turned me in, and today he spoke to me, asking how I was doing. I looked around to see that nobody was watching and then said, "What do you think, we have so many suffering?" He nodded, walked away, and then returned. "What do you think I think?" he said. "You only think the worst."

Later, I saw Elisabeth and Katja saying a few words to the men. I noticed that they speak Croatian with an East German slang. I remember some of it from some inmates when I was in jail. I was surprised when Jakob and Reinhardt joked and carried on like a couple of kids. Elisabeth was laughing, and that was good.

Andrea is speaking more and more English, thanks to Gerda. She says Andrea is a loving child, but very frail. I see her every day, her lump is gone, her skin improved, and the kidney infection has apparently cleared up. Gerda's love and attention has been healing.

The SS men were still here today working on the wiring. Again they had a few friendly words. It feels good to hear kind words, but difficult to know if they mean it. They could be spies. We get the feeling they have found a good job and like hanging around. They do not seem to work very hard. But it was not our business, and the whole episode is rather amusing although I must remember that these men are Nazis killers.

Tonight as I pray, I remember how it was to have real conversations with people, without fear, without whispering. That would be so nice to experience again.

* * *

It is now the last day of January 1943. The time has passed so quickly. After head count this morning, Jakob was back at the clinic, but today he was alone. All morning, he managed to be working close to me and saying little things, friendly things. I had to keep reminding myself he is SS, but he does not seem to have that hardness to him. His eyes are light brown, and they reflect a certain type of goodness, not the cold, steel look of other SS. He has aged some since I first saw him, and he is tall, thin, almost lanky, and has a reddish circular scar below his right eye. His hat over his brown hair is dirty, and his gray SS uniform is too large and very worn. It does not look as though it belongs to him.

At one point he started telling me about the war. I was on my hands and knees disinfecting a cabinet, and he just kept talking in an ordinary quiet voice, as though he were speaking of the weather. He had heard that in Warsaw there was an uprising in the ghetto and many Jews were fighting the Nazis. And he said that the German Army had been defeated at Stalingrad and also in North Africa. In my heart I was cheering, wanting to jump to my feet and run to Elisabeth and Katja and everyone who would listen. But why was he telling me this? Then he quietly told me, "Call me Jakob if you wish. I was an electrician in Heidelberg before duty called." Then he talked about missing his mother and sisters and how he worried if they were safe. Finally he asked me about my family. I got up and went to another chore, shying away, still suspicious of a man who showed kindness and gave me good news about the war. He actually sounded affectionate, as though he wanted to cheer me up, something very strange under the circumstances.

At lunch, I whispered to Elisabeth and Katja what Jakob had said about the war. It was difficult to keep them quiet. They wanted to sing it out, but it might not be true.

After lunch, Jakob cornered me again to talk, this time about how thin I am. Then he quietly pointed to the floor in the corner near where we stood. There was a small package there. Then I was really concerned. What was he up to? I assumed he wanted me to pick it up, but why did he not just say so out loud? He had been talking softly, but not in a manner that anything was a secret. I shrugged my shoulders and finally picked the package up and handed it to him. He took it, but looked a little dumbfounded. Then he went to the little bucket where we keep coal for the oven, deposited the package there, pointing at it again. After that, he casually walked out of the clinic.

I was very curious and went straight for the package. It was meat sandwiches; bread with thickly layered lunchmeat. There was also a little note that said, "You are so skinny. Eat this with a good appetite. Do not worry. I am not a traitor. I did not turn you in before. You can trust me."

I did not know what to think or do. It made my mouth water looking at food I had not seen in several years. But it could be a trap of some kind. I glanced around to make sure everyone was too busy to notice me, and then wrapped the sandwiches back up and put them in the bucket.

Tonight it is very late. I need to rest, and still I sit here, trying not to be confused by this SS man. Is it possible he is just trying to be nice to me, that he likes me? How could he like me? He does not know me. But he acts as though he does. And even if he liked me, he could not be attracted to me. I am skinny, a rack of bones. My hair is still nice, but probably too heavy for my skinny face—it takes several knots to keep it back. But oh it was so nice to think he really liked me. The way he talked, his kind words. It took me back to university life when I was carefree and learning and hoping to be a doctor. But I know better than to take chances. I must forget about it. I must pray to God to help me know if this man is dangerous. God knows, and I must rely on him.

* * *

As March has come, I have sometimes seen Jakob, as he keeps asking me to call him. I have spoken to him a few times, but carefully. Today he appeared at the clinic again, looking as though he was busy doing more wiring, but he seemed to be waiting for a chance to talk with me. When no one was looking, he came up and slipped a ragged yellow dandelion in my hand. It frightened me, and I wondered where he got it. Everyone hates the SS, and I would be looked upon as a traitor if I was friends with him. But he appears to be a kind man. God would not let me feel that he is if he is not. I believe he is a man who hates the war but does not want to be shot. By staying alive he can help others, and maybe he does. I will include Jakob in my prayers. His face and words cheer me—what a blessing, or so it seems.

* * *

Today was another nightmare. At noon break, Gerda came rushing into the clinic. She was extremely disturbed and appeared out of breath. "Hurry, Vera! You must come and get

Andrea right now! We were just told they are starting a transport. They are going from Block to Block picking people. There will be an inspection at the same time. You know what that means."

I knew. They would stick their nose in every corner and crack. "Please, Vera!" Gerda pleaded. "They could be here within the hour! When it is over, Andrea can come back, but there is no way possible to hide her until then." She hurried away before I could think of what to do or say.

Where to hide my Andrea, I asked myself. The guards were searching every Block. Oh, how that little girl pulls on my heart. The thought of her on a transport to be gassed. I dare not think of it.

Frantic, I kept pacing in a circle and pulling on my hair. Elisabeth came up and put her arm around me. She had heard Gerda, and she whispered in my ear like the angel she is, "The guards do not come to the clinic, Vera."

We decided I could hide Andrea in the clinic for a while, but we did not have any empty beds. We looked over the patients and saw one woman who was to be discharged the next day. After being released, she would receive a bed card for her Block. I talked to Charlotte. She talked to the patient. The patient was pleased to help. Charlotte discharged her.

Andrea was so thrilled to get back with me. The commotion at Block 9 had already started before Elisabeth and I took her out. She was frightened and ready to go. I hated to put her back in bed, as she has been up using her legs, but there was no other way. So back to bed she went, trusting me. I wish this were a regular hospital where patients are allowed to walk around, but that is not the case. If you can walk, you are discharged out of here.

More transports leave, but many more come in. The TB Block gets bigger and bigger, so does the typhus Block. They also have triple layers of bunks. The medics are collapsing right and left just trying to keep up. Greta has been transferred to the typhus Block to help out. She reports that it is complete hell there. How can they give decent care to someone on the top bunk? It takes an acrobat to climb up there. Everyone in the typhus Block has diarrhea and is too sick to climb down and make it to the toilets. It is a mess! The SS doctors do not even look up there. Another calculated way of destroying people—just let the women die in their bunks, haul them to the pit and throw dirt over them.

Screaming fills the camp. And there are the gunshots from the executions. The noises alone cause many to go mad. We are turned into common thieves in order to get the bare minimum of supplies. Marschall has another nickname—monster. She is, and she will surely burn in hell one day.

Now they are sending many people to work in ammunition depots. They have tables set up on the street, and one Block after another has to appear. Work leader Pflaum decides who will go, often with his boots or fists. He came from the male camp, Dachau, and loves to beat women. If he chooses one who does not want to go, he pushes her to the ground. Most want to go, anything to get away from here. They hope as long as they are needed, they will not be killed. They are told they will receive a wage for working outside the camp, but it is well known that they never see the money.

In turn, political prisoners do everything to get out of it. Making bullets to kill more people in a war we protested is a huge slap in the face. The SS is aware of our feelings and they enjoy sending us first. Interestingly, even though they hate us, they never call us the filthy names they call the foreigners. We constantly hear them yell, "Jewish swine, Russian pigs, Polish pigs." But they cannot use pigs in context with German, so they call us "Jewels." So sweet.

I do what I can to stay out of the street, hoping that I am worth more here as a medic than I would be making weapons. Tonight I pray to God that I will never have to make a bullet or a gun. Please God, let me stay here and tend the sick. Please God, keep Andrea and me together and safe.

* * *

Tonight it has turned to April and a moon peeked behind the clouds and said hello on a starry night. I spend the night in the clinic and pray for another miracle. Today they began what they are calling a complete general inspection, which is estimated to go on for days. The SS are inspecting every Block, tearing them apart, and they are to include the clinic Blocks. I am at my wits' end. Where to hide Andrea now? Gerda and Maria had their own share of problems. I brought Andrea to the clinic and hid her in the bottom of a short patient's bed, piling supplies on top of the blanket. There seemed to be nothing else to do.

The poor little darling knows she is in a bad situation. She is so tired of being moved and of hiding, but she understands it has to be. My situation is not much better. If they find her, I will be executed. She is my problem, and I have to find a better place for her to hide.

I worried all day and bit my fingernails which I do not do much. I kept watching for the SS to come to the clinic. The wait nearly drove me nuts, but they did not get this far today. But what about tomorrow? I cannot bear the thought of them finding my angel.

* * *

Two days have passed, and Andrea has not been discovered. I have hidden her in the crawl space below the Gypsy Block. I feel dead inside knowing she is shivering and cold. I have taken a great responsibility on myself, and I have to see it through. I pray for more energy, physically and emotionally.

I go as often as I can to check on her. I act as though I am picking something up as I walk by, in order to throw some food in to her. I wish I had the SS man's sandwiches now. It tears at my heart to know she is hungry. She trusts me completely and cries silently, knowing she cannot make a noise. I sometimes hear her whisper, "I love you, Mama." My heart breaks. I want to scream with the injustice of it all. If she has to stay there much longer she will catch pneumonia, and they tell us this latest inspection will go on for days.

Today I went to see the Russian pediatrician, Maria. She was very upset when I told her where Andrea was. Among them, they volunteered six blankets, some bread and butter, and a few slices of potato. They also came up with a bucket for her to use as a toilet. So much better than what she had. I have been eating half rations in order to feed her, but half of the skimpy rations I get are not enough for a child that is growing.

I decided to risk taking her out of the hole tonight for a little while. She was so glad to see me. She realizes this is not a child's game, and everyone must sacrifice to make it. Terribly shy now, she whispers when she talks, and she is very pale and thin. I took her out of the Block to get some air and stretch her bones. She was stiff from lying in that place like a little animal. But she is alive. For all the SS knows, she is in another camp or already dead. I felt awful telling her that she had to stay in the hole a little longer, but she did not complain. When I was ready to leave, she gave me a quick hug and told me how much she loved me. I could not bear the silent plea in her eyes.

* * *

As long as this inspection goes on and Andrea must remain in that hole, I am not much help here at the clinic. I cannot concentrate on the work. All I think and worry about is Andrea. Does she sleep or cry? What does she do? I pray she does not cough or sneeze too loud. I cautioned her to do that into her blankets. I also told her to try to sleep whenever possible. Time would go by faster, and she would not feel the cold and hunger as much. She must be terribly bored lying there all day with nothing to do. Today at lunch, I wanted so much to go see her, but it was too risky. The SS are still out tearing apart the Block next to the Gypsies. I had to wait until night.

It is not easy to see her even then. The searchlights go around and around, much too fast. I constantly have to stop and lay flat against the wall, not breathing. Often the guards of the security tower are drunk and fire at women without knowing if they are legal or not. The whole camp is awakened from these ordeals.

I made it to Andrea's hiding place, again in one piece. I heard her whimpering, "Cold, Mama." I told her to come out, but she did not immediately do so. Finally I pulled her out and she could hardly stand. Her legs were numb. I carried her out of the Block for some air, where she shook one leg and then another, saying. "Already, I feel better."

Then she told me she had heard noises down in her hole and felt things brushing against her. God, no, I thought. Mice, or maybe rats! She said proudly, "But I did not scream, Mama. I know those bad people might hear me if I do." She always says "bad people" when she talks about the SS. Maria has told me that the term SS shocks the children.

Elisabeth had sent half her rations with me, and together with mine, Andrea had food tonight. I made her eat it all before going back to the hole. I did not tell her about mice. When we said goodnight, she said, "I will sleep all right, Mama, and when it is dark again, I know you will come and see me." Dear God, she is a brave little girl.

I did not go to my quarters tonight. The clinic is closer to Andrea and dodging searchlights is scary.

Chapter Nine

Tonight it was late before I got to Andrea. There was one emergency after another at the clinic with doctors coming and going into the evening. By the time I started my trek past the searchlights, my legs hurt so badly that I was limping. When I neared Andrea's hole, I heard her whimpering. I pulled her out and held her trembling body in my arms. "Oh, Mama," she pleaded, "how much longer must I stay here?"

"I do not know my little angel, but you will not stay here tonight."

"Why Mama? What's wrong?" She started to cry.

"No, baby, tonight you will sleep in a warm bed. How about that?"

"Oh Mama, I love you!"

"I love you too, hon." My heart was swelling with love. "It is just for tonight, sweetheart."

"Oh Mama, that is wonderful. Just one night with you and not freezing will be nice." I wished she would not talk like that. Such gratitude for so little, and in her sweet Russian accent—it breaks my heart. She makes a bed sound like a Christmas present.

It was difficult carrying her to the clinic, past the whirling lights with my legs feeling like they would break. When we were inside, I put her in a warm gown. Her feet were icy cold. I wanted to give her a warm footbath, but it was too risky with patients sleeping nearby. I got her a hot water bottle and slipped it under the blanket. She began to glow, her cheeks taking on color, but she was still trembling. I had warm coffee for her, and when she tasted it, she looked at me with such appreciation and love in her eyes. Soon she was sleeping.

I went to the toilet to have a long cry. I know if this continues, I will have a nervous breakdown. Oh God, please help. This is torture for Andrea and for my nerves. What did this innocent child, or any of the children here, ever do to deserve such a life? They do not last long. They sleep under beds or in a corner or curled in a hallway. Why, why? Sometimes they are too weak to fight their way to the food pot after working all day and have to do without. Often they root through the kitchen trash and get potato peels out. Often they just sit in the corner and wait for death. But they are what courage is all about, and if they keep going, so must I.

I did not dare fall asleep, lest I not get Andrea back to her hiding hole in time. At three, I awakened her, wishing I did not have to, but unable to take the chance. Even those few hours had done her good, as she got right up.

When I was helping her with her clothes, she said, "Cold, Mama." I scrounged two more blankets that were dry—better than the cold damp ones she has in the hiding space. I borrowed clothes from a patient I know will be in the clinic awhile. She put the dress on over hers. I refilled her water bottle, and she drank some coffee I had heated. I did all of this hurriedly, and I do not know how. I was so exhausted, so tired and angry. Innocent child. This has to be a hideous nightmare for her. She knows we are risking her death and mine. Those brutes that would kill us are sleeping in warm beds.

As we were about to leave, she whispered, "How come you are a German? Germans are bad people."

"No, my child," I tell her. "Germans are not all bad people, just some of them. Some people all over the world are bad, and some are good. The bad people here are not just bad, but sick in the head."

"You are not sick in the head," she said as her precious face twisted at me trying to understand.

Oh dear, I wanted to laugh and cry and scream out loud. I surely am a sick German—sick at heart. "Okay, we better leave now," I told her. And off we go, back to her hiding place.

When I got back to the clinic, it was nearly time to go to work. I cursed the SS, Hitler, and every German who aided them. I even decided not to be nice to Jakob anymore. He is just one of them, one who kills or helps others kill.

* * *

A happy day has occurred, the ridiculous inspection is over, and Andrea has been out of the hole three days. She is so happy that it makes me happy. I am grateful to have coworkers and patients who do not object to my keeping her here with me. I need her as much as she needs me. The patients here know we are their allies and are grateful to be treated like human beings.

We have a homemade calendar that says it is spring, but this year it does not feel like it. Maybe we got the dates mixed up a little. There has been much snow the last few days and cold winds. The clinic is quieter now than it has been in months, a fact I mentioned to Katja, Elisabeth, and Anna. Anna laughed, reminding me it is the quiet before the inevitable storm. "The SS will think of something," she says.

Tonight I sit in the lounge until I know Andrea is sound asleep. Then I will make my way back to my Block in the snow. There is no bed for me here. I have prayed, thanking God for withholding the snow while Andrea was in the hole. I also thanked him for my dear friends who helped save her. Compared to so many, our luck has been good.

* * *

This morning walking to the clinic, the wind blew mud in our faces. It was a very cold ten-minute walk—Elisabeth, Katja, Anna, and I holding on to each other as always, our hands over our faces. It was very chilly inside the clinic, and the camp is out of heating material for the year. Many of the patients were cold, and there are no extra blankets.

Thinking about a solution, I remembered an old chair in the corner, too old and wiggly to sit on, and no tools to fix. I decide that no one would miss it, so I took off one leg, then another, and made a fire. Charlotte thought my idea was very clever and funny. But soon we heard keys rattling in the door. I took what was left of the chair and threw it under one of the beds, but too late. Nurse Agnes had arrived and saw what I was doing. I had no idea what she would say and just stood staring at her. She came over and quietly said Dr. Sonntag was on his way, and I had better get rid of the smell before he arrived. I am always grateful for Nurse Agnes.

Hurriedly I tried to stick the rest of the chair in the oven, but it would not fit. Part of it caught fire, but I could not push the remainder in. "Hurry, Katja! Water," I yelled. But when we poured the water on the fire, the smoke billowed. Elisabeth and Charlotte were opening windows, but it did not help. Agnes was hiding her face, trying not to burst out with laughter, and finally went into the next room.

There was only one thing to do that I could figure—pour a whole bottle of ammonia on the floor and scrub it. Katja stood there snickering while I sweated. That stinker. Finally the smoke was gone, the floor clean, and the smell of ammonia in the air—spring cleaning, if they asked.

Then I hurried to ask Agnes if Sonntag would be checking the patients. He would not. I breathed a sigh of relief. I would not have to hide Andrea in the broad daylight.

Katja was right. It had been the calm before the storm. Sonntag announced that in eight days we would get huge transports in from the eastern camps—Chelmo, Treblinka, Sbibor, and Belzec. He said they would be healthy women. But then we know what he considers healthy—women who come to the clinic very sick, some closer to death than life, and after a stay of only a few days, they are returned to their Blocks, and then after a few more days, back to work. They are often not capable of work, so it is off to a better camp—a gas chamber. Sonntag told us to discharge anyone who was healthy enough to work. Those who could not work would be sent on a transport with the old and sick. Our clinic was to be emptied and ready.

We knew what they were doing. They were sending us fairly healthy women to work to death and readying our clinic to keep them patched up until it was their turn for the transport. Our only comfort is that those who are transported out are on their last journey of hell. Their suffering would soon to be over.

We were able to save a few lives today, but they were much too sick to work, so they will probably be back, eventually ending up on a transport. Andrea is so sweet, lying here sleeping.

* * *

It is April 20 and Hitler's birthday already. Again Himmler was here with his buddies to do the formal check of Blocks 1 and 2, to praise Hitler and release a couple of prisoners in his honor. Thank Goodness for Rosel, who keeps our Block 1 in good shape.

At the clinic we had other problems to deal with—lice. All the Blocks are full of them, and it has spread to the clinic. Because we have discharged all our patients, Katja, Elisabeth, and I carried an endless trail of blankets to the laundry where they were to be disinfected. I had used disinfectant soap on Andrea early in the morning and taken her to Gerda for the day.

Lice spread germs like wildfire, to say nothing of the itching. The absolute worst is someone with lice who has to stand formation and head count where we are forbidden to move. The desire to scratch the lice is overwhelming. If the SS is so determined to have healthy bodies, why do they do nothing about the lice? Two or three lice combs are shared by all the Blocks, that is all. Often a comrade can be seen in the bathroom killing lice. But you kill a hundred today and tomorrow you have 200. Bodies and heads are red from bites and scratching.

Washing with regular soap does not help, and we have no shampoo. We also have no sanitary napkins, which is a real mess, particularly as many now must share beds. As a medic, I wear summer clothes all year. The lice seem to love the heavy clothing, but not the summer dresses. Yet I have not escaped the pests entirely. My hair is to my waist, even when knotted, and the lice occasionally get in it. In spite of the aggravation, I cannot bear to have it shaved. It has always been my pride, and it makes me sick to think of giving it for a blanket to be used by a soldier with a gun. Besides, shaving off a person's hair is the first way the Nazis use humiliation to break people. Some who have their hair shaved kill themselves by throwing their body at the electrically charged barbed wire. They simply cannot take it and decide that death is better.

When we retrieved the blankets, they were still full of lice, so we hauled them all back again. Anna told us we were going to have hernias from the heavy hauling. The second laundering must have been stronger because the lice were gone. We had scrubbed all the beds with pure ammonia and replaced the straw. It finally felt clean, but we had worked through our lunch hour and were weak with hunger. Charlotte retrieved some food for us, and at 3:00 we sat down to eat.

All of a sudden, Jakob and Reinhardt walked in with their electrical tools. We were embarrassed as they watched us eat our thin turnip soup from tin bowls. But we were much too hungry to stop. And I was still thinking I would rather eat the thin soup than a thick sandwich and end up in a bunker. That is where the most severe punishment is carried out. No one wants to go there, especially to the lower floor where the flogging takes place in the caning room. We hear there is a table where women are strapped down and then flogged until they are bloody while the SS watch with smiles on their faces.

We eat quickly without talking, except Anna, who asked the men kiddingly if they would like a bowl of colored water. The men did not answer, but they watched us and tried to make small talk. Mostly we pretended not to notice them. There was plenty of work waiting for us. We still had to scrub and disinfect the floors and the windows.

A commotion in the street sent us all to the door and the windows of the clinic to see what was happening. The source of the noise was about fifty meters away. The most feared man in camp, Johann Braeuning, was kicking three prisoners on the ground. One was Maria, my dear Russian friend, and two young girls who work with her in the tailor shop. I have watched so many beatings, but I could not stand there and watch my dear friend Maria, the lover of children, a pediatrician, being beaten.

I was about to scream out, when a heavy hand covered my mouth. It was Jakob. He whispered in my ear, "Braeuning will hear you and beat you too." I slowly turned around and there he stood, wiping water from his eyes, something I did not expect from this man, this SS man. I jerked away, still unsure of whether this man is friend or foe. How can I tell?

Upset, I shouted, "But Braeuning is your friend, your ally. How can you stand by and watch? You are filth just like him." Once I said this, I wish I hadn't. Jakob backed away, his face reddened.

I wanted to say something else but he shook his head for me to be quiet. So I just stared at him, glancing up and down his uniform. He knew what I was thinking, and he said, "Yes, I wear this uniform, the great SS rags, but I am not a Nazi swine."

I felt such pain for him and said, "It's okay, Mr. Jakob." He actually blushed. Then I was suddenly aware of the other medics. Thankfully they were still looking out the windows and had not seen my communication with Jakob. Even though they are my very dearest friends, they probably would not understand. The SS is despised and hated without exception. If they thought I was playing up to the Nazis, I would be shunned and worse.

had to find out about Maria. I kept looking out the window until I saw Nurse Agnes walking out of the bunker. I ran out to meet her. She had heard what happened to Maria and the two girls and had gone to the bunker to see if they could be taken to the clinic. The word was "No." While she stood shaking her head and making her groaning noises, I asked her if she knew why they were beaten.

"Oh," she replied, "it was horrible what they did." I could see the disgust in her glistening eyes as she tried to keep the tears under control. They were getting material for the tailor shop and the youngest dropped hers in the mud after she slipped in a puddle. Maria saw this and tried to help, but then the other girl slipped and fell. Braeuning was watching and decided they all did it on purpose. After he beat them, he took them to his girlfriend, head guard Binz, and she smacked them around and threw them in the bunker."

I touched Agnes' hand and then returned to the clinic. There, I repeated the story to my comrades and the SS men. The nurses sat down and put their heads in their hands. Jakob said, "These swine! The day will come for them too!" We all stared at him. Those were not words heard from an SS guard. It was hard not to feel friendship with these men despite them being SS. The other nurses have now seen what I have seen in Jakob; that he is not like the others. Still, they must wonder if he is trapping us.

Without patients, the clinic is clean and fresh, and I will stay here so I can be with Agnes. I weep for Maria, poor Maria, and the two girls. And I cannot stop thinking about the two SS men, especially Jakob. The way he looks at me, you would think I was a beauty. Surely I look like a mop stick. He must be very lonely being with comrades he hates, doing things he loathes doing. I suppose his friend Reinhardt is a blessing. How strange they still come to the clinic. Could they possibly still be doing wiring? I doubt it. Maybe it is because we are nurses. Nurses are expected to be kind to everyone, and they need kindness. Tonight I will pray for them. And I will pray for dear Maria and those two girls. God must take care of them. They are in his hands.

* * *

We are working in the other clinics, still overloaded, while we wait for the big transports to arrive. Four more days, we are told. Nurse Agnes has our medicine cabinet filled. She said for whatever reason Marschall did not protest. She even gave us calcium shots, an obvious indication of her genial mood. We will probably need the extra boost.

ndrea is eating my lunch. Anna has heard a rumor that the SS will be sending a huge transport out of the camp, but they have not prepared a list and are not telling us when or who. She talked with Greta in the typhus Block, who seems to get much information. She said that no one seems to know even where the transport is going. We are all a little anxious and uneasy about it.

Andrea looks pale, but seems to be feeling quite well. She needs fresh air. With the clinic empty, I have been leaving the windows open during the day. Oh how I wish I could be walking down a real street with her, both of us dressed in real clothes and going to lunch somewhere in a nice, friendly city. Hiding and lying is such a terrible way to grow up. She is just twelve. At least she is alive.

* * *

Today we learned that last night 800 bodies disappeared. We do not know if they were transported out or taken to the pit. They simply disappeared. I spoke with Gerda today and Rosel, both of them in shock. In the night, SS guards came in quietly, went silently from bed to bed, taped people's mouths indiscriminately, and then hauled them away. Elisabeth and Katja said they just lay in their beds with their heads covered. Anna said that at one point her blanket was lifted, but that was all. She said Greta woke and screamed, but she was also left alone. I was thankful that I had stayed with Andrea.

The camp was quiet today, and terrified. What next? The only thing we can figure out is that those big transports coming in are packed and the SS is making room the SS way. We work and worry and wonder. What next? What next?

* * *

The transports are arriving, new people from everywhere. These women look as sick as we do. Fear screams from their faces, many bald, all weak and helpless. We are overwhelmed, and Charlotte is angrier than I have ever seen her, rattling French. Some of the words I recognize as profane. At one point she walked into the lounge ready to explode. I followed her and took her by the shoulders. She waved her arms anyway. "Why do they bother to bring them here? Why not take them straight to the chimney? Save so many to suffer."

Another transport from the east is due shortly. We have all stayed at the clinic tonight, waiting. I am praying hard for all those poor souls arriving at our door.

We received eight more really sick women from the night transport. We wonder how many went to the other clinics. The camp is bursting at the seams again. Mostly with Germans, Russians, and Poles.

Among our new patients are two girls from Danzig. One an artist, and one a music student—both very friendly but obviously frightened. We do our best to let them know there are good

Germans. Elisabeth is best at this. It is impossible to look at Elisabeth and feel anything but safe.

Today I finally was able to take Andrea outside. I talked to the other patients about her growing needs, and none had any objections or seemed to feel slighted. They care for her and because she is a child, they know she needs special compensation. One of the patients said, "She needs to be healthy in case she has a life ahead of her." This was a rare exception to our policy of treating everyone equal. I was so grateful they were willing to extend this love to Andrea. Because of her confinement, she was very stiff and had difficulty walking her first few steps. But oh, she was happy to be up and about.

Because of the confusion of all the new people in the camp, it was a good day to mix without attention. We went to see Gerda who was so busy she barely had time to speak. Then we went to the Russian Block to see if there was any word on Maria. A woman pointed to a bunk in the corner. I went there and crawled to the top. There was Maria, hiding. She said they kept the girls but released her. She was afraid to go to the clinic for fear she would be transported out. Her front teeth were missing, and she had an open wound on her shoulder, possibly others I could not see. She said she would hide there until she was well enough to go back to the tailor shop. I promised to try and bring her some bandages and ointment.

Tonight I am very tired and so depressed. Today was long and hard. So many patients, so much suffering. And seeing poor Maria was terrible. A wonderful woman, she has done nothing but good, hiding in a top bunk of straw like a wounded animal. I will return to my Block to sleep.

* * *

It is May 1943, and today Jakob came around again. Earlier I had seen him talking to other SS and I wondered if he was talking about the nurses or me. I still have to wonder if he could not be a spy being nice to us with the hammer to fall later. But I want to believe in him, and today, I saw him nod and I nodded back but quickly moved away when Oltha, another woman in the barracks, saw me. Her face showed she was not quite sure what happened, and I have to hope she will not tell anyone of the nod. One word to save her skin, and I am dead.

After finishing a little early, and after Andrea was tucked in, I went out to the camp road. There was music playing over the loudspeakers. I had heard that Himmler had ordered that music be played. And there it was, making us all homesick, just as Himmler wanted.

Because there were so many people out, I was able to join with a group of Jews without notice. Johanna was with them. She is from Berlin, where she and her husband owned three businesses. They were preparing to flee to China, and had already shipped their jewels and valuables, when the Gestapo came and dragged them from their home. They were assured it was a minor problem and would be handled quickly. Very soon Johanna was shipped to Ravensbrück and her husband to Sachsenhausen.

For two years Johanna has been a prisoner in Block 11 and still cannot adjust to the reality of it. Technically she is a Jew here, the lowest of the low, but she always maintains a flair of class. Not snobbish, she is well liked—a very nice but naïve woman. She still believes their imprisonment must be a mistake. No one has ever come out point blank to tell her she is a Jew and Hitler hates Jews. She probably knows this deep down, but has been too proud to accept it. Unfortunately her lofty demeanor does not endear her to the SS. I was glad to see her tonight. I am always glad to see her. I never expected her to make it this long.

I will stay at the clinic a little longer. Andrea is having trouble sleeping. I need to pray for a while anyway. All those people tonight looking lost, listening to music that made them remember good times and wonder what happened. I will pray for all of them, and for Andrea, and for me. I need more strength than I have.

* * *

We must have more electric problems since Jakob and his friend came by to fix them. I laugh to think of all of the electric needs of the clinic and know that the two SS just want to be with the nurses. Jakob touched my shoulder as I was mopping, and I felt a little squeeze. No one saw that, I am happy to say.

But I could not help myself, and said to Jakob, “All the deaths, and you do nothing to stop it. What kind of man are you? You have no God?” His face stiffened and he started to walk away, but then he said, “I have a God like you. But he has left me behind. He hates me, I am sure.”

These words touched my heart, but Jakob walked away before I could say anything. I wanted to tell him that God loves everyone, even the worst murderers if they only repent, but I must keep the words to myself.

Later, when I went to the bathroom, there was a faded dandelion lying on the dirty sink. I grinned when I saw it although I am not sure Jakob left it for me. But I bet he did, his way of showing he cares.

We have been working so hard, on our feet so much, that my feet and legs are hurting more than usual and itching a great deal. I take cold and hot footbaths and this helps. My toes will never straighten out. They are curled inward from holding on to the sandals in the snow while they were frostbitten. They are red and blue and will always stay that way. I was lucky. Some women’s feet and legs turned white and hard as stone. Some had parts of their feet, legs, or arms amputated. It still happens every winter.

Today I asked Nurse Marschall for some Ichthyol, an ointment that stops the itching. Of course, I did not get any, and she told me I knew better than to ask. I guess I did since kindness is a stranger, missing in action.

Book II

Chapter Ten

It is May 1943. This morning Jakob cornered me behind the barracks as I was washing some soiled linen. I let him do all the talking and he told me about his hometown, Meissen. I could tell he was proud as he said the city was founded way back in the tenth century by a king on both banks of the Elbe River. "We are most famous for the porcelain," he said, "but there is beauty everywhere with the Albrechtsburg Castle, the Gothic Meissen Church, and the Meissen Frauenkirche, the Church of Our Lady. He said Meissen was called the "City of White Gold," and he remembered how his mother took him to the church and then raced off to the porcelain factory where she worked long hours. She had an interest in music composition and when he was born, she picked the name Jakob after the German writer/composer Jacob Gottfried Weber.

He told me his real name was Jakob Gottfried Kortemeyer, but he shortened it before the war in an attempt to evade serving in the German Army. The ploy did not work, and he finally enlisted like so many other young men in Meissen who knew their families would be harmed if they did not.

"My aunt really raised me," Jakob said. "She showed me everything, and I loved it when she took me for walks along the river and bought me ice cream." When I asked Jakob what happened to his father, his face turned sour and he muttered, "He left us and never came back." He said nobody liked his dad anyway since he spoke "a different kind of German," being originally from the west. I could tell Jakob did not like his father and I asked about him no more.

I kept looking over my shoulder to see if anyone was watching us talk, but I don't think they were. Jakob made it look like he was repairing part of the roof while he talked. Reinhardt came by, but Jakob shooed him away so he could keep talking. He said his older sister, Greta, was very smart, and he was kind of smart with good grades and science as his favorite subject. He laughed when he said he had been a good runner on the team and played soccer. And he said he liked to ice skate on the river and then go home where his mom would cook apple dumplings. "I miss her," he said, before telling me that she left to work in Dresden where there was bombing and that he did not know what had happened to her. He wiped his eyes and then he left kind of embarrassed. I bet I did not say five words at all. I just let him talk but I could tell me wanted me to know about him so I would not hate him and I am sure I do not even though I probably should.

Now the day is over and the only food I could arrange was two slices of dry bread with a little margarine and cheese. Not much for five people, but they still cried with happiness. I felt a little embarrassed because I had given my bread to Andrea. She is not an official patient, and does not receive any food from the kitchen. I am always scrounging food, and I just keep getting thinner and more tired.

I always thought May was the most beautiful month in the year because the flowers spruce up the countryside, but no month is beautiful in camp. We now have a camp police made up of prisoners. They run around like scared chickens stirring up trouble in order to be fed. Gerda was about to break apart today. Transports are to be made ready again, and she has to tell the ones who are going. And there will be inspections, she warned, including the clinics. She did not know how soon.

Dear God, here I go again. What to do with Andrea? Maybe the doctors picking the patients will not check them. Sometimes they do not. Agnes never asks about the patients individually, and thus didn't question Andrea being here so long. Maybe she did not want to know.

* * *

My feet are in a bucket of warm water, but I should be out trying to find a place to hide Andrea before curfew. Maybe her old home in the hole would work but I bet the rats have taken over.

On my way to the Jewish Block tonight, my hands and pockets were full—bread, medicine, and dressings. I hurried through the people listening to the music, not as aware as I should have been.

Suddenly there was head SS guard Binz blocking my way. The sight of her was enough to turn my blood cold, and I tried to move around her. She grabbed my arm and pushed me back in front of her. "What do you have in your hand?" she growled, grabbing it, seeing the two pieces of bread.

"Two pieces of bread," I said. "I have not eaten my ration from yesterday."

"What about your pockets?" she asked while poking into them. She saw the medicine, and my heart nearly stopped. As fast as I could talk, I explained the German Block had extremely sick people who could not make it to the clinic. I told her I was taking the medicine over to them. I knew we were never allowed to take supplies out of the clinic, but what could I say? No matter the reason, what I did was considered camp theft. What I wanted to do was scream in her face that the Jews were living worse than stray dogs, but my hands were shaking too much and I felt frozen.

Binz shouted at me to tell her my Block number. I thought the whole camp could hear her since she was so loud. Then she pushed me along in front of her toward my Block. Rosel, Blockeldest, turned white as a sheet when she saw us come in. Binz barked at her that I was a thief and was to report to Suhren in eight days. At least she did not beat me, not yet. Then she marched out.

Rosel held me while I cried. But I did not have time to cry much. I had to find a place for Andrea. Rosel said she heard the inspection could start tomorrow. Quickly I ran to the Russian Block. Poor Maria did not look a lot better and they had a new Block-eldest who was terribly fearful of the SS. With the inspection and roundup for the transport about to happen, Andrea would not really be safe anywhere.

Trying to think clearly, I stood outside and prayed for guidance. Then I went to see Andrea's hole under the Gypsy Block. It was much smaller than I had remembered it. I took out the blankets. They were heavy, soaked with moisture, and foul smelling. I would try to get new ones down there tomorrow.

Then I went back to the clinic to tell my comrades about Binz. Elisabeth and Katja cried and cried. Anna told me I would be okay, that I was tough. Charlotte talked in French and threw a tube across the room. When I went into the lounge and sat down, Elisabeth followed. "Vera," she said, putting her arm around me, "they did not throw you in the bunker. And you are reporting directly to Suhren, the commander, instead of the SS in charge of assigning punishment. That must mean something. Perhaps you will get off. We will all make a plea for you. We know how valuable you are to the clinic. They will see that."

"Dear Elisabeth," I said, "it is Andrea I am worried about. This inspection could happen tomorrow, and I have no place to hide her except back in the hole."

"Then she must go back in the hole. When the inspection is over, she can come out again. If you have to stay in the bunker for a while, we can take care of her." I was crying so hard I could barely hear her tell me, "Please do not cry anymore tonight, Vera. Tomorrow it will look better."

I stayed in the clinic after the others had gone. It was late, but I had to talk to Andrea. I had to get her into the hole by 4:00 a.m. Sitting on her bed, I told her she must return to the hiding hole for a few days. She looked scared but said, "I heard others say you are in trouble. What is the trouble? Is it me?" She is such a brave little girl. She did not even cry. Maybe she was too tired and could not understand when I explained the trouble.

Back in the lounge, I talked to God. Besides Andrea, the worst thing facing me was the possible end of my time as medic. It was not always the easiest job, but better than a lot of them, and I had found many friends and helped many people. But I would take any kind of punishment willingly if only little Andrea could be saved.

* * *

It is May 22, and I woke this morning in the lounge. It was 3:30 a.m. Andrea seemed okay about going under the floorboard. I managed to find extra food, fresh clothing, and three blankets that had holes in them but were clean. I did not tell her everything about my personal problems. She had enough worries on her own. I could not tell her all of the fears I had for her. Maybe they would throw me in the bunker today. Maybe no one would be there to empty her bucket, or to feed her. I did not tell her that we needed a miracle.

I was too weak to carry her and the supplies. It seemed to take forever, and the searchlights seemed much faster. Finally we made it. She crawled into the hole without crying. "You come and see me, yes?" she pleaded. I promised. All the way back to the clinic I prayed I could keep the promise. I saw Jakob standing by a bunch of rocks watching me. Had he seen Andrea? I could not tell but hoped not.

* * *

SS guards including Reinhardt were at the clinic today sorting people out to go on the transport. This means Andrea can return to the clinic tomorrow. I will work there as long as I can.

In the afternoon, we carried the lousy blankets the transport left behind to the laundry. I do everything like a puppet, always wondering why I have to report to Suhren, Hitler's handpicked Aryan blonde god. It makes me wonder if there was a spy involved in catching me. The spies report directly to Suhren, I am told. Could Jakob have made them wise to what I was doing? Would he do such a thing? Can I trust him or has he been setting a trap for me?

I am grateful few people know about Andrea. When one of the patients woke up as I brought her in, I acted as if she was just admitted. And Andrea knew how to play the game of acting sick. She had learned how to lie to stay alive. I tell myself that no matter what happens, I will stick by her. But when I am gone, who will look after her? What if I die? Many women going to jail never come back. I cannot think of that right now. I should be sleeping, but I cannot.

I still think about Jakob. I saw him today and he never mentioned our quarrel or anything about telling of his time in Meissen. He told me he had heard about my trouble. He tried to get me to smile. He has such kind eyes. Could he really be an SS officer? He said he might even be able to help me with my punishment, but I surely doubted that. He and his friend Reinhardt have been very kind, but they do not know about Andrea, and I cannot tell them. They would be shocked if they knew I had hidden a little Russian girl this long. It is better they do not know. I have to remember they are the enemy and could have me shot, and Andrea too. I also have to remember what my comrades would think of me if they ever saw me friendly with the SS. I would be labeled a traitor and collaborator.

Before Jakob left, I could not help myself and blurted out, "God loves you." He shook his head no, but maybe he will think about my words and not feel his guilt for being associated with killers. Before he left, he said, "We were one of the few Catholic families around and my mom took too me to church, but I did not understand Communion and the priest made no sense. I no longer have a god, but if I did, he would surely hate me." Then he showed me a yellow dandelion in his left hand. "I used to pick these near Heinrich's Fountain in Meissen, and by the convent and brewery house. Some people think they are weeds, but I think they are beautiful," he said. I took it quickly so no one would see. For the first time, we smiled together. I will sleep with the dandelion beside my head tonight.

* * *

Good news. Elisabeth told me they will keep Andrea at the clinic, but it is such responsibility, a constant vigil, and they are always so busy. Many things could go wrong. Tomorrow I will go see everyone I know in the camp who might possibly be able to help. Perhaps camp-eldest Betty; she has always been so helpful. Can I tell her about Andrea? Maybe I will have to.

* * *

Today, bad news. I went to see Betty. She was in her office putting things in a box. She had tears in her eyes, and her tall frame was slumped. I have never seen Betty anything but calm, tall, and straight, and it shocked me. I stared at her for a moment, and then went to her and took her hand. "What is it?" I asked her. She slumped into her chair to tell me, "I am going to Auschwitz." They had told her she is needed there to work, but she is not sure. She was angry, saying there is nothing but propaganda and lies from the SS. She believes the SS plan to exterminate all political prisoners. For a moment she had forgotten I, too, was a political prisoner. She apologized, saying she did not want to alarm me.

I decided to tell Betty about my arrest, and about Andrea. The risk could be worth it. She had many connections in camp. It was a mistake. While she talked to me, she stroked my hair, as though it might help, but I left her office feeling more depressed than ever. She said that being ordered to report to Suhren was not a good sign. I was probably set up, so there could be an example made of me by the SS. As for Andrea, she said that the children were all lost causes. The quicker they were exterminated, the less they would suffer. How could she say such things? Being sent to Auschwitz has taken all her hope away. I feel so sorry for her.

I was so frantic that I went to see Maria again and cried on her bandaged shoulder. She told me that I had to tell Andrea everything. It would not be fair to the child not to know the truth. She would go with me, in case there was a need to translate something. Poor Maria; she can still barely walk.

Andrea's eyes got big, and she turned a ghastly pale when I told her that her Mama might be going to jail. She did not throw a fit or become hysterical, which I had half expected, but tears rolled out of her blue eyes and down her beautiful face, and she grabbed on to me. I wanted to hold her and cry like a baby myself, but I needed to be strong for her and bit my lips. Maria talked to her in Russian in a soothing voice and that alarmed Andrea. She pointed to Maria's mouth, asking her questions I could not understand, obviously wondering what happened to Maria's teeth.

Finally she asked me in fearful English, "Where do you take me now? I do not want to be in that hole when you are in jail. People maybe forget me. Can I go with Maria or with Gerda, and when you come out you take me to the clinic and all is good?"

"Yes Andrea, all will be good when I get back out," I said. "You will stay with me at the clinic for three more days. I am still looking for the right place for you while I am away."

Three more days, God, just three short days before I must report for punishment. Elisabeth and Katja cannot look at me without crying. Anna keeps trying to cheer me up, but she knows it is useless. Charlotte is angry and starts talking again in French like she does when she gets excited. I love them all so much. Can I possible expect them to take on the responsibility of Andrea with all their concerns and worries and care of the sick? Oh God, I just do not know what to do. Please provide a miracle. I believe in miracles. You have shown me there are miracles. Please show me one again.

* * *

Jakob does not know of my pressure with Andrea but he tried to cheer me up today with tales about the porcelain factory in Meissen. I was so tired and worried, but I listened to him by the back door while others were working toward the front. He said the porcelain came from rich deposits of china clay called kaolin and potter's clay, and that the porcelain was painted with flowers and landscapes and animals. He said his mom's friend Alfreda painted florals and that she was a distant relative to Johann Joachim Kaendler, the most famous sculptor of large animals. "You can tell the Meissen porcelain," he said, "by the signature logo—crossed swords on tableware where there are Red Dragon patterns. I have some pieces, and after the war I want to give you some." When he said this, I burst out crying and left him standing there wondering why I was so upset. I heard him say, "I am sorry. I am sorry. I just wanted to take your mind off punishment."

Later, Charlotte called me aside. She took me into the lounge to talk with me. She said nurse Agnes had heard about my arrest. She was very sympathetic and believed that I was turned in by a spy. She also told Charlotte that she has known about Andrea for some time. She believes that could be why I was turned in, and Andrea could not stay in the clinic if I had to go to jail. It would be too risky for everyone, and Andrea would surely be found.

I was so scared and went begging to Gerda. She took me by the shoulders. "Vera, you are going to have to be calm and brave. Yes, I will try to hide Andrea as long as I can. But I have some very old and sick people in this Block, and the SS did not take all of them this time. They will be back, and probably soon." I began to cry, and Gerda put her arms around me. "Be strong, Vera. You must take care of yourself. Maybe you will get eight days jail and get out. Eight days is the usual punishment for theft."

I went back to the clinic after seeing Gerda. Andrea needed comforting—she just sits and stares out the window, probably wondering what will become of her. I told her a story about when I was in medical school, and the wonderful children the students took care of, and how brave they all were with their illnesses. I mentioned one little girl I remember who had a terrible disease but would not give up since she said God was looking after her. I can only hope it helped a little even though Andrea does not know much about my God.

Katja and Elisabeth took me in the lounge and gave me a piece of bread they had saved for me. "Vera," Katja said sternly, "you have lost way too much weight. Please eat everything you can while you are gone. We want you back here strong and in one piece."

I think and pray. I have been crying since Katja and Elisabeth talked with me. Surely they both knew I would not be allowed to return as a medic. They are just being kind and hopeful. Oh I can hope too, but I know it is just a hope.

All morning, the clinic was a madhouse, and I worked and tried not to cry. Every time I went to Andrea's bed, she took my hand and squeezed so hard it hurt. At lunch, my coworkers made sure I ate everything I was given. They gave their half-rations to Andrea.

At mid-afternoon, Jakob came to the clinic alone. He walked right into the lounge and caught me weeping. I was embarrassed. I was sure he thought I was fearful about jail, about being imprisoned for helping the Gypsies and the Jews. I fought with myself about telling him the truth, telling him about Andrea, my little angel of a child, but I could not get a word out. I was frozen. He did not say anything but continued to look at me as though he was waiting for me to talk to him—an SS guard, and I a prisoner. I dared not, but he must have seen me fighting with myself.

In a really warm tone, he said, "Please tell me, what are you feeling? Is it something besides the fear of jail? You can trust me. I will tell no one. Have I ever given you a reason not to trust me?"

No, he had not, and Lord, I just busted out in tears and told him the whole story about Andrea and everything. I knew I was out of my mind, but it was all so hopeless anyway. When I was out of words, he looked at me with a strange look on his face. I thought, "Oh God what have I done? What will he do?" A long time seemed to go by, but it was probably only a minute or so since my heart was beating so fast with fear. Then he took my hand and squeezed it, patted me on the shoulder, and said he would be back in a while. Then he was gone. I had to wonder if he was on his way to the commander. Everyone believes I was set up for the arrest. Maybe it was Jakob.

I sat down for a while. I was so dizzy. Would Jakob come back? Would he come with the SS? I was sick with worry. What had I done? What choice did I have? I prayed and prayed. Elisabeth came in the lounge and found me on my knees. She stroked my hair and left me alone. I could not tell her what I had done. She knows Jakob is not like the rest, but cooperating with the SS is considered a mortal sin. Even my friends would not understand.

Why had I been so weak? I was so nervous my stomach was churning and I threw up. Later, I tried to sleep a while but when I did, I dreamed a nightmare where Andrea and I were standing with Jakob, and Braeuning was with him. They called us out and began beating me, and Andrea was screaming and crying. Then they marched us to the wall, and the guns were cocked before I woke up sweating. Oh my, I am sure we are dead. What have I done? Why was I so stupid to have trusted an SS guard, the enemy. I must have been out of my mind to do so.

I was on my knees praying when Jakob returned. He was with Reinhardt and that put more of a lump in my throat. Now I was sure they had come to arrest me.

Too many moments went by, but then Jakob motioned for Reinhardt to wait outside the lounge. Luckily no one was around and Jakob smiled and helped me to my feet, slipping a package in my hand, whispering, "For the little Russian babe." I took it, my heart almost blowing up. Then he handed me a note and told me to read it right away, and then destroy it. "Do not worry so much for her," he said. "Things will be all right."

My eyes went to his uniform, and he said, "You forget about what I wear, you hear? I might even have one of these," he said, pointing at his heart. Tears were rolling down my face, and my nose ran embarrassingly. I nodded and asked if his friend knew. "Yes, I told him everything. Do not worry. He is a good man and can be trusted. But now go and read. I will see you later and find out what they will do with you. So long, little woman. No more tears," he said.

"God does love you," I said as he began to walk away." "Maybe so, just maybe," he said as he handed me a fresh yellow dandelion. I touched my lips and then his hand and then he was gone. I raised my hands and thanked God for the miracle.

I ran to the toilet to read the note. It was a long one.

> My friend and I will pick up your little girl tonight at the clothing chamber. I will have a small man's prison suit. We will take her to the men's camp next to Ravensbrück. There the SS has a place where they raise feeder pigs, and that is where we will hide her. We will take care of her. She will not be hungry or cold. There are little piglets that she might like. Not a wonderful place, but a safe one. We will keep her there until you have a chance to take her again. But tell her everything that is going to happen. She cannot scream when she

> sees our uniforms. Meet us at 11 p.m. Be careful and destroy the letter. So long and good luck.
> Your friend, Jakob.

I sat down on the lid and put my hand over my heart. It was beating so loud I could feel it in my ears. Was Jakob really going to help? Could it be true? Was this the miracle I asked of God? What if my comrades asked where I was going to hide Andrea? I could never tell them that I was handing her over to the SS. They would think me really insane, and maybe that was the truth. But I had to tell Gerda. She expected me to bring her Andrea tonight.

Gerda looked at me like I had smacked her. I cried and pleaded, asking her what she would have done in my place? She must have realized how much I was going through to take the help of an SS. She said sadly, "Well, all we can do is wait and see if this is real. Or whether we will all be shot at the Death Walk."

I took Andrea into the toilet to tell her what was going to happen. I sat on the lid and held her. She cried. The idea of receiving help from the SS was terrifying. But I told her she had to trust me, as she always had. She settled down. Like me, what else could she do? Then I gave her the little package from Jakob. It was a sandwich, like the one he had brought me before. I told her it was from the nice men and they were going to take care of her. Her eyes wide, she asked, "Can we eat it?"

"You can eat it, and right now," I replied.

"No, I will eat some and you will eat some," she said, her eyes shining. I did not argue. Maybe it would take away my dizziness.

Gerda and I sat and watched the clock in her little room for the Block-eldest. Andrea sat on the floor fidgeting and talking up a storm, some in Russian, some in broken English. As much as I loved her I wanted her to shut up. I kept thinking about how many things could go wrong. If Jakob was really helping me, he was taking a huge risk. If he was caught, he would be jailed or shot.

"It is l0:30," Gerda said, jumping up.

Andrea looked worried. I said, "It only takes ten minutes to the clothing chamber! Can I wait a little longer?"

Gerda answered, "Yes, but we are not taking a stroll. We have to sneak from Block to Block.

I looked at her, surprised. "What do you mean, we?"

"Well, I am going too," she said.

I was so grateful that Gerda was going with us that I had to sit for another moment to still my heart. My wonderful friend, thank you Lord for my wonderful friend Gerda.

We removed our shoes in order to walk silently. Andrea carried hers, along with some other things Gerda gave her in a small bundle made out of a shawl. I went out first to see if everything was clear. Then came Gerda with Andrea in hand. We stopped to let our eyes see in the dark and to listen. There was no sound except the monotonous machines at the tailor shop.

Slowly, first me, then Gerda with Andrea, we crept along. The searchlights were whirling, but then they stopped on something for a moment. We all held our breath. Finally they began to move again, and so did we. I looked back at Andrea. She actually smiled at me. "Little child," I thought, "you are smiling while two grown women are ready to wet our pants."

Then we saw the shadows and heard the footsteps. Two uniforms came out of the dark. Were those our SS men, or was it a trap? It was so dark we could not make them out. We stayed glued to the wall. The men came closer and closer, oh so slowly, ten meters, then five, and there they were, in front of us. "Hello, how are you?" Jakob whispered. I asked him quickly where the men's clothing was, and he put his finger over his mouth and said that the clothes were at the men's camp. Then he reached out and gave me a hug with one hand, and grabbed Andrea with the other. I whisked her cheek with a kiss, and they were gone.

Gerda and I returned the way we came. Back in her little room, we sat shaking. Finally we calmed down and Gerda said, "You know, it is dangerous to be friends with you. You even get mixed up with the SS."

I then had to go and get the blankets out of Andrea's hole. If they found the hole, the whole camp would be punished until they found out what was going on.

Andrea is gone. Please, God, keep her safe, please! And keep Jakob safe, and give him a place in heaven when it is his turn.

I know I will not sleep. I have to believe my little girl will be okay, but I feel as if I am on death row. What will happen tomorrow? I had to be strong for Andrea, and now I must be strong for myself. Maybe I will only get eight days as punishment. I will go now back to my bunk in Block 1. Lying near Elisabeth, Katja, and Anna will make me feel better.

* * *

Some time after I climbed into bed, a young prisoner who works at the office of punishment came to our Block. I was not yet asleep, but Elisabeth woke up startled. The young woman apologized for scaring us, and then told me that I would not have to report tomorrow. Everyone at the office had to go somewhere and left orders for tomorrow's calendar to be moved to the day after. She wanted to tell me so I would get some sleep tonight.

* * *

In the morning, Elisabeth and Katja made me stay in bed. They told me I was not expected at head count anyway. I did not argue. I was too tired and too scared. The second time I woke, it was nearly ten. I dressed quickly and went to the clinic where again Katja and Elisabeth had instructions. There was no way they would let me work today. Charlotte and Anna joined in the chorus. "You rest this day. You will not work."

It was strange not to work, and I sure did not need to think. I sat in the lounge until lunch. After we had eaten and washed up, I decided to beg Charlotte to let me work. I found her in a corner huddled with Anna, whispering. When I asked if everything was okay, they took me into their circle and continued to whisper. They said they did not want the patients to hear. Agnes had told them there was a big bust of several SS officers last night. No one knows who they were, at least not yet, but it is believed they were shot for treason.

My knees gave out from under me, and I sank to the floor. Charlotte and Anna helped me up, not understanding that what they had said had anything to do with why I collapsed. "You are not going to cave in now," Anna said. "You will be brave. You are representing the medics." They helped me to the lounge and sat me down with a pillow.

My head was screaming out. Had I caused Jakob and Reinhardt to be shot? What happened to Andrea?

Elisabeth came in with a wet cloth and a pot of water for my feet. "Are you going to make it, Vera?" she asked. "We are all counting on you, the bravest of us all." She gave me a faint smile, and I nodded numbly. When she had gone I cried out loud, "Oh poor baby, what have I done?" I knew that I would kill myself if something had happened to Andrea. But maybe I would never know. Oh, that would be the worst. Never knowing. I wanted to run and tell Gerda, but I could not move. I was struck dumb with a panic like I had never felt before.

After a while I took my feet from the pot and got up to stare out the window. The fresh air helped, but I was shaking so hard it was difficult to stand. What did I see? A uniform was coming toward the clinic. I sat down again quickly. Were they coming to take me away? Did they find out that I had hidden Andrea? They would shoot me too. If they had killed Andrea, I did not care what they did with me.

The lounge door opened, and there was Jakob. I just stared at him and he at me. Finally I got to my feet again. All I could do was stand there and wait to hear what he said. He did not say anything, but he reached out and pulled me into his arms. I wanted to hang onto him and sob, but why was he here? Then he pushed me away, put a note in my hand, and was gone.

I was in the toilet in a flash, ripping open the note. It began,

> I learned at the office that you have another day, and I would be able to contact you. Your little girl is okay.

I sank onto the toilet lid and wept for several minutes before I could read the rest.

> We have made her a soft bed out of straw and given her lots of blankets. We also gave her plenty of food. Reinhardt is with her now. We had to tell a male prisoner, the one who feeds the pigs, but he will keep quiet. We can trust him completely. He lost his little daughter in the camp, and he treats her like his own. Reinhardt had her clean her face and hands under a hose and gave her a comb and little mirror. There was much distraction last night, which made it easy for us. But it was sad. Two SS guards who could not take the SS slime made a break. They were captured and shot. I will ask Katja when you will be back out of the bunker, or maybe I better check myself. Your friend, Jakob.

I turned the paper over, but that was all.

I could feel my chest get lighter, and I just sat there breathing deeply. In a minute I tore the letter into pieces and flushed it. Andrea was safe. Jakob was safe. I said a prayer for my little darling and those two brave men. And I said a prayer for the two men who were shot. No one could blame them for trying to break out of the SS.

So tonight I will sleep and try to dream of angels. Tomorrow I will report.

Chapter Eleven

On the morning of May 28, my number, 2985, was called over the speakers.

I was not taken to Suhren but straight to the office of criminal sentencing. Suhren was there, waiting for seventeen of us to stand before him, seventeen of us caught by spies for aiding the Jews. First, we had to listen to a salvo of insults. Mine were not much different than the others. "You stupid rotten bitch, you thought you were smart enough to get by with stealing expensive medication for those Jewish pigs," he bellowed. "We knew you had been doing it, but we wanted to catch you red-handed. Then you lied to the SS guard, telling her the stuff was for your Block. It was for the Jewish pigs. Do not deny it. Tell me, was it for the Jewish pigs?" I choked out a "No." I was not going to say much of anything. The whole camp knew the worst thing to do was talk or get mad.

I did not know what to expect for a sentence, but it was the same for all of us—twenty-five lashes, four weeks in the bunker, and hard labor at detention for a period of time not specified. As he told us the sentence, my heart stopped.

After Suhren was through yelling at us, we were walked over to the jail. Before the jail door opened, I turned around once more to look at my clinic. "Goodbye," I said silently. Although it was a camp, it had been my home and my place of work. People had loved and respected me there. People made me feel needed and worthwhile. But someone turned me in.

The door closed behind us. I was inside now, and there I saw Jakob, standing a little aside. He was trying hard to look casual. I heard him ask the jail guard, "Mrs. Moebius, are these the prisoners who are sentenced to be here, or will they just work here?"

"No, these are all the rats who thought they were smarter than us, the ones who were caught helping the Jew pigs."

"What did they do exactly?" he asked. It was obvious Jakob was trying to find out about my sentencing."

Although we were not allowed to talk when not asked, I still answered fast. "I, for one, was sentenced for theft, because I stole some food for hungry Jews and some medication because this is denied them by headquarters. I was sentenced to twenty-five lashes, four weeks in here, and some detention afterward with hard labor. I will get a warm meal just every four days. Now you know what a jewel like me has done to be here."

I received a big kick from Moebius, and was told to shut my dirty mouth. I looked over at Jakob, his face in a knot. He could not say or do anything but lifted his head as if he bid his last farewell. I was grateful that he came. I was thankful for all he had done and risked for me. I could face anything knowing Andrea was being taken care of.

I was led to cell 10 on the top floor. It was chilly for June. They never opened the shutters, and it was dark. I had a long-sleeved sweater, and my summer prison dress under that. The cell was ten feet long and six feet wide. It had a bunk that was not let down and a table. Both were screwed to the floor and the wall. The window was so high I could not reach it, but it was shut anyway with just a crack of light coming through its side. In the corner, there was a toilet. There was also a tiny radiator, cold. The floors were bare stone.

Moments later, I saw what was stuck in the window shutter. It was a dandelion, bright and yellow. "Oh, my Jakob," I said, realizing for the first time that saying his name almost sounded like saying God, the Holy One's name. Sinking to my knees, I pressed the flower to my chest. "Thank you, Jakob," I said, "thank you."

I had to tell myself to try my best to survive this. I wished so much they had let the bed down. I walked back and forth until I became dizzy and lost complete track of time. Finally I heard a voice in the hallway, "Mrs. Moebius, is it time to get the meals?"

"No, we just have ten to eleven," she scolded.

That meant I had been there about forty-five minutes. I could have sworn it had been hours. I sat down at the table and wrapped my arms around myself to try and stay warm. I must have fallen asleep. When I came to, my upper body was lying across the table. My arms had fallen asleep, and my feet were completely numb. I crawled off the stool and onto the stone floor. I needed to rest my back against something, and the wall would have to do. And so I sat, staring at the opposite wall, shivering with cold. I was drained, completely. After all that had happened, my body was demanding to rest.

I woke to the sound of keys making a loud echo. My legs refused to move. The lights went on, and I was blinded. In a moment I saw Moebius standing there. She did not holler at me like I expected, but just said, "Sat on the floor the whole time, huh? Well it's your own fault." I did not answer. I had sworn to myself that I would not say anything unless asked. I wanted to get the whole thing behind me as fast as I could. I would not lick boots either. I had never done that and would not begin at this late date.

Moebius let my bed down. It was made of wood with some straw on it. She put a pillow and two blankets on it. On the way out she checked the cold heater, I supposed to make certain it was cold, but did not comment. I wished she had turned off the lights. I wanted to sleep. I was about to crawl in the bunk, when I heard a voice at the door. "Hey, how are you doing? I heard they put you in ten. That is one cold cell. I had better turn on your heater for a while. You dummy, see where generosity has gotten you?"

"Whoever you are you are generous yourself, turning the heater on," I said. The voice sounded vaguely familiar. I went to the door and looked through the slot. At first I did not recognize her, and then she smiled. It was Liesel. "Liesel," I gasped. "We never knew what happened to you. So you recovered after all."

"Yes, after all that snow and ice, I was glad to have a job inside, even if it is in the jail."

I felt so much better immediately. There was someone who cared. I remembered when the dog attacked her when we first arrived, and how we worked in the bitter cold. "Oh, Liesel, I am so glad you are here. And thanks for turning on the heat."

"Do not get used to it," she laughed. "After a while I have to turn it back off. Moebius checks the cells sometimes, and if she finds it on, I will be on the other side of the door again."

"Can I go to bed?" I asked.

"No, you better wait until you hear the siren. The guard might check. You can stay in bed on Sunday. I better go now." She was gone. In the distance I heard Moebius' voice, but she did not come.

It went on like this for four or five days, until I got my first warm meal. There is not much I can remember about those weeks. One went on like the next. Liesel would always turn on the heat a little, or ask me how I was doing. I tried to rest and not think of anything, particularly Andrea. There was not a thing I could do about anything. But I did think too much about the rest of my sentence. I would receive the lashes after the confinement and hard labor. I wondered which came first.

Finally one day Liesel told me the four weeks were over tomorrow. That night I did not sleep. What would happen next?

The next day around noon I was removed from my cell and taken over to detention. I had often heard this place was hell itself. I wanted the ground to open and swallow me. That did not happen. I was taken first to the office. My comrades who knew me as a medic were very sympathetic when they saw me coming in. But there was nothing they could do. "We are so sorry," one said. "We sure would like to know who told on you."

"So do I," I answered. "One day we might know. The worst thing is losing my job in the clinic where I was of some use."

I was assigned to the wing where I was glad to see Gertrude who was the room-eldest. She was a political prisoner like me. She said everyone was shocked at my arrest and that they were all still trying to find out who the snitch was. She also told me that no one knew how long I would be here. They were never told. This made me worry about Andrea again. They could not hide her forever, and thinking about her brought tears to my eyes. Gertrude thought it was about being in detention and worrying about the lashes I still had coming. She tried to comfort me. It was awkward, because I could not say anything to anyone about Andrea or trusting an SS officer.

The next morning we had work formation and were going out the door when Gertrude pulled me back. "No, I'm keeping you here for an inside job. Would that be okay with you?"

Who was I to get any preference? "No, I would get you in trouble," I told her.

"Do not worry about me," she said. "You will have a lot better recovery in here from the bunker. You are awfully skinny." Despite the kindness from Gertrude, I felt a little ashamed. The other woman at the formation looked just as bad. At least the bunker had meant a little rest for me. The other woman got a pint of watery soup and had to work for twelve hours—and hard at that. Also, I knew they were cut off on rations if they slipped just a little.

Gertrude assigned me the top bunk with two other German political prisoners, Rosemary, and Heike, both tall and fair. They had been recently released from the bunker and looked as emaciated as I surely did. Seeing my red triangle, they welcomed me.

It was three weeks before I saw real work, and Rosemary and Heike had been working two weeks already. Their SS guard for work formation was Belling Bergmann, one of the cruelest and most hated guards in camp, and she had constant punishment for them. I had seen them stand for hours in the rain or burning sun without supper. I had to join them. I was embarrassed to have dodged the work.

The next day I lined up with them for work formation. I stood on the end, fifty bodies strong. Bergmann marched us out of the camp to an area near Lake Schwedt being prepared for a building site. We were to haul dirt. All we had for that were wagons, spades, and shovels. No tractors, no heavy equipment. We dug out the dirt, loaded it on the wagons, and hauled it down to the lake and dumped it in. Bergmann snarled at us all day and cracked her whip. I kept hoping she did not recognize me from our last confrontation, when she had kicked me for watching her beat that young Polish girl.

Just as we were about to return to the detention center, I saw Jakob leaning against an old tractor a few yards away. I looked at his face and felt a sudden urge to run and grab him and tell him I loved him. How silly and stupid that would have been. As we marched away, I saw that the thumb on his left hand was pointing up. I hoped it meant little Andrea was okay.

That evening I had a terrible headache. I was not used to the sun and had no hat. I also had a terrible thirst and wanted to drink more than my allotted water, but I did not. I knew better. My comrades were not any better off. I had to just suffer. My first day outside had not been rosy except for seeing Jakob.

On my fourth working day, my headache was not any better. Neither was my thirst. A little Gypsy girl of fourteen, Wanda, had bad diarrhea. She had drunk from the lake. Bergmann, grinding and twisting her whip, watched her each time she went to the outhouse. Finally she yelled at the girl, something I could not hear, and the girl sat on the ground crying. Bergmann laughed at her, but she did not beat her.

We did not get supper that night because we were told we did not work hard enough. We were too sick to eat anyway.

My twelfth day at the detention Block was a Sunday—no work, but it was a terrible day. In the morning, Heike was caught stealing Ilga's bread. Heike stubbornly denied it, saying she had saved from the day before. She was not believed, and a big commotion started. Gertrude, room-eldest, yelled, "If you must fight, do it outside and not in here!" But that did not stop it. Two boards were broken off a bed and Heike was worked over by Ilga. Rosemary, I, and a few others tried to stop it, but Heike was badly injured, all over a piece of bread.

The whole Block had to stay in formation until midnight without supper. I stood there for hours thinking how happy it would make Hitler to have seen comrades turned to animals over hunger, hurting their own. I also prayed for Ilga's soul, and I prayed that the grueling work schedule would soon be over.

There was one day that went well. Bergmann was off, and the substitute guard was new and obviously naïve, a fact we made good use of. At noon when the sun was hottest, we asked her if we could go to camp and carry back some water. "Of course," she said and picked three women to go with her, one being me.

We marched back to the gate. After she signaled the tower, the gate was opened, and we marched to the kitchen. When we asked the staff for drinks for fifty women, they looked at us as if the sun had messed up our heads. But seeing the SS guard, they did not argue, and gave us two large pots of unsweetened tea they had already made for supper. We took the tea and marched back through the gate, feeling like royalty.

We were so happy. It was like a holy day. We worked a little better and faster than usual, just like kids—the nicer the teacher the harder they try. We hoped the guard would stay permanently. She was not particularly friendly, but she left us alone.

Jakob walked in today. He could not speak to me, but gave me thumbs up. I patted my heart, hoping he would understand I am so grateful. He has saved my little girl. He also made me laugh since there was a wilted dry dandelion stuck in his helmet. Bless him, bless him.

For several days we worked in the rain, slogging through the mud, always wet and miserable. In the early afternoon of the fourth day of rain, we heard the siren go off. Through the electric barbed wire we could see SS guards running frantically around the camp. One of them walked to the fence and yelled at Bergmann. Three women had escaped the "free Block." Immediately she called for a head count formation. Bergmann counted us five times.

For three hours, we stood in the rain. Women fought their bladders and some peed their pants, thankful that it was raining. We just stood and stood. Then suddenly there was a commotion near the gate where SS guards with dogs had three women cornered. They were crying, their clothes ragged and hanging on their skinny frames. The SS began pushing them back down the camp road. They stumbled and fell. Then they disappeared from view. We never learned what happened to them but guess the worst.

The next morning, Gertrude called eight numbers, including mine, and also Rosemary's. All of us were political prisoners. When we asked what was wrong, she told us we were to report to the clinic for a checkup. Since we were not sick, we wondered if we were being chosen for a transport.

At about nine, we marched to Revier 1. Marschall greeted us with her wicked grin. It was a strange feeling to be a patient there. Everything seemed so different. Nurse Agnes came in and smiled at me. "Vera, how nice to see you. Everyone misses you so much." I told her I missed them as well. She made her groaning noise, and her hazel eyes filled. "We worry and pray for you Vera, especially Elisabeth and Katja. I will tell them I saw you, but they will not be happy about the reason." And then she was gone, leaving me to wonder what she meant.

Then Erika came in. She walked straight up to me and gave me a big hug. Oh it felt so good. She had such a strong presence. "You are much too thin, Vera," she said. "You must learn to be more selfish about yourself." I just nodded obediently. Erika is always right. Then she said, "Today is a sad day for you, but you will make it."

I felt a knot in my stomach and hurried to say, "We are just here for a checkup, Erika."

"Oh Vera, you do not know?" I just stared at her without breathing. She said, "Dear Vera, you are here so Dr. Sonntag can see if you can take twenty-five lashes." I gasped, and she patted me on the back. "Be brave, Vera, this time for yourself. We are all counting on you." She gave me another hug and walked away.

By now the other women knew too. They were murmuring and whining. Most of us had nearly forgotten about our lashes. Deep-down wishful thinking, I supposed, that maybe the SS had forgotten too. Well, there we were, and I decided to raise my head and be proud. I advised Rosemary to do the same—we had done nothing to feel guilty about. She said, "Raise your head high and soon enough you will hear the angels singing."

Then the door to Sonntag's office opened and we were ushered in. "Put your pants down so I can take a look at your bottoms," he hollered. One after another we had to pass by him and show him our backsides. When he saw mine, he said, "Not enough to make even a bony soup." It was humiliating to be looked at and insulted by a doctor I had worked with as a medic. Then we were weighed. The scales showed seventy-nine pounds.

Then the show was over, and we were marched back to our Block. "When do we get our lashes?" I asked Rosemary. "Did you hear?"

"Yes, Tuesdays and Fridays are official beating days," she answered sarcastically. I hoped it would have been today. I wanted it to be over. But they surely want us to sweat as long as possible."

I told Gertrude why we had been ordered to the clinic. She knew. She said she did not want to have to tell us. She grabbed me by the shoulders. "You will make it. I know it is humiliating, but in your heart you know you have not committed a crime. We all know that."

Later, Jakob showed up and we talked behind the barracks where no one could see. His eyes were moist as he told me he had tried to stop the whipping but could not do so. "I am so very sorry," he said, "I have let you down." I grabbed his hand and held it tightly and told him it was not his fault, that he had given me such a gift by saving Andrea. "You are my shining light," I said. "You are a good man."

"No, I am not," he said. "No, I am not."

When I asked about Andrea, he told me she was fine, that she had adopted a little piglet as her own, calling it Vera. I could not hold back the tears, and had to wipe my eyes with my dirty sleeve. Then Reinhardt showed up and the two men left me standing alone. "I will pray for you," Jakob said, "the first time I have prayed since I was a kid."

On Friday my number was called. I prayed to be brave. I prayed that I would live. I told myself I had to live for Andrea. Eight of us were marched to the bunker where we had to wait for nearly an hour. Finally SS guards Binz, her lover, Braeuning, and Dr. Sonntag came out. "After me," Binz shouted. We followed, some crying. I proudly raised my head, telling myself I would not be humiliated.

Dr. Sonntag and Braeuning went into a room and shut the door. Binz ordered us to remove our clothes immediately, and then she went into the room. We took off our clothes, eight women, one child, shaking and whimpering and crying. Then the door opened, and Binz called the first number. It was the child's, a little Gypsy girl, thirteen, who had been caught stealing carrots. Binz pulled her inside and slammed the door behind her. First we heard nothing but a mumbling. Then there was a scream, and another and another and another.

The second number was Johan, a Jehovah's Witness. She did not move fast enough for Binz. "When an SS guard yells, you move!" she hollered. Then they took her in the room and we heard the screams again. When they threw her out, she was unconscious.

Next was Rosemary. She screamed louder than I believed anyone could, and then her screams became muffled. What were they doing in there? I was trembling so hard I could not keep my ears covered. My stomach was convulsing, trying to throw up food I did not have. When Rosemary was thrown from the room, I got on my knees beside her, just as my number was called. I was paralyzed, and Binz grabbed me around the waist, picked me up and threw me into the room.

Sonntag's white coat was a blur as I was slid onto a table, my knees on a bench. My hands and legs were tied down in seconds. I heard Binz saying, "Number 2985, twenty-five lashes for camp theft." Then she said something about counting. I had to count? I saw a hand go up. What was that? A clobber! Then I felt the pain on my kidney. The first lashed ripped at my back, followed by the second, a bolt of fire, then again the clobber on my kidneys. I heard myself screaming, "Help!" Then there was a blanket thrown over my head and the fire continued striking my back. I kept trying to scream, but knew I was being suffocated.

I remember the straps being loosened and being thrown out the door and landing on Rosemary. I remember we lay there and watched each other. I remember Rosemary muttered, "Hansi from Berlin," several times. I later learned that was the name of the woman doing the lashings, a name I would remember.

Five days later I returned to my block. Black and blue streaks lined my buttocks. I could not lie on my back, sit or stand up. Finally, I began to walk again.

Thoughts of Andrea kept me going. One evening, Jakob showed up again with thumbs up. How I miss my little girl, how I wish I could see her. But she is safer without me, and I know she knows I love her.

After Jakob left, Gertrude said, "that guard sure likes it here. Or maybe he just likes someone who lives here." I smiled. Gertrude is smart but she will never tell on me.

Chapter Twelve

It is mid-July, 1943, and ten days have passed since that black Friday. I have healed faster than my comrades and already do a little work inside. The black coloring on my body has changed into a reddish purple with some yellow.

Jakob came by to see me today. He told Gertrude he was there to check for faulty wiring. I was so happy to see him. He smiled at me, and I formed the word "Andrea" with my mouth. His face grimaced, and my heart sank. He gave me a note, and then hurried away. It read:

> Close call, but everything looks like it is okay. One of the prisoners saw the little child and told me he would turn her in unless we helped him escape. Didn't know what to do, but then he disappeared. Have not seen him and must believe he was transferred. Assume he did not tell anyone about little child since it has been two weeks. Moved little child just in case. She says to kiss you for her, but I dare not do so even though I want to. Jakob.

Imagine that, Jakob wanted to kiss me despite me looking like a ghost. It has been so long since I kissed a man, and that man was just a boy, really. A wonderful boy I met in the underground, too young but so caring. His name was Otto. He was tall with broad shoulders, brown curly hair, and a cute dimple. He said sweet things to me as we lay together for the first time, and he squeezed me so much I thought I would burst. But I loved that, and I loved him.

Otto worked for the railroad and wanted to be an engineer. I wonder what happened to him. He was supposed to be at the apartment with me in Berlin, but he never showed up and then later the SS stormed into the room and dragged me by the hair to the dungeon. I wonder what happened to all those who fought in the underground. What courageous ones they were. So many were silent, but they spoke up.

That night, I dreamed I was dancing with Jakob. It was after the war at a big hotel in Berlin. He was dressed in a black tuxedo and I wore a white flowered dress. An orchestra played a tune I like called "The Summer Waltz." We danced all night, two young people in love. Dreams are great, but they usually don't come true. Will mine? Will I one day be with Jakob? Is that meant to be?

* * *

August has come now, and Rosemary and I have been working outside again for nine days. We had seen the questioning looks of the other women at head count. They seemed to be asking how long it would be before we healed. I talked to Gertrude about it, and she said, "Nothing doing. Let them look, you stay here a while longer." But after a few more days, we went to work. Bending and stooping are difficult, but our wounds closed. It is hot, and the work hard. Bergmann is happy to see us suffer.

I feel so worn out. The heat is getting worse. It was maybe one hundred degrees today, and we worked outside like field horses without any water. "Hurry, hurry," was all we heard. More than once, I was ready to throw my tools away and just fight Bergmann when she came at me. Fortunately, an inner voice always held me back. It, and hearing so many stories of women being shot on work crews.

I think of Andrea more than ever. It has been too long. Is she still at the pig farm? Does she think I have forgotten her? I have not seen Jakob since he came by the Block. Maybe he and Reinhardt have been transferred. Maybe that prisoner told on the little one and she is dead. Oh, Lord, let me know if this is true.

* * *

My number and fourteen others were called this morning. "What now?" I wondered. Rosemary was frantic. She was sure it was the transport. Gertrude told us that we were not to work today and to report to her at noon. When she saw how nervous we all were, she told us it was a "good surprise." A good surprise seemed far-fetched, but at least we stopped fretting.

It was a great surprise. I am free! Not really free, still a prisoner, but free from detention. I cried. All of us did. The best part is that I am now back in my old Block, Block 1. My comrades were happy to see me. They hugged and kissed me and cried as much as I did. Elisabeth, Katja, Anna, and Greta all had presents of food, and Rosel had arranged it so I could have my old bunk with them. Oh how wonderful to be with my dear friends again. My job as medic is gone, of course, something hard to accept. But I had to feel optimistic. Elisabeth reminded me of something I said when we arrived at Ravensbrück. She said, "We will get out of this school alive." Maybe we will after all. There are rumors about the war. Nothing specific, except that Hitler has lost some battles.

* * *

Today, just as head count was over, a woman in a green triangle picked me for a work crew. I recognized her as Strecker, from that first winter of working in the snow. Rosel, our Block-eldest, saw her and grabbed me by the hand, shoving me. Loud, so Strecker could hear, Rosel said, "Would you wake up and stop making mistakes. I have told you which group you are to report to!" That was not true, but I knew what she was doing and kept quiet. Strecker just shrugged her shoulders and moved on. Rosel pinched my cheek. "You have worked enough. You will stay inside for a while." I felt like kissing her. Working for Strecker would be like being back in detention.

At night, I heard someone tell Gertrude farms outside the prison might be closed. Does this mean the one that Andrea is in? Oh, no, that would be it, for there is no other place to hide her. I have to hope the rumors are untrue, and I wait to hear more. Where is Jakob? Why doesn't he come by to tell me what is happening? Has he betrayed me? I wonder now about him. Maybe Andrea isn't even at the pig farm. Maybe he just whisked her away and had her shot. He is a Nazi first, and maybe I made a mistake by being a sucker. When I see him next, I will tell him how I have been a fool to believe he would help me. But, no, Oh Lord, why do I think such things? I must have faith. I must believe in him, but where is he? Why doesn't he let me know what is going on with the little child?

* * *

August is ending, Strecker was back this morning, and there was no way out. Rosel was not around at the time. Again I was given a shovel and pick. We dug a four-meter deep ditch, close to the SS headquarters. We stood to our calves in water. It could have been a lot worse if it were winter. Whenever we threw a shovel of dirt, some of it fell back and resulted in mud. The work had to be exact by the inch. It seemed to take forever. We have no idea what the ditch is for.

There is a civilian in charge. Strecker stays behind him the whole time. She is probably afraid we might start a private conversation; maybe even tell him about the camp. We do not know his name, but he does not seem interested in private talk. It is obvious that he just wants to get done here and get out of this weird place as fast as he can. It seems to bother him to have a guard behind him at all times and that women are doing this kind of work. Who is he?

Sometimes the man takes a break. Maybe to be good to us—we really do not know. When he first took a break, he said aloud, "Break time for ten minutes!" Strecker then said, "No break. Keep digging." But he told her that if we got too tired, the work might not be exact and that would mean trouble with headquarters. So she let us take breaks, but we could tell it galled her to see us rest, and she surely felt the grinning behind her back.

In the afternoon, the man asked Strecker if we could wear rubber boots. She called him Dolf and told him there were none. I knew better, and told her that there were fifteen pair in the tool shed. She gave me a dirty look and said they were being used. I knew they were not, and so did she, but I said nothing else.

* * *

I have worked at this job in September for two weeks. Tomorrow is Sunday. Maybe I can get my clothes washed and dried. Our clothes are always wet from the ditch, and whether we wash them at night or not, they do not dry, because we have to make them into a tight square bundle. And we only have one set of clothes, so we have to wear them in the evening. What is the use of getting cleaned up if we have to climb back into smelly, dirty clothes that can be washed only on Sunday?

* * *

Finally, news. Jakob came by this evening to change the light bulbs. He didn't even seem to care that it had been so long since I saw him. I gave him a bad look, and he knew I wasn't happy.

When he came close, I did not say hello. I did not even look at his face, but then he said in a soft voice, "I was sent out to round up prisoners. I could not tell you."

I waited a minute and looked around to see that no one was looking at us before I spoke to let him know of my being upset. Then I said, "Where is my baby?" He gave the thumbs up.

I knew despite my being upset, I was relieved to see him, but embarrassed by the way I looked and smelled. He smiled at me, his eyes so bright. He had something to tell me and spilled some of his tools, telling me to help him pick them up. He said there was a close call with Andrea. I stared at him and waited for him to say more, while he put his tools back in the box. He said the farm will remain open, but an SS guard sat down very near where Andrea was hidden. He was there and watched him. After several minutes, the guard left. Andrea was too smart to pop her head out.

I think Jakob told me the story so I would know he is taking good care of her. I asked him if he had any news of the war. He did and spilled more tools to tell me. He said Mussolini had fallen, and Italy was again an ally of Britain and the United States. He said the Russians were also putting up a good fight. Then he patted me on the shoulder and said, "We Germans may get lucky and lose this war."

When he left, I went into the toilet to pray all that he said was true. Tonight I pray again. Please, God, help the English and the Americans and the Russians and the Italians. Help the world get rid of Hitler. And I pray for God to watch over Andrea. Keep her smart and safe.

I also prayed to ask God to make me have more faith. I should not have doubted Jakob, but I did. I am so weak. I wish I had a Bible so I could read James. He always talks about trouble and how to handle it. I miss my Bible, the one taken from me when I was arrested. Many thought I was a Jew, but I was a Christian who loves the Lord. I saw a Bible once when new prisoners came in, but it was taken away, and I never could read it, the Lord's Word. How I need it now to keep me sane.

* * *

It rained today and my clothes did not get dry. I had hoped to go out on the street, even if it was raining, but there was an announcement on the speakers that everyone was to stay in their Blocks. We did not know the reason until noon. Someone had broken into the SS magazine and stolen groceries. As soon as it was discovered, all kinds of SS guards took off with their dogs to find the "evil" person who would steal food. We all worried, wondered, and hoped whoever it was would not be caught. There was always one who would steal vegetables or a piece of bread, but breaking into the SS magazine was new. Who could be so stupid? It had to be someone starving. They would surely be shot or beaten to death.

There was a silence throughout the camp. Everyone sat around leaning on their elbows and whispering. Elisabeth and Katja hoped that whoever it was would escape. Anna tried to be funny about it. She said that whoever did it should share with us because we would end up without dinner. Greta had nothing to say, as usual. She has become even quieter since I have returned. I wonder if she is well. I want the thief to get away with it, even if we do not get supper. Anyone who would break into the SS food supply had to be desperate.

In the evening, when we did not get supper, everyone began to noisily debate the issue, taking sides as to whether they hoped the thief would be caught or not. We were all grateful that we did not have to stand in formation hungry.

In the middle of all the debating, Rosel came in. She was laughing. "They found the thief!" she hollered. We all looked at her as if she was crazy for laughing about it. Then she told us that the dogs had not found the thief—the thief had been found by the kitchen storage chief, Kurt.

We asked where and who at the same time. "On top of the storage closet, still eating!" she laughed, "The thief was not even registered here!" She was slapping her side, whooping it up.

"Not registered?" everyone shouted. A chill went down my spine. Andrea? Now the questions were flying. "Well, if it was not a prisoner, then who was the civilian?" someone asked, "Who would be so stupid and break into the camp instead of out?"

Rosel shouted, "Would you believe it was a monkey?" We all looked dumbfounded. "Yep," she said, "A monkey. He was the SS official mascot. They discovered his empty cage and figured out the rest. They found him on the storage closet, hidden in the back corner, the bugger."

Everyone laughed, a load off our minds and hearts. A monkey. The last thing we expected. Oh, how we carried on. We pictured the SS chasing a monkey. Everyone had a funny scenario of what happened. It was difficult to know if it was that funny or if we all desperately needed something to laugh about and just took advantage of the situation. It did feel good to laugh and be silly. And it was such a relief that no one was beaten or shot.

We received supper after all. It was late, but we even got an extra slice of bread, some lunchmeat and margarine. We could hardly believe it. Could the SS possibly be embarrassed? Whatever—we did not care. All of us are so skinny.

At free hour tonight, Elisabeth, Katja, Anna, and I went over to the Russian Block to see Maria. She cried when she saw us. Of course, she had many questions, many about Andrea and some about why I looked so wet and muddy. She told us that the children of the camp were all in terrible shape. She asked us to go with her to the Gypsy Block where she said things were the worst.

Steffi, the Gypsy Block-eldest, very short with coal black hair, greeted us with a smile, but she had the look of a heartbroken woman. After the Jews, the Gypsies were the least liked by the SS. Steffi said the children in her Block have no underwear, rags for clothes, and not enough food to keep them going. Many die of starvation, even before they were hauled off on a transport to be gassed. She said they had to stand in formations and head counts, just like the adult comrades. And they worked long hours side by side with the adults, until they cannot. Most of their parents had already been killed, but she did not have the heart to give them the bad news.

When Steffi stopped wringing her hands, she said, "It all just breaks my heart, but what can I do?" We told her we would try to find a way to help.

After we returned to our Block, we sat down and put our heads together. Elisabeth came up with the idea of letters. The problem was the language. When Susie, a gal from Vienna, an artist, happened along, we incorporated her in our plot. She knew a lot of Slavic dialects. So we gathered up paper and began writing letters to the children from their parents. We decided to add the names later. Susie drew a cute picture on every letter. We had so much fun, and while we were doing it, we talked and shared experiences. Katja and Elisabeth had lots of stories from the clinic. Anna was telling one joke after another—I do not know where she heard them all. Greta helped with the letters but had nothing to say. She looked healthy, at least compared to me, but she must be terribly depressed. Without telling them where the news came from, I told them about Hitler losing some battles, and Italy being an ally of the Americans and Britain. They were so glad to hear the news, and we said a silent prayer for all those against Hitler. It was so refreshing to have moments like this, particularly after being hollered at or kicked or made fun of all day.

* * *

It keeps raining, and the water in the ditch now reaches our knees. The weather is cooler, the water colder, and after hours of it, we get the shakes. We all look so pathetic. Every time we shovel, some of the dirt falls back in our face. There is lightning crackling in the sky, and it terrifies me. I remember when one of our barns at home was hit by lightning. It burned, with all the livestock in it. It's the only time I saw my father cry.

Today there was more lightening than usual, and I was so nervous, always looking about. Suddenly there was a pair of black leather boots beside me. They belonged to our camp commander, Suhren, the Aryan god. He was dressed warmly in a raincoat. We did not know why he was there but hoped it was to give us orders to go back to our Blocks and out of the lightning. He could see we were wet and muddy in summer clothes. Instead, he told us to work harder.

After work, Jakob came by to check the wiring again. I was in my bunk, so he came back and puttered around in the corner. He gave me some sandwiches and told me to eat; he was worried about my health. He said he wanted to be sure I was around after the war so he could know me better. I did not know what to say. It is too hard to think of anything beyond the day we are in now. I wanted to ask if he had more news on the war, but Katja came, and he left.

On our free hour we took the letters we had written to the Gypsy children over to Steffi. I also gave her Jakob's sandwiches. She was so thrilled. We added the names and passed them around. Oh God, I hope you saw their faces.

Tonight I prayed hard for those little children, so innocent. Please God, can't you see they are innocent and helpless? Give them strength and courage, and please keep them fed.

* * *

Today was a very lucky day. We had all turned in our shovels and were heading back to our Block in the rain when I ran into Friedel, a political prisoner from Hessen, Germany. I had met her a few times while I was still a medic, when she and Erika both worked in the kitchen. She was good about giving me food for the Jews. Today she had a wonderful story to tell about her brother, Sepp. They had been arrested together, and he was sent to Sachsenhausen and she to Ravensbrück. She had just learned that he, too, was now here in Ravensbrück, sent to do construction. She was happy and beaming, and I was happy for her, but I was wet and muddy and terribly cold.

When she realized I was shivering, she looked me over and wanted to know what I was doing to look so bad. I told her, and she said, "How about reporting to my group to work? I am now work leader in the kitchen basement, where they keep the vegetables in storage. We work pretty hard, but inside, and the SS leave us alone. And sometimes we get extra food, and dear, it looks like you could use some food. I heard that someone turned you in. They must have starved you in jail."

I told her the detention was worse, and that I would really like to work for her, but if I did not show up, Strecker would come after me with a club. She just grabbed my arm and said, "Come on! I can fix all of that. I am a group leader now. But we have to hurry, before the clothing chamber closes. You cannot work in my group in those clothes."

We hurried and made it on time. I received a new, even-fitting dress, new shoes, and new underwear. They gave me a towel to clean myself a little before I put them on. Oh it felt so good to wear something dry. I had almost gotten used to those muddy, wet and itching rags. The comrades at supply enjoyed my happiness. "Just leave the dirty stuff here. We will have it laundered and drop it off to you." What good people they were; how blessed I was.

Friedel, satisfied with her accomplishment, told me to go to my Block. She would arrange for the rest. Friedel sure had nerve. I think she learned a lot from Erika when they worked together in the kitchen. Erika used to say to her and to me, just act the coolest possible, do not show fear and they will believe every word. I remembered her philosophy.

Back in my Block, I took a shower in cold water, but a shower. I scrubbed myself and washed my hair with soap. The clothing people had let me take the towel, which was nice, because we never had anything but moldy, dirty towels. Elisabeth and Katja raved about how good I looked. "And smell," Anna laughed. They were so happy I had been reassigned. I could not tell them about Friedel's little scheme. I had to promise her that.

As I lay here in my bunk tonight, I feel so good. How wonderful it is to be clean and looking forward to a job inside.

* * *

But now my world was about to end. Oltha, the woman who saw me nod to Jakob, told one of the nurses she knows I am a traitor. When I heard this, my whole body shook. Nobody trusts Oltha, but somehow she was standing nearby when Jakob came by my bunk and she smelled the sandwiches and watched us. My friend also told me that Oltha found parts of one of the notes he gave me in the toilet and has the notes. The only reason she hasn't turned me in is because she is waiting to go to Binz and make a deal to be released. When I heard this, I fell down on my bunk and was scared. Now everything will be exposed, including Andrea. And Jakob and I will be shot.

I was crying when Gerda walked by. I hated to burden her, but I told her about Oltha. She tried to calm me, and said something will work out, but I knew it would not. My night was spent staring at the walls and crying and wondering what to do.

While I awaited the SS coming to get me, I worked at my new job. The vegetable and potato carving was not so easy, but it was so much better than working outside in the wet and cold and lightning. Trucks arrive constantly with vegetables—potatoes and turnips, our number one food here. We also get cabbage, and sometimes carrots and onions, which have to be put in a special place because they are for the SS. Potatoes are put in a space called the peeler kitchen. Our basement is situated next to the SS kitchen and under the prison kitchen.

When the trucks come, there are about thirty women to carry in the goods. The SS drivers are always in a hurry, which means we are too, up and down the basement as fast as possible. We are glad when the loading is over. Then we have a huge mess in the basement to put away, and all the rotten vegetables to pick out. Friedel gives us regular breaks. She says it means we work longer, but it is easier with a break. We all sit and chat, all in a good mood and grateful for having Friedel as our group leader. She has the job because she gets the work done on time without trouble. She is a good woman.

I eat plenty of raw vegetables. They are not cooked, but I do not mind. Raw vegetables contain lots of vitamins. I never realized how good raw cabbage could taste. Sometimes we even get a few carrots, which are meant for the SS. Friedel knows—she eats them too. We sit chewing like a bunch of rabbits, laughing at each other for how funny we look. We also have several sacks of tapioca, but it does not taste good raw. At times, when supper is ready, we snatch some hot potatoes, which we eat as fast as we can.

Only political prisoners work in the basement. We are kind of isolated. All we see through our little windows is the peeler kitchen, the place where the trucks are unloaded, and part of the jail. We can hear the screams every Tuesday and Friday when the lashings are scheduled. I cover my ears. I was there.

We are not always through working when everyone else is. At suppertime, we go back to our Blocks, but afterward we frequently have to return to the basement to unload a truck while our comrades are doing free hour. It would be nice to have fresh air, but I appreciate having vegetables to eat and not having an SS guard looking over my shoulder, cracking her whip.

I am so thankful for my good fortune in getting this job. I feel healthier already. I will pray tonight for all those whom I love and am grateful to. And I will pray for Andrea and Jakob. And for Oltha, who keeps looking at me as I wonder what she is going to do.

When Jakob walked by, I motioned him to a safe place. I told him about Oltha and how sorry I am, and his face got red. He is a brave man, but I know he is worried. He told me that he will do something and gave my shoulder a tug before he left.

Chapter Thirteen

It is later in September 1943. Tonight, on my way back to my Block a woman stopped me that I did not know. She was a political prisoner and said she worked at the sewers. She introduced herself as Mavis. I wondered why she had stopped me and was so friendly. She said a few casual things, and then out of the blue added, "I am supposed to tell you that your adopted daughter is well, but her so-called godfather wondered if you could manage for a change of clothing. Also stockings?"

I knew the color left my face, and my knees went weak. I did not answer. She smiled and said, "Do not worry, I will never tell." Then she told me how she knew. One day the workers needed a special tool at the sewers. They knew it was available at the pig farm next to them. She went to the farm for the tool, and Jakob was there. He gave them the tool without any hesitation and was very friendly. After that, she went often to the pig farm because the sewer work needed to borrow more tools and Jakob made it easy. But each time he engaged her in conversation with lots of questions, as though she was being interrogated. After he felt he could trust her, he told her about a little Russian girl who was hidden by two SS guards. She was not sure what to say but finally told him that it was nice of the SS guards to do such a kind thing. A few days later, he told her he was the SS guard hiding the child, and he could use some help. She ended the story by saying, "So, here I am."

I shook at the news and began to weep. I thanked her and hurried to my Block to pray. Oh God, thank you! Now I can know more of my little Andrea. And that Jakob! What a caring man he is, still risking his life to help. Maybe in some ways Andrea was sent along to transform him, to let him see the light. If so, God surely had a hand in this.

More good news occurred, or bad, I guess. Oltha is nowhere around. I wonder where she is, but when I asked Gerda, she shook her head and walked away. I do hope nothing bad happened to her, but I am happy she could not squeal on me. Later, Gerda knew I wanted to know and all she said was, "Auschwitz." How this happened, I do not know, but I believe either Gerda or Jakob answered my prayers. Now I will pray even harder for Oltha; that she may be safe at Auschwitz.

* * *

Today after work, I went to the clothing chamber. I remembered how wonderful they were and decided to ask them for some clothes for children. They looked at me like I was asking too much, and I started to leave, but one of the women called me back. She was from the Russian Block, and knew the desperate problem of the children. She said she could give me a few things, but only once. I was so happy. Hopefully I will see Mavis soon and pass them to Andrea.

Tonight on our free hour, Elisabeth, Katja, and I went to Block 9 I did not want to see anyone. when I was filthy and muddy. Elisabeth had passed the word that I was out of detention and would come as soon as possible. She was so happy to see us she cried; all of us did. She said I was a beautiful sight, and then added that I was way too thin. I told her I was gaining now that I was working around the vegetables. She made me show her my scars. I did in the washroom, where I was also able to tell her about Andrea. She began to cry again, either because of the scars, or maybe with happiness that Andrea was doing okay.

* * *

Our working days are mostly the same, but today it was different. About noon we were told to take potatoes to the SS kitchen next door. Friedel and I did and noticed eight male prisoners and two SS guards. We rarely see any male prisoners and probably stared a bit at how bad they looked in their prison cloth, but we could not have looked much better.

We were barely back to the basement when the two SS guards brought the prisoners down. This seemed very strange. One of the SS guards spoke quietly to Friedel. She then told us that the men would be with us for the next four weeks. They were surveyors, and the basement was to be enlarged. One of the men had been an architect in civilian life. "I was told to tell you that while they are here there will be no private conversation between any of us, and particularly none with the men," she said. Friedel was grinning, but I knew it was an order straight from the SS.

Friedel was pleased because she was sure that through the prisoners she could stay in touch with her brother, one of the 300 male prisoners from Sachsenhausen here to do construction. The prisoners' markings were the same as ours, so we could tell they were a mixed group. Despite our orders, we did start to talk to each other after a while. Before the day was over, we knew that the man from Czechoslovakia was Benno, a captain from Prague, and a German, Werner, was from Breslau. We also found out that the men's relationship with the SS was much better than the women's. We found that strange, as women were supposed to be kinder and more feminine. We told them the SS women here treated us like animals.

The men told us about some of the other camps and things about the war. Some of the construction prisoners had been working in different places and heard a lot of news. They told us that at Auschwitz there was a doctor called the "Angel of Death." His name was Josef Mengele, an SS doctor. He is young, they added, and possessed with a passion to please Hitler. He carries on savage medical experiments, including injecting dye into prisoners' eyes to see if he can change the color. I asked them to stop talking about it. I did not want to hear anymore.

About the war, they confirmed that Hitler had lost a lot of ground, and that the Americans and Brits were gaining strength. That was news we all wanted to hear. This gave us hope.

After work, Mavis was waiting. I got the clothes from under my straw and gave them to her. She said that Andrea sent a big hug and a kiss to her mama, and Jakob wanted to know how I was. He had heard I had a new job. I was so thrilled to hear news directly from Andrea. But I do miss seeing Jakob.

* * *

The male prisoners were back today to work on enlarging the basement. The SS came in occasionally to check on them, but never stayed more than a minute. Friedel received a note from her brother, Sepp, which brought tears to her eyes. He is a communist, and the SS here in Ravensbrück would call him a red pig if they knew. We have learned here at the camp not to have any prejudice. To me, communists are much better than those murderers out there called the SS. At camp, a good heart counts, not what nationality and conviction. No prisoner is better than the next. It was sad that Sepp and Friedel could not see each other, but at least they were close and could now stay in touch.

* * *

Today, October 5 or 6, Werner, the German prisoner from Breslau, passed me a little note. I was shocked. It was kind of a love letter, my first ever. I had been raised very strict and had not had much experience with men. It was a bit exciting, but it made me uncomfortable, although I felt like a silly schoolgirl just thinking that a man cared for me. I did not know what to think so

I did nothing about it. Wonder what Jakob would think? Would he fight for me? How silly to think of such things.

After work tonight, I met Mavis. She had such happy stories to pass along from Jakob. Andrea loved her new clothes and sent many kisses. She wanted to know when she could see her mama. She sent me a little stone that hung from a piece of leather made with the help of her godfather. Mavis said Jakob said Andrea was in good health, but her hair was a terrible mess. She no longer had a comb. I told Mavis I would find one and pass it to her.

* * *

Today Werner came to me with a request. He wanted me to write a letter to his mother in Breslau. He said he had no paper, pencil, envelope or any place to write. If I would write it for him, he could have it mailed out by one of "his" SS men. Paper and pencil were not a problem, but where would I get an envelope? Friedel told me I might get one from one of the Block-eldests. Sometimes they had plain envelopes. She said I should say that I want to write a field letter. Some of the prisoners had brothers, sons or fathers in the fields as soldiers. Sometimes this was allowed.

Friedel was right, Rosel had an envelope. She warned me to be careful. Written letters could get me put back in jail, or worse. I hated hearing that. I really did not want to write the letter for Werner, but how could I refuse? He wanted to let his mother know he was alive. I was so sympathetic to that. Maybe I should try to contact my father. No, if I had not gotten him in trouble already, I surely would with a letter.

* * *

Tonight I saw Jakob on the street. He passed by me and gave me a signal to go to my Block. I did, and soon he was there with his electrical tools. He told me that Andrea was very good. She always asks about me. Her hair is much better with the comb I sent. He said she kissed it several times. He told me all of this while he was under a bunk looking as though he was wiring something in a corner. I just stood nearby listening. When he came out from under the bunk, he was not wearing his hat. It was the first time I had seen him without it. He looked very handsome, and I must have stared too long. He looked around, and when he saw no one, he grabbed me and kissed me like Otto used to do. I could not believe he was doing it even when he was doing it. I wanted to kiss him back, but I just stood there frozen like a chunk of ice. If we had been caught, oh God, it would have been curtains for me, being close with the SS. And Jakob would surely have been shot. It really scared me.

Now I think I wished I had kissed him back, or at least let him know that I felt something very deep for him. He has been so kind, and I am very grateful.

Also today I wrote the letter for Werner. I did not feel comfortable about it at all. Everything here has to be so secret and difficult. To make it more uncomfortable, a prisoner we call "Rosey" looked over my shoulder while I was writing and wanted to know where it was going to.

"It is a field letter," I said.

"To a woman?" she asked.

"All right," I snapped at her, "so I write to a woman!"

"How do you think you can get that out?" she asked.

I told her not to be so nosy and finished the letter quickly. Later, I passed it to Werner. It felt like it was burning my hands.

* * *

Now it is November and winter is here. Work goes on more or less the same each day. The construction men are gone. It was interesting to have them to talk to. They gave us hope about the war, and information we did not normally get. I felt sorry for them with their shabby uniforms and dirty hands. How lonely they seemed. Men do not do well without women to nurture them. At least we women have each other. Men seem to suffer alone. As much as I enjoyed their company, I was glad when they were gone. They made me nervous with their small talk and constant flirting. It was risky to have them around, knowing the SS would have loved to catch us communicating like regular people. I still pray for them, and I honor them. They, too, have refused the evil Hitler doctrine.

Occasionally I see Jakob. That always makes me feel good and scared at the same time. Such a risk he takes hiding Andrea. He continues to send me messages through Mavis when he can't talk to me. It is a blessing to have this kind of communication with her. Poor child, she has to live with the pigs in a pile of hay.

Chapter Fourteen

1944 is here. Seveal days ago I was released from jail. Sixty-one days of horror. On December 3, 1943, my number was called out at head count. I was told to report to Johann Braeuning. I was terrified. Before I left, I wrote a note to Elisabeth and asked Rosel to give it to her.

I was trembling in front of Braeuning. He was yelling, "Which SS man took your letter out of the camp?"

"What are you talking about?" I could hardly believe what he was saying.

"You wrote a letter for a prisoner, Werner, and gave it to an SS. I want to know his name, and I want to know right now!" He was in a rage. My fears had been substantiated. I should never have written that letter. And I had no idea who the SS man was who took the letter. Werner did not tell me, and he obviously did not tell Braeuning either.

"I do not know what you mean. Really, I do not!" I pleaded.

He said he would give me time to think about it in the bunker. And I did think about it. I was paralyzed with fear. What if one of the spies had seen me with Jakob? Was he suspected of taking out the letter? He did not know of it, of course, and was completely innocent. Oh God, had I somehow implicated Jakob? Was he also in the bunker?

It was winter-cold, and there was no heat. The lights were never turned on. My bed was not down, and I received no food. In the night they would come get me, drag me to Braeuning's office, and he would start with the same questions, much more concerned about who the SS man was than the letter. On the fifth day, close to unconsciousness, I knew the end was near, and I was about to die. With all the strength I had left, I rolled over onto my knees and prayed through tears for God's mercy. I had been foolish to write the letter, but I knew God did not think it a sin.

I had almost given up, when the door was opened. I could not get up, and I could barely see. There were black boots in front of me. My eyes finally made it to the top of the uniform. It was Commander Suhren. There was someone with him. He introduced himself as a Swedish officer of the International Red Cross. I managed to state my name. He said he also needed my number. It took me a minute to remember it. Then he asked why I was there. I told him the accusations but admitted nothing. Then Suhren asked me how I felt in a voice that did not seem like Suhren. He sounded friendly. It was the wrong thing for him to ask, because I found a little strength and told him exactly how I felt. "I have had no bed, food, air, or heat for the last five days. I am so sick that I will die soon." It took all I had to say those words because then I fainted.

The next thing I remember, Liesel was in my cell and it was warm. The heat was on, my bed was down, and Liesel had a tray of food like I had not seen in years. It was food the SS were fed—meat, vegetables, potatoes, bread, butter, margarine, a thick slice of lunchmeat and a big hunk of cheese. There was also a big pot of good coffee with sugar. Liesel helped me get up to the table and balance on the stool then whispered she would return. The door was shut, and I stared at my meal. I was about to die of starvation, and I was nearly too weak to eat. I knew if I ate too quickly, I would be sick. I picked slowly.

After a while, Liesel came back. Quietly she told me that Commander Suhren had given her personal instructions to bring me the food. He had also asked her who ordered that I go without food or heat or lights or bed. She told him it was SS guard Moebius, and her order came from Braeuning. Liesel said that Suhren was really upset. He did not appreciate being made a fool of and a barbarian in front of the Red Cross officer. The Red Cross was very popular because of the war, she said. This was something I did not know. She said although they were civilians, they mainly handled military affairs.

For three days I had heat, the lights were on, the bed was down, and I was allowed to lie down when I wanted. All I could think of was Jakob and Andrea. If a spy had seen Jakob with me, he would be suspected of taking out the letter he knew nothing about, and then Andrea might be found. Please God, I prayed, please make it not so.

The food, rest, and heat did not last long. I was called out of bed at 11:30 at night for another Braeuning interrogation. He asked me the same old question, "Who was the SS man?" I gave the same old answer. Every time I said I did not know, he slapped my face. He threatened me with Auschwitz. "You know what that could mean?" he screamed. Blood ran from my nose into my mouth. I was terrified at the word Auschwitz, but I continued to deny everything. "Get the hell out of here," were his last words, and I was back in my cell, praying that Jakob was not receiving the same treatment and interrogation.

It was Christmas before he brought me to him again. He was smiling. "I will let you out of the bunker to go back to your comrades," he said very fatherly. "Wouldn't it be nice to spend Christmas with them?" I was staring at a Christmas tree with lit candles in the corner of his office. Wow, how ironic, a Christmas tree, the symbol of love and peace in an SS office. I nodded, continuing to stare at the tree. That tree made as much sense as me believing in Braeuning's friendly face. And then I saw Jakob looking at me through the window. Our eyes met, and he looked so sad. But he was free, not in a bunker! My worries were unfounded. I was so grateful, I almost did not hear Braeuning say, "Well that can be arranged, as soon as you tell me who the SS man was." I knew he was going to say that.

"I am sorry, sir, I do not know."

I was already in the hallway, when I heard him shout, "Merry Christmas, you stubborn bitch!" Reinhardt was near the door. He passed by me and gave me a thumbs up. I felt better, so much better. I knew Andrea was safe, and Jakob and Reinhardt too.

It was about 11:00 in the morning when I was next picked up to see Braeuning. He had on the nasty and victorious grin he is famous for. "I have a little surprise for you, or let us say a late Christmas gift." He waved an envelope under my nose with my handwriting on it. My pulse hammered in my temples. He enjoyed it so much. "You thought you had outsmarted me. But no one outsmarts Braeuning. Now for the last time, who was the SS man who took this letter out of the camp?"

He had the letter, so I told him I had written it for Werner, for his mother, but on God's name, I had no idea who had taken it out. He stared at me like the devil himself, but I could tell he believed me.

That day I was transferred once more to detention. Moebius took over. She told me that my twenty-five lashes were coming. I cried, but was then surprised and happy to see Erika. She is now the Block-eldest of detention. She gave me a big hug and a very sad smile.

I have been here now for several days. I have a card for inside work. I have a terrible kidney infection. One side always hurts, the side where I was clobbered during the last lashings. Gertrude is still here as room-eldest. She told me, "I am not exactly glad that you are here, but it's better you are with me than somewhere else."

Then Gertrude told me something so shocking I thought I might faint and had to sit down and put my head to my feet. They found out who the spy was that turned me in for taking food and medicine to the Jews. It was Greta. I just could not believe it. Greta, a political prisoner, a medic, spying for the SS. Gertrude said she admitted it and asked for forgiveness. The SS had promised to free her for any information she brought them. As I thought back, I had often wondered why she was so quiet, so withdrawn. Guilt, I supposed. I wonder how many others were beaten, lashed, and jailed because of Greta.

But then Gertrude told me the horrid part. When word got out about Greta, some of the women ran her into the wire surrounding the camp. As she hung there, they threw dirt on her. Dear God, what a terrible end for Greta. It made me think about what might happen to me if I were caught with Jakob. I must be particularly careful with that very kind and generous man.

I asked Gertrude if it was known who turned me in this last time, for writing the letter. She said it was believed to be someone in the basement kitchen, but no one knew whom it was. I suppose I knew. Considering what they did to Greta, I think I will keep it to myself.

And it was a stupid thing to do, writing that letter. I am embarrassed to be back in detention. Helping out Jews was a different story. It was a crime in the name of humanity. But what is done is done, and I have to live with it, if I am allowed to live.

Our only hope is that the Russians are apparently coming closer. We know this because there are often alerts when the planes fly over Fürstenberg. All the lights have to be turned off in the camp. Some whisper that it could be Americans. We do not know. Whoever is in those planes, will they bomb the camp? Is that why we have to turn off the lights?

* * *

I have worked outside now for a couple of weeks. Every morning we are hauled to the port, about eighty women. Daily transport ships come with shingles and coal. With boxes and wheelbarrows, we unload the coal and take it about a hundred meters. It is hard work. Ton after ton of coal. It seems to never end.

The shingles are harder to handle than the coal because of the rough edges. A line of women is formed about 100 meters long, and we throw the shingles one to another. The last two women stack them. It looks easy, but without gloves, our hands bleed. Again, comrades are whipped and kicked when their fingers get so cold and numb they cannot hang onto the shingles. If they stop to blow on their hands, they wish they had not.

Sometimes two boats come at once and have to be unloaded at the same time. We always have to hurry.

Erika became more and more upset about our treatment, our bleeding hands, and that night she went into action. She could always arrange for the most impossible things and she did it again. In one hour she had bandage strips and iodine. Soothingly, she nursed all eighty of us. We were so grateful, so happy she was our Block-eldest. She was still very upset. She did not think the bandages would help that much, but we assured her they would.

The next night we found thirty pairs of mittens. Some had holes in them but that was okay. Erika must have used every trick up her sleeve to get them. She told us that we had to share, rotating them daily. We did just what she said. None were selfish.

Yesterday my number was called at head count. Again, we were on the way to the clinic for a checkup. It was Tuesday. Would they do the check-up and the lashing in one day? Such punishment for a letter, but that was how they saw it. It was my day to be lashed and beaten. I wondered if my kidneys could take it. Nurse Agnes wondered too. When she gave me a pat on the shoulder, she told me I was walking crookedly. I just nodded. I wanted to scream and tell her that at least I was walking, and soon I would not be walking. Is there no one who cares enough to stop what I have to go through for writing a letter for a friend to his mother?

Standing in front of the bunker waiting for Sonntag and Binz, two SS guards suddenly approached. They were dragging a prisoner. It was Friedel! No, not Friedel! Could she be in trouble for my letter? As we were marched to the beating room, she told me. They had been working late in the basement kitchen last night. Everyone was exhausted from unloading trucks. There had been a report of a plane, but it did not materialize. Friedel saw an opportunity to give her crew a rest and turned off the lights anyway, thinking the SS would not know the difference. A guard found out and reported it today. They charged Friedel with sabotage and brought her straight to the bunker.

Friedel was first in line for the beating. She screamed louder than any woman I have ever heard scream before.

Again Binz told me to count, and again the horrible pain of the clobber, followed by the lashes. At one point Sonntag grabbed my wrist to check my pulse. He said, “Keep going!” That’s when I lost consciousness.

They must have had a hard time carrying me up to the top bunk. I was surely a lifeless bag. Finally I passed out again.

Good news though—Jakob came by today with his electrical tools to check on me. The barracks were nearly empty, except for those of us recovering. I hated his pathetic look when he saw me. I must have looked like a very bad ghost. There were tears in his eyes. When he could, he gave me some bad news. Andrea had to be moved. The place where she had been hiding in the straw was cleared. While he was telling me this, I started trembling. My vision blurred. Quickly he told me he had worked it out and not to worry. He said that he had to tell others at the pig farm about her, but it would be okay. How could I not worry? Too many people know about Andrea. But what can I do except pray and trust God to care for her? I do pray, with all my strength. But I have so little strength. It’s been a week since my beating, and my skin has closed again. The rest of my back is swollen and black and blue. I have terrible cramps from what is left of my kidney.

At noon, Gertrude and Erika gave me the news of my dear friend and comrade, Friedel. She is dead. I will pray tonight for her soul. She was a good woman who always tried her best to help others. I wonder if her brother, Sepp, knows. Or maybe he, too, is dead.

* * *

It is already March, and last night was a torture for me. Erika had told me that if I did not get better soon she would take me to the infirmary. I told her it would be useless. They would not treat me. But Erika was not sure of that, and knowing Erika, she might convince them. She had been rather prominent in her civilian life—a deputy mayor and a state delegate. So those uneducated SS guards sometimes felt rather stupid talking to her when she gave them one of her sophisticated speeches. Somehow, she had a way of looking at them that caused them to shut up. No one knows exactly what it is with her, but whatever it is, we are so glad we have her on our side. I think even the SS are glad Erika is here. With just a few quiet words she can handle almost every situation when the SS cannot.

Erika just told me that if I am not better in two more hours, I am going to the infirmary. When I complained again that they would not treat me, she exclaimed, "Yes they will!" I admired her confidence, wishing I had some of it. I knew if she took me to the infirmary I would listen to a bunch of insults, but if I must go, at least she will be with me.

* * *

The result was awful. I had typhus. I was not taken back to the detention Block, but to the typhus Block—an isolated Block for typhus patients only. It was overflowing. I had never seen anything like it. I had not realized there were so many who had caught this disease. It must have been an outbreak. There were over 1,000 women with typhus and more patients each day.

Later, someone brought me some turnip soup. “Good night,” she said and left. After drinking the soup, I was too tired to sit, and finally lay down on top of the blanket.

After the whole ordeal, I was only skin over bones. My fingers had blisters and itched badly. I could only hope I did not also have scabies. But I did. Two days after my release from the typhus Block, I was transferred to the scabies Block.

Now, once again I am back at the detention Block. Through my ordeal, I had little strength to worry about Andrea, and when I did, I became noticeably sicker. So I tried to leave it to God to worry. Now I am worrying constantly. Is she all right? Has someone squealed on her and has she been shot? I hope God is protecting her from the vultures. Little Andrea needs me.

Just as I was thinking about Andrea, Jakob came by. He always seems to know where I am. It was wonderful to see him, but I looked around nervously to see if anyone was there. I did not see anyone, but still I worried. So many spies are around. When he gave me a big smile, I relaxed a bit, and smiled back. He gave a thumbs-up. I breathed a big sigh, and he came closer with a drooping dandelion for me in a porcelain vase like the one his mom used to make.

“When this is over, I want to see you and learn about you,” he said. I watched his eyes as he said this. They were so caring and sincere, I had to smile again and tell him that I would love to know him better as well. He looked pleased, and I had to reach out and touch his hand. He held onto it, squeezing, until I pulled it away, whispering something he may or may not have heard, “My little Andrea angel, saved by the enemy, also an angel.” At least so far, I said to myself. A strange miracle, but maybe miracles are all strange.

* * *

It has been three days since I returned to the penalty Block, three days since I have seen Jakob. This morning I was ordered to report to Dr. Sonntag's office for a kidney check. I hated to have to go to him, the person who participated in damaging my kidney. He obviously enjoys the embarrassment of women having to expose themselves in front of him naked, skin and bone. I remembered Erika telling me not to care. There was nothing I could do anyway.

He told me what I knew. I was healed from typhus, the scabies were gone, and my buttocks and back were healed. I should drink lots of water for the kidney infection. He knew that I knew it was not an infection. It was the pain of living with a crushed kidney. I could still hear him in the lashing room telling them, "Go ahead!" The man could not possibly be human. The only thing he said that I did not know is that I weighed seventy-two pounds.

On the way back to penalty Block, I ran into Elisabeth and Katja. It was like a vision, a mirage. I could hardly believe that I was seeing my dear friends after such a long time. The both hugged me at the same time, hanging on. Oh God, it felt good to have their arms around me, but I could feel how small I was in their grasp. They carried on about how they missed me, but I could see the worry in their eyes. I suppose I do look a fright.

Elisabeth said they had kept up with me through Gerda and her connections. They started to tell me about Greta, but I shook my head. I did not want to hear it again. Katja was asking me about how bad it had been in the bunker, when an SS rounded the corner. We dashed in different directions. I was glad I did not have to tell them about the horrors of where I had been all this time.

Tonight I thank God for letting me see Elisabeth and Katja. Knowing they are alive is a blessing to my heart. Feeling their warm hugs was like having a wonderful meal.

* * *

Today at head count, Mavis happened by. She whispered to me that Andrea sent her love, and that she had been moved to another pig stall.

That thought stayed with me all day. Andrea, an angel of a child, living, hiding to stay alive. Sometimes when I cannot shake off a thought, and it continues to plague me like a bloody scab, I wonder if I am losing my mind. Some of it is because I am so weak and still unable to use my muscles. I receive mild shocks twice a week for my circulation. The SS seems more cautious about health lately. Polio is the latest disease people have here.

I also learned something I had missed all that time I was in the Bunker and sick with typhus. Heinrick Himmler had ordered brothels built at the men's camps. He said the men would work better after having some fun. For a stay of twenty minutes, the lady was to be paid two Reichsmark. Our SS gentlemen, including Mr. Himmler, had turned into pimps.

But it did not stop there. The SS decided to have that privilege for themselves as well. And more women, not just prostitutes, were hired for that kind of job. They were brought before Dr. Sonntag and high SS officers to parade naked. Those who were picked were fed, so they would not look so bony. They were bathed, scrubbed with a good smelling tincture, and even treated with a sun lamp to get a tan. They were given nice silken underwear, perfumes, and jewels, all taken from newly arriving prisoners. Some women thought it might be worth it, because of that little bit of kindness and special treatment, and particularly because they were promised to be released after a few months work. There were plenty of volunteers. They should have known better. Many had come back to the camp with VD. That meant an automatic assignment to a transport.

* * *

Today again at head count, I saw Mavis. There was no chance for a quick whisper—just a thumbs up. This made me think of my dream last night, my dream of Andrea. We were walking in a field near my home outside Berlin and all at once, my pony Champ was there. I helped Andrea up and she rode him around in a circle with her hair flowing in the wind. She was so happy, and then a group of silly schoolgirls joined us and we began to celebrate her birthday.

Jakob was there and he had the chocolate cake, and the girls danced and played and laughed and teased each other. All the while I stood watching as Jakob, dressed in a smart-looking bright red shirt and black trousers held my hand. "Light the candles," I told him and he did and then Andrea blew them out as the girls squealed in delight. Right before I woke up, I was wiping chocolate from Andrea's mouth and holding her tight against me. This morning, I smile every time I think of the dream. I must take care of myself and get through all this so such a dream may be possible.

* * *

It is Thursday now and several prisoners were called out this morning at head count. My number was among them. *What now*? I had to wonder. Some women had been discharged for Hitler's birthday in April. Maybe more were to be discharged—at least that was the hopeful thoughts of some. I was not so optimistic. But maybe I would be discharged back to my old Block. That would be so nice. But I did not care as long as it was good news.

Erika knew how nervous I was, but she could not help me. When head count was almost over, someone from the camp police told us that the numbers called were to report to the camp office the next day, together with our belongings. A defining day is ahead, and I fear the worst, but my faith is strong and I am determined to live so one day I can help Andrea ride Champ, wherever he may be.

Chapter Fifteen

It is June and eighteen days later. When I reported to the camp office, I was not released, but put back in jail. I was accused of taking carrots and smoking by a snitch who was lying, but it probably bought her extra food. I cannot think again about the pain of jail. All of the details are the same—nothing new to say, except my body is older and more tired than it was. The only saving grace was talking to my God, and also one day when the tray of food had a dandelion stuck under the tin plate. How Jakob managed that I do not know, but certainly the flower, or weed as some may call it, is the true symbol of our love. For hours I held it in my hand and thought of better days when the war is over and I am free. What a wonderful word that is, and I said it over and over and over again. Yes, one day I will be free.

I am too excited about tomorrow to recall all those horrid yesterdays because I will be released from detention tomorrow. I do not know where I am going, but hope it is back with Rosel, Elisabeth, and Katja, or perhaps Gerda.

One great piece of news. I overheard one of the SS say, "Hitler is losing. The Americans and Brits are winning. The war will be over soon." Could that be true? Oh God, make it be true. Tonight I pray my release from detention means my life will be easier. I need so to see my little Andrea. Maybe that will also be possible, somehow.

* * *

Today I reported to the camp office. There were five other women there, three Gypsies, and two Jews. We waited for about half an hour not knowing what to do. Then Edith walked in, the new Block-eldest from the Gypsy Block, with about a hundred Gypsies. All were there with bundles like me. A few minutes later the Block-eldest from 11 joined us, with about the same amount of Jews. What was going on? I had no idea.

Suddenly Dr. Sonntag was there, followed by Commander Suhren. SS head guard Binz came clomping up in her big boots, followed by Braeuning. The worst people I could imagine, besides Hitler, all together to meet two hundred Jews and Gypsies, mostly young girls and children, and one German. I was shivering, wondering what was happening.

Braeuning saw me, and gave me a grin like the devil he is. He was probably thinking how skinny and unhealthy I looked, and how proud he was that he had made me that way. I tried to stop shivering and act as though everything was going my way, like Erika had shown me. What happened would happen anyway, I told myself. But what was happening? They just stood there whispering among themselves.

Then Binz yelled out to all of us, "Everyone follows me to the bath!" The bath! The bath! I was screaming inside. That would mean we were going to die, either here, or in a gas camp. Dear God, could this really be the end of me? Will I never see the outside? Never see my family? Or Andrea? Or Jakob? Oh no God, you wouldn't let this happen to me, would you?

At the bathhouse, Binz said, "You all will take a shower because tomorrow you will be transported to another camp!" She hurried away, leaving us to talk among ourselves. Next to me was a young Gypsy girl I did not know. I asked the dreaded question. "Do you know what camp we are going to?"

"You do not know?" The girl smiled and then said, "Good news. We are going to Auschwitz." I started to say something to let her know of our certain death, but why should I break her good mood. Obviously, she did not know of the horror we faced.

My heart turned over. I knew then it was the end. That is why Braeuning gave me his devilish grin. He was the one who made sure I was picked, the only German among the Gypsies and Jews. Had he not punished me enough? My mind felt like it would explode. What could I do? Run away? Maybe I could get away from the bathhouse and hide somewhere. Maybe I could hide in Andrea's old hideout. Someone would give me some food, surely. I did have enough friends. But I was the only German, handpicked by Braeuning. I would be obviously missed. The dogs would find me quickly, and the whole camp would suffer. Would the gas chamber be better than the dogs?

I took my shower with my mind swirling. Then Binz was back. Now what? She told us all to sit down on the ground and wait. So we sat, clean, waiting for the inevitable. A seventeen-year-old Gypsy sat down next to me. She was smiling too, like the woman who had told me we were going to Auschwitz. I asked her why she was happy. She spoke German well enough for me to understand her.

"Not too long ago" she began, "the whole Gypsy Block had to step out on the road. Braeuning, Binz, and two doctors were there and asked us if we wanted to go to Auschwitz. They said none of the rumors were true. We were all going to be saved, and best of all, if we would agree to a minor operation, we would all get to see our female relatives.

"What kind of operation?" I asked.

"Oh, it is nothing special," she said. "Just a little thing. We do not need an anesthetic; there is no pain involved. It is called sterilization. I do not know what it means, but it cannot be bad if there is no pain. Most all of our families are at Auschwitz, and after the operations, we will all be discharged together. God has answered our prayers!"

I sat staring at her in disbelief, and she went on. "Some were afraid they would not be able to go because we had to sign papers, and many cannot write, especially our young girls. But luckily all they had to do was make a cross and someone else signed as a witness. It was wonderful! I cannot wait to see my little sister, Lydia. It has been so long."

I could not say a word. Most of us had heard the rumors of experimental surgeries at Auschwitz. Or maybe they would be sterilized and let go. Perhaps they had run out of space for the living as well as the dead. And if Hitler was losing the war, he would want as many Jews and Gypsies sterilized as possible. Even after the war they would not be able to bear children. What did that mean for me? Would I be sterilized? No, Braeuning probably sent me along on this load to Auschwitz to be gassed. Or maybe we were not really headed for Auschwitz. Maybe we would be taken to the woods and shot. The SS lies are all we know, just lies and lies and lies. I just wanted it to be over. I had lived too long already. It seemed Braeuning agreed.

As I sat waiting, I wondered if Jakob knew of my fate. I had not seen him and knew I might not before I left. And Andrea, how would he tell her I had left her? She was just a little girl and would not understand.

At noon, Binz came back and marched us to the building that used to be Block 6. It is now called Sky Command, a place to hold prisoners for transport. We were given rations for our trip to Auschwitz and then locked in. We each have a half loaf of bread, forty grams of margarine, and two small cheeses. Binz said we would get warm meals and plenty to drink on the way. I remember those promises on my last train ride. I knew many would starve before we arrived in Auschwitz. Or maybe they planned to shoot us en route.

I wandered back and forth, from one locked window to the next. If I broke a window, it would be noisy and discovered immediately since the building was surely surrounded by SS. I feel like a caged animal, and I was. Oh God, I cannot pray anymore. You have abandoned me, God. This is how it feels to know I am going to die.

* * *

It is Sunday morning. The siren lets us know it is time for head count, but not for us. Our heads have already been counted. We have all slept on the dirty floor. The two toilets are running over. When will they come for us? Today we are going to Auschwitz, or at least starting a journey there. Good-bye Ravensbrück, good-bye all of my friends. Maybe I will see you all in heaven.

I know that I will never see Andrea or Jakob again.

* * *

I am not dead yet but only because I am German, and because I am a medic. This became clear when one of the SS at Auschwitz, a tall, stern man with a hooked nose and fiery eyes, asked me my nationality and what I did at Ravensbrück. When I told him, he yelled out, "Medic!" and I was escorted to another SS while the others were marched off in the opposite direction. He said, "Work here is piling over our heads. Do you know anything about sterilization? Well, it does not matter. They will teach you that in no time."

And that was that. I was assigned to a political Block for prisoners with special assignments. The only good thing about it was that I did not die. It has been several days, and my mind still has not cleared from the torturous ride, the hectic arrival, and the filth of this place. But they let me keep my shabby life. They let me live to help sterilize innocent young girls. My heart is all I own.

The work I am doing here is so hideous, so filthy, so depressing, that I may lose my mind any minute. People do, just lose their minds completely. Many women begin screaming and pulling out their hair. It is not a problem for the SS. They simply haul them off to be gassed. All I have to remind me of a will to live is a small crumpled up piece of paper with Jakob's handwriting on it. Just before I boarded the train, Mavis pushed her way to me and hugged me and kissed me on the cheek and put the note in my hand. I did not dare open my fingers until much later and then read the note

> My dear Vera, do not fret. Andrea and I love you and I will take care of her. After the war, we will all be together. Just keep thinking of the dandelions, and every time you see one, think of me. You know I love you, and I will find you wherever you are. Jakob.

The trip, as I had expected, had been a nightmare. Women shoved around and too many to fit in the train car. We only had one bucket for all of us, and none of the guards cared. Outside before I left I had seen a jasmine bush, thick with its luscious greenery and beautiful blooms. A beautiful bush it was, innocent of its surroundings.

I sat on the floor in the corner and fell asleep. When I woke up a little Gypsy girl with red marks on her cheeks and light green eyes was looking at me. Her name was Wilhelmine and she moved closer. Shyly, she asked, "Can I sit with you, please?"

"Oh, please do," I said, putting my arm around her, looking at the innocence of her twelve-year-old face, remembering Andrea. "It is going to be a long trip, Wilhelmine. You will need to be brave." I said it, but I hated those words. I had heard them over and over and had said them over and over. Why, God? Why did we have to ask little children to be brave when they should not be here?

Even with my bony bottom bouncing on the floor, the monotony of the train ride soon had me asleep again. Wilhelmine's head was in my lap, both of us leaning against two other sleeping women who were leaning on others. I do not know how long I slept, but I woke suddenly when the train stopped. Everyone did. We heard a lot of commotion outside, loud voices. It sounded as though we were at a station. And then the door opened, and there were lots of sighs from the fresh air. Someone said that we would probably be fed now. Two soldiers were passing by and I heard one say, "How long will the train be here at Potsdam?" So that is where we were, Potsdam. Then some station employees began hooking another box car on behind us, probably more military equipment.

After a very long time, the train made another sharp stop, causing everyone to topple over. We could see all the signs out the windows. We were in Berlin, still in Germany with much longer to ride, and without any idea if, or when, we would get to eat or drink. Being in Berlin made me think of the old days, of Otto my boyfriend, my love. Where was he? I hoped he was okay.

We caught a breath of air again, as the guards left the car and slammed the door down. The women began to grumble among themselves. I consoled myself with the idea that the longer the ride, the longer it was before I died. I would never have believed I would prefer what was happening over death. I was so miserable and had been so miserable for such a long time. But I always thought my death would happen only when God ordained it so. He had saved me many times already. Perhaps he would do it again. And then one day my daughter or son would say to me, "I am so glad you held on, Mama, or I would not have been born." But now I am convinced that if we do not starve to death before we make it to Auschwitz, we will die soon after. And even if I live, children are probably out of the question. My body has been ruined.

I still had some rations and took out a slice of bread. Wilhelmine, watching me, took a tiny bite of what I had left. I knew she was starving but still sensible, despite her age. My heart broke seeing this poor, poor child. She had never hurt a soul and was imprisoned just because she was "different," because of her ethnicity. She could not pick the country to be born in or her parents, and probably loved them and was proud of them. I wondered if she knew what sterilization was. All she could think about was seeing her sister again. I left her with that hope. She would find out soon enough, and everything would be easier for her until she knew the truth.

Hour after hour we rode. The floor got harder, and sensation began to leave our bodies. Finally, I had had enough. Grabbing the little child, I squeezed through some women and made my way to the guards. The two saw me and knew I wanted to say something. They looked at me kind of funny, as though they were wondering how I would have the nerve to talk with them in their pretty blonde curls and well-tailored uniforms—privileged dolls.

"Ma'am," I began, "we are two hundred women. Our bucket is full and running over. Also, we were promised warm meals and plenty to drink. Our rations are long gone. We were told that you two ladies would take care of us, and that we would not suffer anything, as long as you were in charge.

The guard I had heard called Bormann snapped at me, "Who said we had to take care of your little problems?" I did not give her a chance to insult me and continued. "Commander Suhren had told me that I should keep things together, and whenever the need would arise, to report this to you. You are guard Bormann, if I am not mistaken?" I had only just heard her name, and the commander had not told me a darn thing. I was lying and went on with it. "Commander Suhren said that guard Bormann will arrange for meals and sufficient drinks and all the other necessities."

She wanted to know my name and number and I told her. "You are the only German here, aren't you?" she said as I noticed a small scar beneath her left eye.

"Yes, to make sure they are taken care of as Commander Suhren instructed me to do," I replied. "Here to help you in any way."

Bormann did not say anymore except, "Sit down!" I made my way back to where I had been, hoping my big mouth was worth something. Some of the women thanked me for speaking up.

Now we all waited for the next stop to see what would happen. It wasn't too long. When two SS men opened the door, Bormann talked with them. Two Gypsies were called to empty the bucket. The SS wrinkled their nose when they went by. It made me happy they smelled what we had to endure. After the women came back with the empty bucket, our guards left.

In a while, Bormann came back with an SS man. I was waiting. She said to me, "This station does not have much, but we have some fresh coffee."

"That's better than nothing, ma'am," I said.

"Well, why don't you come down with someone else and go to the kitchen."

I told my little girl I would be back, grabbed another woman, and we followed Bormann to the big restaurant belonging to the station. The woman working there said that she only had two pots of coffee. It was such a letdown—one pot held only ten liters, not nearly enough for 200 women.

Bormann looked a little embarrassed and said, "Well, we will take that for now. Do you have a few cups? I will bring them right back."

A small chaos broke out when we showed up with that little bit of coffee. Everyone wanted some. I did not take any, and many others did not get any either and were really angry. Bormann saw this and said, "I saw a water pump. If you are that thirsty, perhaps water will do."

We went several times to fill the coffee pots with water. Everyone had enough to drink, but still, they all were disappointed. We had hoped for food. So I tried again. "Ma'am, is there any way you could make a phone call to our next station? Maybe they could arrange for some rations ahead of time. We have many children here, and they are much harder to convince to keep quiet. I am sure Commander Suhren would be pleased with all that you are doing."

That really made Bormann mad. She hissed at me, "Let this be my problem. You do not need to tell me what to do. Who do you think I am?" I wanted to say what I thought she was but swallowed it. Then she jumped down into the arms of a huge SS man, and the huge door slammed shut.

I hoped I had not messed things up. We waited and waited, hoping something good would happen. Finally the blonde dolls returned, each with a lantern in their hand, which they put next to their straw bales. SS men helped them up, the door shut, and the train took off. We had been given water. I hoped it kept some alive.

The train stopped often after that, but we received food only one time, at Krakau. We were there for eight hours. They gave us lots of white beans. We ate like a bunch of wolves and were even given second helpings. Some people got sick, but I was careful when I fed my little Gypsy girl. She smiled and smiled. Maybe after the war she could meet Andrea and become friends.

It was the dead of night when we reached Auschwitz. We had been on that train two weeks and three days. There was not a train station, just a bunch of tracks on an open field. As we fell out of the car, they began sorting us out—Jews and Gypsies, young, old, healthy, sick, most unable to walk. Little Wilhelmine came about three steps toward me saying, "Now I get to see my sister. I am so glad!" And then the SS pulled her away. This is when I was asked if I was a medic.

That first short night in my new Block was strange. Strangest of all, sometime in the night, I woke to see a woman standing over me in a long silken gown and robe. I pretended not to see her and kept thinking it must have been a dream. I did not go back to sleep again. The rest of the night I prayed and thought about Andrea and Jakob so far away.

The next morning, the Block-eldest, Yvette received me. She was from Luxembourg. The first thing she did was hand me a bundle of civilian clothing. She said, "Prisoners in the special assignment Block are allowed to wear civilian clothes. We have many to choose from."

I looked at the bundle of glittery things and felt queasy, saying, "I can't work in those."

Somewhat relieved, she smiled. "I'm glad. Lots of folks fight over garments like this. I can understand they are tired of their old rags, but it looks grotesque seeing them running around in formals or working in them. I wanted to find out about your attitude. Now we will find something decent. Why not look like a woman for a change?"

"I guess so," I said. I had almost forgotten what it would feel like to wear a pretty dress. She brought me a black dress with a little white collar and jacket. It looked really nice, except for the white cross sewn on the back. I asked Yvette, "Where did this come from?"

"You will not wear it if I tell you," she replied.

I knew then that it came from a dead Jew here at Auschwitz, just like all the other clothes. I did not want anything to do with it. "Just give me a fresh prison dress," I said.

"You sure are a tough customer," she laughed.

"Why are you wearing a prison dress then?" I asked.

"For the same reason," she said. "If you wear civilian clothes and fall out of favor with one of the guards, they will make you wear warm winter clothes in summer or a dancer's robe to work in."

We talked for a few minutes more and I learned that all the civilian clothes were marked with a cross on the back—a dark one for light clothes, and a white one for dark clothes. This was for security in case of a break out. Yvette said that some of the other camps were doing the same thing because the prison clothes had run out. She also told me that the most beautiful clothes, furs, and jewels were worn by the SS women. Sometimes the Jews who were not yet dead recognized their belongings.

Yvette was nice but in a hurry and left me to get settled. It was difficult to know if my nausea was from the long trip or what I had just learned.

That first day, I did a lot of reminiscing. I felt so far from those I loved and so lonely. I lay on my bunk and tried to tell myself that I had done the best I could; that it was not my fault for being sent here. Helping the Jews could have been avoided, but I would have not felt human ignoring their pleas. I was so naïve—a child when they arrested me. Now I was so old. Maybe God had a purpose for me here.

Of course, I wonder if Andrea and Jakob are alive. I feel like I am a million miles away from them, and I wonder and wonder. Will they be saved? Will I ever see them again?

Book III

Chapter Sixteen

It is August 1944, and I am terribly lonely and depressed. I lie here in my bunk at night, dreaming of being back at Ravensbrück, where I was beaten and lashed again and again, starved in jail, suffered with typhus and scabies, and worked my hands bloody. But my heart is there because my friends are there. I miss Erika so much and Gertrude and Rosel and Elisabeth and Katja and Gerda and Mavis. I feel lonely and forsaken, and ashamed that I feel this way. "Be tougher," I tell myself. To die would be to let them win. No, I will not let that happen.

Today, I met Lilo, an old comrade from Ravensbrück. I did not know her well. She had worked at Sky Command. She is a member of the Auschwitz camp police that is made up of prisoners. Twenty-four years old, she is a tiny woman with a sunny smile and good-natured. She told me, "The tough ones make it through here, and the scared and the shy ones might as well be dead. You have to choose which way it is going to be."

When I asked her to define *tough*, she smiled. "Well, do not show fear. Act like no one can bother you, and if so, you can take care of it. As soon as you show any weakness, they step all over you, and you end up doing the hard labor. I know it is a poor way to earn respect, but that is the way it is. I had to learn it the hard way." Lilo must know. She has been here for two years. And she is camp police and therefore allowed to go wherever she desires. Compared to her, I am locked up.

Lilo helped me get assigned to cleaning up the clinic. I tried to do my job and not think about how terrible the conditions were. The woman in charge reminded me of Marschall at Ravensbrück, at least by her looks and stature. She wore the red triangle, like me, but seemed more SS than prisoner.

My only friends here are Lilo and Yvette. They are very different from each other. Yvette is such a fragile thing, and Lilo more of a tomboy. But they are both honest and understanding. Two friends are better than none.

This morning at about ten, SS officer Hoffman came with about twenty-five Gypsy kids from twelve to twenty years old. Everyone knew why they were there. Hoffman seldom comes himself. Usually he sends the kids with someone else. Somehow he had seemed rather friendly for an SS, almost sorry he was participating. But Lilo told me he was an evil man and to stay away from him. She is the only one I can talk to and let my feelings be known, which I did today after work. Later, she walked over and brought me some flowers. "Here is something to cheer you up. I know what a tender person you are."

The flowers were short-stemmed clovers, no big thing normally, but here at camp, worth more than roses. It was the kindest thing that could have happened to me. I could not talk. I choked up and cried when I thanked her. I loved her for doing that. I never will forget the little gesture as long as I live. She is a true saint.

Later, as I looked at the clover, I thought of Jakob and his dandelions and the vase. I managed a smile, something rare for me these days.

* * *

Today, August 19, is my oldest brother's birthday. I thought of him all day, wondering where he was and if he were alive. Even if I could, I would not tell my brothers what is going on here. They were such hotheads and so protective of me, so it is difficult to know what they would do. Maybe they know about this place anyway. They might even be here. Oh God, I cannot think of them being here. Help me sleep, God, and not think anymore today.

* * *

There was a blessing today. It came out of the blue, and I have no idea how it happened. I started to sit down in the clinic, and there was a note on the chair. I looked about to see who put it there, but no one was around. Quickly, I shoved it in my hand and went behind some shelves. I opened it and could not believe my eyes. It was from Jakob. It said, "Andrea is okay and so am I. We will see you soon." My heart soared. Oh God, what does it mean? Was Jakob here? Surely not, but how did he get a note to me all this way? He kept telling me Hitler was losing. Maybe he is. Maybe the Russians or the Americans are coming to rescue us. Dear God, let it be true. Do I dare hope that I will see my little Andrea again? Do I dare dream of Jakob? Please God, give me hope.

Even with my note from Jakob, I am sick at heart. Will these crimes ever stop? I want to take a gun and use it on the butcher who is slicing up these children. Today it was little twelve-year-old Wilhelmine's turn. Those pigs! Why? Why? A twelve-year-old child! I was able to exchange a few words with her before she was brought before her butcher. "I have not seen my sister," she said, "but they told me I would get to see her after the surgery. I hope they hurry. I miss her so much my stomach hurts." All I could do was nod and smile and hurry to the toilet far away so I would not have to listen to her screams.

How perverted. How terribly sick these people are. I try to understand their sick motives, but it is a waste of time. And time is so precious here, every little minute of it. We never know when it will end for us. Every day could be our last one. All we ever hear is, "Hurry. Hurry, work makes you free." It was Hitler's favorite saying. Lots of people were free all right. Free of life from being worked to death.

A transport left here several days ago with a group of eighty women who were picked to work at an ammunitions depot, a factory called I. G. Farben. The women were pleased. They did not want to be a part of producing the deadly bullets killing their countrymen, but some factories produced other things—like medicine for the Army hospitals. Whatever, the women were glad to get away from this place where death lingers everywhere.

* * *

We are in October now, and this evening, Lilo asked me if I wanted to join her on her patrols. I have never seen the whole camp, so I said I would. Yvette joined us for our little tour. Ravensbrück looked pretty bad, but it was nothing compared to Auschwitz. Everything is run down here—broken doors, windows, bugs everywhere, and filth and dirt.

Auschwitz has only 28 Blocks, Yvette told me. Seventeen to twenty thousand women occupy them. They come and go quickly. Many of them go straight to the Birkenau, our sister camp and its gas chambers, but just as many come here. The process is always the same. They come, they die, and more come, and more die. Lilo said, "It is easy to understand why so many women here are apathetic. One does not have any tears left to cry." I thought about it and could not remember when I last cried.

Tonight as I laid in my bed praying, I wondered if the whole thing was just a nightmare, and that I will wake up soon. Or maybe it is hell. I have already died, and I am in hell. But God would surely not let me go to hell. Tonight I need to pray hard for my sanity.

Chapter Seventeen

While I was scrubbing some tables trying to make them clean, I looked up and could not believe my eyes. Standing before me was Reinhardt, Jakob's friend. He had his right arm in a sling and a bandage on his left cheek but I knew it was him right away. I wanted to grab him to say hello but others were around. He motioned me to the back by some barrels and said, "Vera, I so hoped to find you. I was transferred here two weeks ago. Jakob was supposed to be too but we got in trouble for helping some new arrivals and he was punished. Nothing too severe and he will be okay but I was transferred when they made a mistake. I don't know if he knows where I am but I know he would want me to tell you Andrea is okay. She had to be moved several times at the pig farm, but she is doing alright. We are hoping the war will be over soon and then, we can take her with us when we leave and make sure she is safe."

Before Reinhardt had to leave, I took a chance and squeezed his arm. I told him how happy I was to see him and hoped he would be okay for the rest of the war.

This afternoon, there was some exciting news. There were some new arrivals, communists. They were telling everyone that the Russians were coming closer and closer, and they were winning. Was our dream to come true? God, please let the Russians win. It is difficult to want my beloved Germany taken over by another country, but anything would be better than Hitler. Germany could be good again without Hitler and his people. We could be free again. Oh, how I love that word.

The communists said that fewer and fewer people believed in Hitler. Most just drag along behind him for fear of their lives and their families, like what happened to Jakob. I hope what the communists are saying is true. It makes sense, considering they are letting Jews work in the ammunition depots now.

Today I met two cousins from Meissen who live in this Block. I told them I knew a prison guard from there but they did not know Jakob. They are political prisoners who work in the kitchen and have been here at Auschwitz since the gates opened in 1940. Before that they were imprisoned in a regular jail, as I was.

The cousins were convicted of being Social Democrats. Ten years is a long time to be locked away. In five months, I will have been imprisoned for eight years altogether.

The amazing thing about these women is that they have done the impossible. They have survived four years here at Auschwitz. They gave me some badly needed courage. When they arrived, they decided they would survive, no matter what it took. It reminded me of what I told Elisabeth when we arrived at Ravensbrück; that we would survive. Oh Elisabeth, I pray you are still alive.

These cousins have done very brave things to survive. And they have established connections at the main office. Whenever their names appear on a list of who will be killed, they have themselves written off as already dead. They also do it for friends or people when they can. They told me I have been on the list, but they never tell anyone when this happens, otherwise our faces and actions might give us away. They say this would not be possible if Auschwitz were better organized. The SS here really do not care who dies and just pick names at random.

Two transports will be leaving tomorrow for the ammunition depots again. The Nazis must be desperate for weapons. We are still hearing rumors of the Soviets coming closer. Everyone is whispering about it. Yvette keeps warning us to watch our tongues. “They may get cut out!” she says. Yes, I better watch my tongue. I have to. Maybe we will be freed. If the SS knew my thoughts, I would be chased into the chamber.

* * *

A signal went through the camp today. Huge transports are to be sent off with all nationalities, except Aryans. These transports are said to be leaving for another camp. The Soviets here are exchanging looks, happy ones. I talked with a Russian today and asked her why she looked so happy. She said, “The end is near, the end of the war. We can feel it!”

“Oh that would be so wonderful!” I told her. She asked me if that would not be hard on me as a German if they beat my country. I said, “I do not care who beats Hitler, as long as someone does—anyone!” And then I told her that I never thought of any prisoner here as the enemy; that we were all in this together. The SS tried everything to make us feel hatred for one another, but we never had.

The woman said, “You know I believe you. Come over tonight and I will show you something.” I promised I would and was very curious what it could be.

This evening I went to see her. We crawled under her bunk where there were a bunch of wires and metal parts. She said, “Watch, and if you want, you can help me. I am building a receiver and transmitter.” I watched every move of her hands, so that I might be able to do the same if I needed to. She told me that if it works they can receive and transmit messages, letting the Russians know where we are, and at the same time find out what is going on there. I cannot remember when I was so excited. And how excited they would be when they heard their countrymen’s voices and found out that they were on their way to help them. Such smart women! If the SS just knew how smart! I hoped I could get to see their faces when they discovered they had been outsmarted. I just hope the Russians will hurry, and that they will make it in time. I also thought of Jakob. I wish he were here. With his electrical training, he would know how to help make the transmitter work.

I pray tonight for those brave and smart Russian women. God has blessed us with them. Maybe we will get out of here alive. Oh God, please let us survive, just like I told Elisabeth so long ago.

* * *

Maybe there is another good sign—the SS women have quit wearing the dead Jews' furs, as they had been doing. They all seem nervous. I hope they are just half as scared as any of us have been. Maybe I should not feel this way—for it is probably not being Christlike—but I want so much for them to have a taste of their medicine. They must know more than we know. They have radios and papers. Of course, Hitler probably would not let out certain things to the media, but they certainly have better sources than we have, and they must know the end is near.

I wish we knew how close the Russians were. Maybe the Russian women know by now. I hate to ask too many questions, for fear they might be discovered. But I have so many questions. We all do. Are the Russians coming alone or with the Americans or the British? I do not think Hitler ever liked the Americans. I remember when the Olympics were held in Germany and an American runner had won a gold medal. Hitler would not shake his hand as he was supposed to do. The man was a Negro, and Hitler probably thought a Negro should not have been allowed to participate. The American handled the situation well while Hitler made a fool of himself. I am so glad there are no Negroes here. I could imagine what Hitler would do with them. He cannot be a real man. He has to be a devil. I pray tonight for the Russians and for the Americans, if they are helping. Please God, let us be rescued before it is too late.

* * *

My heart bled today when I found out transports were leaving today for Ravensbrück. Word is they are trying to clear out Auschwitz. How much I wish I were on that train with the others. As horrible as the train is, I want so much to see my friends again. There are some nice people here, too, but I have never gotten close to anyone except Lilo and Yvette. I would give so much to see my little Andrea, and Jakob, the best friend anyone could ever have. It is still so difficult to believe that he is SS. But really he is not. Not in his heart. He is just staying alive and doing what he can to help us who are suffering. I hope the comrades going there will preach the good news about the Russians. They could use good news. Ravensbrück is so much farther away. The Russians will likely be here in Poland first.

Lilo acts so hard-cored and tough, but I know better since she is such a caring person. I laugh when I think of her nickname—she is called the Auschwitz Herald, like the newspaper, because she always knows what is going on.

* * *

Another alert! More transports are supposed to leave for Ravensbrück, but the train has not shown up to take them. The whole SS is nervous. Lilo says Commander Mulka is hysterical. Maybe the Russians had stopped the train or blown it up. I hope I get to see him frantic and nervous instead of being the calm butcher. I hope he hates the shoes he is wearing now. What if the Germans lose the war and the world finds out what has happened here? Hitler and his SS deserve everything the devil himself would do to them in hell. Again, I know I should not feel this way but I do. God forgive me for hating. It is a terrible emotion.

* * *

Today the train finally arrived. Nothing had gone wrong, as some had figured. It was just late. There are many soldiers to be transported all the time, and prisoners from one camp to the other or to the factories and depots. I can imagine the trains are always behind and filled to the brim.

Today I learned they are sending German women on the transport. Although I am still not on a list to go—maybe because those cousins marked me off as already dead. I hated to ask Yvette about going so I asked Lilo to talk to her and she did. Then Yvette came by and said with her eyebrows raised, "What did I hear, you do not like us anymore?" My stomach had a knot, but then she grinned. "Don't worry, I understand very well. You need not be such a chicken to talk to me. I had the feeling you might want to go back to Ravensbrück, particularly as Germans are going too."

I told her what her friendship had meant to me, but I wanted to see my other friends once more and a little girl who called me mama. Yvette said, "Enough of that cute, sad story. If you want to be on that train, you better get your affairs together. They will not send out an invitation or reserve a seat on their first-class train." Lilo had tears in her eyes for the second time as she went on to say that she would add me to the train list. Yvette said she would get some rations for me from the cousins.

Yvette brought food, and Lilo had gifts. She said, "Here my friend, a gift from the Auschwitz Herald. You better remember me always!" She had big tears running down her cheeks. It was too much—tough Lilo crying. Then Yvette and I also began to cry. It had been a long time since I had shed tears. I opened the gift. It was a beautiful scarf, the one we Germans wore with our native costumes—little roses and strings all around. It could be worn around the shoulders or head. There was also a little bundle of pressed flowers and leaves. I wrapped them carefully with the rest of my belongings—my towel and toothbrush, but no soap—especially not from here.

The three of us sat and talked all evening about my trip and what might happen if we were all freed. I swore that no one would ever tell me "Hurry, hurry" again. I would work at my own accord willingly, without a whip, pistol, or dog to tell me to hurry. Lilo said the best thing about being free would be not to smell burning flesh. Yvette said she never wanted to hear a scream or a gunshot. We sat with our arms around each other. I was glad this was my last night in Auschwitz, but I wished I could take my comrades with me.

Finally I had to leave them. I hope that Lilo and Yvette make it out of here all right. They are such fine women. All of us deserve to be free and to eat and be healthy. I weigh just seventy pounds, and they do not weigh much more.

I pray hardest that the rest of the little children will get out of camp. Most of them have lost their parents and families, but maybe someone will take them in. Even in a civilian orphanage they would have some chance—food, clothing, and warmth, and no more worrying of being killed.

Dear God, please stay with me. I nearly died on the last two train rides. Please make this one easier. Please take me safely back to my dear friends at Ravensbrück.

Chapter Eighteen

We made it! Oh God we made it. October 1944 is almost over, but we made it.

I have already been here at Ravensbrück three days, but I am a bit sad that this is not the organized Ravensbrück I had left. It is like being in a huge storm—everything terribly crowded and chaotic. Transports were sent here from everywhere. There was no more space at the overflowing Blocks, so all of us were put into a huge tent, one that is way too small for us. We were just too many. As a bed, we use a little straw they had thrown in, and as a toilet we use a banged-up bucket. Everyone is under and over each other, just as it was on the train.

No matter, I am thrilled to have managed to sneak out each day and see friends. They are all so wonderful, each one so happy to see me alive that they cry. But some are gone, no longer there. Anna was the most obvious. Elisabeth held my hand and told me Anna died of typhus not long after I left for Auschwitz. We cried together, something they had already done many times.

I have told them all about the rumors we heard at Auschwitz, about the Russians being there soon. They have also heard many rumors from all the people coming on transports. Everyone knows something is happening, or we would not all be crowded into this camp like a burrow of insects.

Where is Jakob, I wonder? I have not seen him anywhere, and I keep looking. I dare not ask about an SS guard. I have also not seen Mavis and there is no word of any kind about Andrea. I am so confused and worried.

Again I was able to sneak out to see the comrades at the old Blocks. Elisabeth gave me her bread. I thanked her under tears. For two days we had been given nothing. I go around begging from my old friends and get a little here and there. Because there are too many people, the food is down to plain survival for all, but the tent has been forgotten. And we have kids. I told this to my comrades, and they put up a collection for the little ones.

My dear friend Gerda from Block 9 managed some fresh underwear for me. I am so grateful when she gives me a hug. She said that next week she will try for a dress. I hope not one of those civilian dresses like they had in Auschwitz. I have already seen some women wearing them here—with the crosses on the back. I told Gerda I would rather wear what I had.

After I saw Gerda, I went to the old Gypsy Block, which now has many nationalities. It was so crowded with wall-to-wall bunks that I had a problem finding Andrea's old hole. But I did, and there were my writings and the porcelain vase painted with the flowers, carefully wrapped in a towel and covered with dirt. When I got back here, I thanked Elisabeth. What a wonderful friend. Once again, I told her, "We are going to survive this, Elisabeth." Big tears came to her bright blue eyes.

The sirens blare now more than ever. We are forbidden to leave the tent, but I still go. My dear and wonderful Erika is now with the camp police. She watches out for me.

All I know is that my heart is hollow. I have cried and cried over losing Jakob and Andrea. Nobody knows anything about either of them. God and I have made up since I know he does things for his own reason. I am mad at him but do not hate him. Today I was able to stay at my old Block 1 for almost four hours. It was heaven to be with my good comrades. Rosel gave me my first warm meal in a long time—turnip soup. Elisabeth and Katja brought me a fresh towel and a basin of water. Elfriede, the woman who turned from SS to political prisoner, is now in

Block 1. She had a dress for me. It was full of lice, but otherwise clean. She went with me to help scrub the daylights out of it.

* * *

Commander Suhren and Dr. Sonntag were here today to check out the tent. I wondered if they might recognize me but of course they did not. They saw us in our misery and that our straw was wet. A pipe had broken and all the water ran along the ground. They also saw that we do not have water to drink or food to eat. Suhren acted like he had known nothing about this, but still did nothing to help us. They probably want us to starve to death.

I tried to find Mavis today but no luck. It is so hard since while I was gone people were moved and transferred.

* * *

November has reached us and each day is worse than the day before. It is so cold, and we are about to freeze to death here in this tent. Everyone lies close together, but we are all still cold. We did not get new straw, and it is still wet. At times we lay on icicles.

Once in a while we get a warm meal, always the same—turnip soup. There is never enough to go around. I take pains in making sure the children are the first ones to get theirs. But our women are just as hungry. Some get hysterical. I tell them to eat slowly, but they are afraid someone else might get theirs.

Erika really is an angel. Before I fell asleep last night, she came and gave me a plate with fried potatoes. What a delicacy. She had kept her potatoes and had fried them on the Block's iron stove. She even parted with her margarine—such a kind gesture. I thank God every day for my precious friends.

The power of prayer paid off as today I found Mavis when I was on the way to the old Block. She and I threw arms around each other. Then she said something that caused me to almost bowl over—"Andrea sends her love." I stepped back quickly. "What—you have seen my little one?" I asked. "Yes," she answered. "Just yesterday."

I grabbed her arm and held tight and cried and cried some more as Mavis said Andrea is safe with the pigs. She knew that Reinhardt had been transferred, but was not sure about Jakob. My smile was as big as the sun—how happy I am. Mavis promised to tell Andrea I love her and find out about Jakob. God, I am not mad now. Forgive me, please.

Transport after transport leaves for the ammunition depot. The SS seem to have lost all track of order; everything is in chaos, much like Auschwitz was—no organization. The rumors persist that the Russians are winning.

* * *

Beautiful! I am back at my old Block as I had prayed. I came yesterday. My comrades are so wonderful. For my welcome, they actually made a cake. It was not a real cake, of course, but it was to me. They had taken three slices of bread, piled them, and cut them in the shape of a heart. Then they whipped the margarine and jam from Sunday together and frosted it. I was stunned. It was the last thing I expected. But that is why I wanted to come back to Ravensbrück. Not because of the camp itself, but because of my friends, the way they are.

When they knew I was coming, they arranged for a new dress and underwear. They had given me those things when I came from Auschwitz, but I had become a stinking mess living in that tent. I was embarrassed to walk into the Block smelling like I did. But Elisabeth grabbed me first and gave me a big hug, and the others all followed, not one of them wrinkling their nose. Rosel beamed at me and held up a brand-new pair of shoes. I do not know how she did it. They even fit perfectly. Gerda was there for the occasion. I kept thinking maybe I was dreaming, or I had died in the tent and this was heaven. Katja gave me two fresh towels, and Elisabeth gave me a piece of soap. "You can use this type," she said. "It is not what you think!" I headed straight for the washroom. Rosel was right behind me with a bowl of warm water.

When I came out all clean and smelling better, we shared the cake and had coffee and talked and talked. Rosel said, "Tomorrow you will not go to head count. We already arranged that. You will sleep as long as you can!" I was so happy. They were like family to me, all of us helping each other get through this time we had to endure. Now I think I will probably make it. They have really brought some sunshine into my life.

Today I rested all day with the memory of last night in my heart. I pray for all of my dear comrades. May all of our wishes come true. Please God, let them come true, and take care of little Andrea, and find Jakob. And thank you so much for getting me out of the tent. I feel like a real person again.

Chapter Nineteen

God, no, no, no! It cannot be true. Mavis told me today that Jakob is alive, but got in serious trouble for something. Mavis thinks for helping someone, but maybe not Andrea. He is in the bunker. Oh mercy, no, not him. I do care for him so much. I know now that I must really love him.

Each day I am picked from head count to do odd jobs, most of them outside. They are all hard, and it is cold, but I see what is going on in camp. This morning transport after transport left for the ammunition depots or factories, where they send people to make weapons. Work leader Pflaum selects the ones that are going. His helper, Heckendorf, is the same way. Next to them, Schreiter and Boese help out. The devilish "four-leaf clover," as we call these evil men.

No dent in the population is occurring even by sending people to the factories and through the slaughter of more people each day. So many are sleeping on the floor in washrooms, under beds, and about everywhere there is a place to lay their weary head. And there is still the horrible tent. The prison kitchen cooks all they have to cook, but still many women and children go without food and water. Most of the sinks do not work anymore. No one bothers to fix anything in this chaos.

Tonight the word was passed for a unity meeting. This was something we could have dared not do before the chaos, but now the SS was too busy killing to care what we did inside the Blocks. When we came together, one of the women counted and twenty-three countries were represented; an amazing number, but not surprising. Every country had picked a representative person.

Erika arranged the meeting and was the leader. She said there was so much happening it was important everyone was up with the latest news and information. There may come a time soon when we would all need to do something together as a unified body of women. Everyone agreed but felt tense, as though we were nearing a crisis.

Then Erika announced that we were going to be allowed to receive packages. I do not know how, but I have a feeling she may have been responsible for that. But even if she did convince someone, it was probably because the SS wanted to show their generosity during the final days. Everyone agreed it was wonderful, but why would anyone be sending packages to us. No one knew where we were. Erika said, "Packages from families are received every day but taken by the SS. Most are addressed to several different locations out of hope they will be delivered." It was quickly decided that except for gifts of sentimental value, everything was to go to the children.

The meeting was both wonderful and terrifying. Wonderful because we are all a team; terrifying because it feels death may be closer and faster if the Nazis decide to exterminate all of us.

* * *

Tonight, another meeting was held. Erika had a wonderful idea. We would not give the children any of the packages being received. We would save them for Christmas. These poor kids have not had a Christmas for so long, and some had no idea what Christmas was. And some would die before Christmas, but those who were still with us, assuming we are still here, will have a real Christmas.

We began to plan. Erika said there were still about three hundred children we could gather. We would divide up and tell them Christmas stories and sing with them in their own language. And we would spread the word this was to happen—something to look forward to that could give them spirit, help them live. We would tell them they were very special and Christmas would not even be Christmas without children. We would tell them about the little baby Jesus and that we were going to celebrate his birthday. The Jews would tell their own story. It was to be very democratic. Hitler had us all locked up here because our beliefs were different from his. No one wanted to exclude anyone with different beliefs.

After we did the planning, we had a joint prayer, "Oh God, guide our way and let us help these children. Let us make this a special Christmas for them they will never forget. Protect us and help us to have nothing go wrong so we can celebrate with the children as promised." We left for our Blocks feeling good in our hearts, and hopeful.

Tonight I pray it will all happen for the children. Oh, how I wished Andrea could be here. Maybe that will happen. With your help, God, that could happen! And dear Jakob, please let him be released. At least he is still alive.

* * *

But then, another miracle. A note came from Jakob that Mavis gave me in an envelope with a dried dandelion he must have saved from the summer. I held it as the moonlight glowed in the clear sky. But then my heart sank as I read that while Jakob had been released from the bunker, there was an order to clean up the pig farm, to clear it for troop arrival. He wrote, "We will need to move little child back to you for a week or two while the cleanup takes place, no more. Let me know when you are ready by giving Mavis a note."

Oh my, what was I to do now? I quickly talk to Erika and we decided we could hide Andrea in the old places, under floorboards and in closets. But the inspections are tougher now—we will have to be clever.

Two nights later, we met Jakob and my little angel behind the barracks #6. It was dark, but my little one's eyes were bright, and I hugged her like never before. She has sprouted up some, a young woman now; how beautiful she is. Jakob hugged me too, and I so badly wanted to kiss him but I did not.

Moments later, we heard footsteps along the path, and we all froze in fear. The sound of a lighted match broke the silence, the aroma of a cigarette filled the air. Then we heard nothing until there were boots hitting the ground as the soldier walked away. I nearly fainted, but all was okay. I grabbed Andrea's hand, and we scampered back toward my barracks. I quickly hugged her again and gave her a big kiss before leading her to the closet behind some mops and brooms. The smell is bad, but she will be safe until morning.

December has come and it certainly is true that giving is more fun than taking. What a strange time. The camp is in chaos, so many sick, so many being murdered, yet we are all in such a good mood planning for Christmas. We have something to look forward to—a gift to our children. People who work in the clothing chambers have given material—wool cloth, silk, everything they could spare. The tailor shop has given us scissors, thread, and needles. This could never happen if the SS were organized, as they used to be. And God is surely helping, giving us liberties to plan for his Son's birthday. We work hard during our free time to make clothes and special gifts out of everything we can get our hands on. It really is a glorious feeling.

I pray that we will be able to make this happen. I pray we will live at least until Christmas. This plan for celebration has united everyone and little Andrea is excited too, even though she cannot be outside. Each day we move her from under a bed to the closet to under the floorboard. No one seems to be paying too much attention; so many are so weak and hopeless they do not care anymore, only that they somehow survive. One day, a surprise inspection almost caught us, but luckily Andrea squeezed her way back in the closet so the SS could not see her. She is so brave, my little angel.

We all work so hard, and we sing together. We try not to look at the SS or remember that they are here doing their terrible deeds. We found lots of straw, and the French women are making shoes with it. They are so clever. The Polish make straw dolls and little animals. Nail cleaners and letter openers were made of toothbrushes and whatever one could think of. We used the silks to make blouses, or little slips and underwear. Everyone has some kind of talent to contribute. And most wonderful of all is that the kids are coming out of the shadows and sitting at our feet. They wonder about Christmas and ask questions. I am sure they sense the joy in our planning.

It is a miracle of its own that no one has been caught taking supplies. The SS seem to be so busy figuring out how to kill us all before we are rescued that they have no time to police what we are doing. And what we are doing is completely against their doctrine of hate and prejudice—all the nations working together out of love for all our children. How special that is, people loving people, just like Jesus did.

* * *

Christmas comes closer and closer. Only two days remain until Andrea can return to the pig farm. Sometimes I think we should keep her here, but I know that is not good. She will be safe in Jakob's care, better than here. He came by again today and held up two fingers for two days. And then he smiled and I smiled, and I felt like I could touch him even though I could not.

Piles and piles of gifts are almost ready for Christmas. There will be something for everyone. Every Block has worked hard and stashed their gifts in hiding. The medics have contributed much as well. Because of the chaos of the camp, the Jews are able to smuggle things under their clothes and get away with it.

They bring vitamins, cold medicine, dextopur, calcium, cod liver, whatever is possible to get. Elisabeth came in today taking things out of her apron and from under her dress. She said, "You know Saint Nick came by and left these things for us." A little girl heard her and said, "I do not know who he is, but I can tell he is not a Nazi!" We all broke out laughing. It was sad but glorious the way it came out of that little mouth.

Next Katja walked in with more medicines. She said Marschall had forgotten to pull the key out of the medicine cabinet when she was called away in a hurry. They were able to take supplies from the back, so the front still looked packed. Even though no one is permitted to have a conversation with the SS. Katja said they flattered Marschall the rest of the day about her new hairdo, distracting her further.

The medicine is so desperately needed for the children. They will not appreciate it like they will the toys, but most will not see another Christmas without it. I pray tonight for the courage of all these women working together. And I do not forget those who are being gassed, or shot, or who are dying of typhus or TB.

* * *

Tonight was transfer night. I walked with Andrea along the darkness and then to the special building where they keep the shovels and rakes. Jakob was late but then showed up out of breath. A scare happened again when an SS with a flashlight and a growling dog passed near where we were. Why the dog did not sniff us, I do not know. God must have shut off his nose When the danger passed, Jakob simply took Andrea's hand and led her back along the path to the gate so fast I could not even kiss her goodbye. Tears came to me as I saw her go. Will I ever see her again?

* * *

We have decided to go one step further with our holiday plans. We are going to try and have a Christmas party for the little ones. No one has figured out how this will be possible, but everyone is thinking about it and coming up with ideas. We only have eleven days to prepare. There is a lot of whispering going on everywhere, with an eye out for spies. I would pity the spy who got in the way of our Christmas planning. And I am not sure the SS has time for spies these days with all they have going on.

I cannot stop thinking about Andrea. Is she all right there without Jakob? I wish Reinhardt was still looking out for her? Another Christmas for her in a pigpen, but if not for the pigpen, she would not be alive. If she can hold out a little longer, she could celebrate her next Christmas as a free person.

* * *

Many days have gone by, but God answered my prayers again. At head count this morning, I was picked to work at the sewers, all set up by Mavis, who is their group leader now. It was so cold in the morning, icy wind in our face, but worth it. In the afternoon, Mavis said we had to go to the pig farm to borrow some tools. I was so excited. There was an SS guard there, a woman with long hair and a gruff voice, but Mavis distracted her, and I went to find Andrea.

The smell as I walked through one of the barns was awful, but I was on a mission. There was straw piled everywhere, but I kept looking around. Several SS guards looked at me oddly, but I didn't care. Then I walked around a stall where the pigs were oinking and there she was, little Andrea. I ran to her and held her in my arms and cried; we both did. She looked pretty well, aside from rings under her eyes. She said that she does not sleep well, because men sometimes come in the night, and she has to crawl deep into her straw and listen. Thank God she is so smart. Her hair looked like a wild animal's, but that was of little concern.

Suddenly, she bolted away and ran to the other side of the barn. Then she came back holding a piglet in her hands. "This is Champ number three," she said. "My friend."

Before I left, I told her that her countrymen were on their way, and she would soon get out of there. "Is that really true?" she gasped and grabbed me around the neck again.

"Just hold on a little longer, Angel, and then you can leave this place forever! And do not forget your prayers, okay? I am here today because I prayed so hard."

"No, I never forget. It always helps me."

"I might be able to see you soon, but I cannot promise. We will both pray it will be possible."

"I understand, Mama, but you try, please!"

Then I saw Andrea's face light up. She was looking over my shoulder. I turned around, and there was Jakob. He walked up quietly holding some tools. "Thank you," I whispered. He smiled such a beautiful smile. I wanted so much to hug him, and may have, but I saw the guard approaching, and Mavis coming from another direction. Thankfully, my smart little Angel had seen the guard first, and disappeared into the straw.

"What in the world were you doing here so long?" she yelled at me and then Mavis. "You know you are here to work and not to goof off! You better get your butts out of here before I kick them out for you!"

Jakob spoke up. "Ma'am, this was not the fault of the women. They had to wait until I fixed the tools. It took a while, as one was badly broken. But they are good now." He handed a couple of tools to Mavis, and one to me. We thanked him and were on our way. He gave the guard his great big smile, and she wiggled away. It was a close call, but the best thing that has happened to me in a long time.

In our unity meeting yesterday, we decided that we should take the chance and ask the SS if we could have a Christmas party. It would be better if they knew than if we were caught. It was decided we should ask Head Guard Binz. She is a bad woman, but she knows the Russians are coming, and the end is near, and most important, she knows that we know. She was overheard talking about it to another SS. We hoped she would want to show us another side of her before it was over. It was risky. But it worked. We will be allowed to have a party, but no gift-giving. So what, we could give the gifts out later. Now it is going to be a real Christmas!

* * *

Today we celebrated Christmas. We picked out a Block where we would have the party—Block 2, with the fewest bunks. There, we made a stage of boxes and then we decorated the whole place. Lanterns were made of paper. Elfriede painted nativity scenes with paint she took from the SS garage where she works. Everyone made some sort of decoration. Someone even managed to find a whole box of candles.

When the children walked in, it was such an event. They gasped and sighed, as though it could not be true. They had never seen anything so beautiful! With big eyes they stood there, their pale faces turned pink, their eyes were shining. We stood crying and singing Christmas carols. Someone started and the whole Block followed. Has anyone ever heard children from twenty-three countries sing "Silent Night"?

It was the first time in my eight years of imprisonment that I heard children singing, laughing, and really being happy. It was as if God was right there among us, and some women told jokes, some did tricks, and some did skits, which the kids loved most. I contributed a lot of tears, but mostly in the toilet by myself. I just bawled like a baby, I was so happy.

Erika is the most incredible woman! Her gift to bring people together and make things happen left us in awe. At the party she told the children stories. They all gathered in groups of their own language, and someone from each group did their best to translate what Erika was saying. Everyone's eyes just hung on Erika's lips. All the misery and sorrows were forgotten at this point. We had all worked to make these precious children feel they were important. A little girl asked me, "What if the SS find out we are having a party?"

I told her, "The little Lord Jesus has softened the heart of the SS for today. Also, St. Nick had told them they better let us have a party or they will not get any gifts this year."

"Oh!" is all she said, and her eyes were right back on Erika our storyteller.

We made heart-shaped bread pieces into cakes, like they did for my welcoming home. Everyone had saved their bread, and Elisabeth went from Block to Block to show them how to do it. Many of the packages received at the camp had been special kinds of food treats, enough that we were able to make a little refreshment buffet. Most of these kids had never tasted candy or cookies, and you should have seen their faces and heard their "Aahs!" and "Oohs!"

Tonight I lay here and think of little Andrea out there with the animals in her straw manger, like the baby Jesus. I received a note through Mavis today that Jakob had received a big package from his family and was going to stay with Andrea and share her Christmas.

Chapter Twenty

The Christmas party kept everyone in high spirits for many days. It was such a special time, one we will keep in our hearts for as long as we live. We gave all the gifts out in each Block. The children experienced joy that day they had never had before, and so did every adult who shared it with them. As it turned out, there were several spies who turned us in, but since we had gained permission, nothing came of it. We found out who the spies were, and they are now completely isolated from everyone's conversation. I feel sorry for them and not hate since they are just trying to stay alive. God will judge them, not me.

For ten days now I have had my old job back. I am a medic once again. I do not work at the clinic often, but float back and forth between the TB and the Typhus Block. Sometimes I have to go to the tent, and I dread this the most. They still have no water, no lights, and are using the same wet straw. Women are still led from there to the woods, but more often dragged, as they cannot walk. They die like flies daily in the tent. Christmas is just a memory, and the cold cruel days are with us once more.

I keep praying and praying. Seeing Andrea that day with Jakob is the memory I go to sleep with each night.

Two more transports left today for some factory depot. Pflaum, the SS in charge, beat up some Polish women because they refused to work in a German ammunition depot. "We will not help to destroy our country," they told him. That brought a big smile to Pflaum's face, and an opportunity to do what he does best.

* * *

We are in February 1945 and hope every night the Russians will come soon and stop this whole mess. Four hundred women have arrived from Auschwitz. It is hard to believe any of them are alive. They are filthy, their clothes and shoes torn and ragged. Every one of them has terrible frostbite and is barely alive from starvation. But the Nazis cannot destroy one thing in people—spirit. Some people will simply not let their spirit die, and when I see this in their eyes I am inspired. We will never know the why's of all this, but for many who survive, they will look back with knowledge they never gave up their will to live. How many people can say that—too few I am afraid.

Hundreds of miles those women had walked, only able to ride on trains a few miles here and there. The trains are now needed for the Army and ammunition depots. Of course, the SS did not walk. They were driving right alongside with their vehicles, shooting people who could not keep up.

Some of the women told me what was happening at Auschwitz. They said that parts of the camp were already destroyed and the SS was going to blow it all up before the Russians moved in. They said that as many as possible, thousands, had been gassed and burned. I asked about Yvette and Lilo, but they did not know them.

I pray tonight for my two friends. Please God, let them be spared, and thank you for helping me out of Auschwitz in time.

* * *

The first huge transport left the camp today for Uckermark. The selection was inhuman. When the eldest of the Blocks were not able to come up with sufficient numbers, Suhren had the white coats do the picking. Among those selected were fifty to sixty women from the TB and mental Blocks. Every woman was afraid. The rumors have been horrid about Uckermark. Strong young SS men whipped and beat old, sick, and weak women into a transport. The SS heart is hollow and there are two few like Jakob who try to help where they can. How will all of these men be judged after the war? Will there be court martial trials? What will happen to Jakob and to Reinhardt?

This afternoon, Jakob appeared near the typhus Block where I was headed, my head down against the wind. He motioned for me to meet him in the yard where no one goes, and I did. Without warning, he grabbed me and kissed me, like he had done once before. Then he told me he loved me. I blurted out "I love you too." And then we just stood there looking at each other for a minute, but it seemed like an hour. Oh how crazy this was, but no one saw. Then he said, "Don't worry, I will find you after the war, and Andrea too." Then he was gone. I walked away like I was on a cloud.

God, is this okay with you? I wonder. Loving an SS man—one who is with those who kill Jews and all others against them? Am I sinning—breaking your law? Should I hate Jakob instead for what he does? Are my eyes closed too much? Am I stupid to love a Nazi—an SS—one who doesn't fight back and lets deaths occur? Suddenly I am ashamed and decide to tell Jakob we are no more. But then I think of Andrea—he has saved my precious child.

I am exhausted again. My head is burning, my eyes are watering, and my chest and back aches. Often I get weak in my knees, especially when I have to carry a sick woman off to the clinic. I stumble and fall. I become weaker by the day, and my coughing gets stronger. I do not dare complain that I am ready to be a patient myself. My excitement over possible freedom has ended. We probably all will be killed after all.

Did Jakob wink at me when he walked by today? I think he did but cannot be sure. Maybe he knows I am questioning my interest in him. I simply smiled. I am more careful than ever with death all around.

I felt worse than ever today. My body ached so badly. I could hardly move, and I was dizzy from all the coughing. I knew the fever was in me, but I could not tell anyone. I know what being sick means here. I took some pills, but they hardly helped. I decided to ask the Block-eldest to let me rest a little bit. "Oh please, Rosel," I begged. "I will be back for head count." She understood and nodded. My head was spinning when I laid down, but it helped me quite a bit. I wonder if I have TB. My symptoms are similar. If that is the case, I know they will get me in no time.

An hour after the last truck left today we knew that people had not been taken to Uckermark as promised. We saw the black smoke coming out of the chimney, and it smelled already of burnt flesh and bones. Crying and sobbing, we all watched the clouds of smoke. I will not be able to forget this day. It is hell on earth.

I am so grateful that Andrea is not living at the camp. She is much safer where she is since the whole camp looks like a graveyard of walking dead. Everyone is afraid to say anything. The smell of burning flesh, the screams, I am sure to lose my sanity. Many already have.

The mass murdering keeps on, day and night. Even in the middle of night they come now. We hear the screams and commotion on the street, the doors slamming and tires squealing. No one looks out the window. I pull my blanket over my head and hold my ears and breath. I cannot hear well anyway. I also cannot breathe well. My lungs feel as if they are going to burst, and I can feel the blood hammering in my temples.

The SS must be nervous, all of them moving fast, hurrying. Do they know something we do not? We hear rumors that the Russians are in Poland, maybe even Germany.

* * *

Every day now, as many as possible are ordered to walk before SS Pflaum, and Binz to see if they are healthy enough to march when the camp is evacuated. Every day some are sent off to their deaths, and some taken to work in the factory depots. But the Germans have to be careful since some women disrupt and sabotage the work there. What does Hitler think he has accomplished with people turning against their own country, hoping Germany will lose?

The Block-eldests have little control over anything anymore. Before, they were each in charge of 150 to 200 women. Now up to 3,000 each. Despite the constant murders, we still have that many. The eldest have to see that everyone has food, blankets, clothes, markings, and that everyone is present at head count. This is not easy with so many women. Every one of them tries to do their best to keep their Blocks in shape. They try to comfort those whose friends or family have just been carried off to die. The eldest are more like robots than humans anymore. We all do our best to help them. But no matter what, every day more die.

My bad mood caused me to yell at Jakob. He came by with a jolly smile, but I said, "How do you stomach your SS killers? You let them kill old and young?" He stepped back two spaces. His face got red. Then he said, "If we leave SS, if we don't follow orders, they will kill our families." He started to walk away but I grabbed his shirt. It ripped in my hand. Both of us jumped back. Then I looked at his eyes—close to tears. How sorry I was for what I said. I squeezed his hand. He kissed my check and then he was gone. I am so sorry for what I said. God forgive me.

My health is at its lowest point. Today I decided that I had to go to the infirmary. Mada and Zdenka, the two kind women from Czechoslovakia who worked there, had been civilian doctors back home. I knew they would help me and not turn me away, also not turn me in. But at the door, I saw an SS white coat, and turned right around. No way was I going in there.

I wished I could talk to Erika. I know she would think of something. I have not seen her for a while. It was hard to find anyone in this chaos. If I could just breathe a little better, that would help. I know a lot of women are worse off than me, and Erika is probably busy with someone else. She has always done something for someone other than herself. God, please let her still be alive.

* * *

Thank goodness Jakob and I made up because today ends my time at Ravensbrück. I was picked this morning by Pflaum to leave. I do not know the truth as to why. Maybe I did not march well enough? Has someone noticed me not standing erect? I did not go to the clinic, even though I am sick. My chest feels like someone is sitting on it, but I did not dare tell Pflaum—he would have sent me straight to the woods.

After everyone was picked, he told us we were to go to a factory, to Sudenburg he said, where thousands of my comrades already worked. We are to leave tomorrow, seventy-five women, the exact number I came here with so long ago. I am not sure it is true that we are really going to a factory, but if so, it is better than being killed. Although I think another train ride in my condition will kill me anyway. Or maybe they intend to make us walk. I know I would not make it then. Maybe we will run into the Russians on the way and be saved.

Elisabeth and Katja were also picked, and Elfriede, the woman who was once SS. They cried and cried, like everyone did. Elisabeth held on to me and asked, “Vera, do you still think we will survive this?” Some were glad to be picked, but still they cried because we cannot trust anything the SS tells us. They may be sending us straight to be gassed. Pflaum told us to take today and get our things together.

When I returned to my Block, Mavis was waiting. She gave me a hug. She had been told I was picked. Then loudly, so others could hear, she said I was needed today at the sewers. They had a problem, and as I had worked there before and knew the situation, I would have to help her.

God bless Mavis. One more time I saw my dear sweet Andrea, and Jakob. Even Reinhardt was there, transferred back from Auschwitz. While Mavis distracted the guard, I told them where I was supposed to be going. Andrea and I drenched ourselves in tears. Jakob and Reinhardt had wet eyes too. It was terrible. I feel like it was final, but Jakob kept saying, "We will find you, Vera. We will all make it." Then he told me again that he loved me, right in front of Andrea and Reinhardt.

I told Andrea that when her countrymen came for her to tell them what Jakob and Reinhardt had done for her. "It will be your turn to save their lives," I said.

I never thought leaving a man would bother me. But Jakob has been so kind. I will miss him; I love him so.

* * *

This morning Pflaum told us we would leave at noon and to remain in our Block. Then Binz came about nine and took us all to a building behind the jail. One at a time we were sent in to have our heads shaved and now I am bald. Me and all of my German comrades. My hair has always been my pride. We all look so horrid, and me the worst because I am the skinniest. There are no mirrors, but I know my cheeks and eyes are hollow and probably black from the sickness, and my clothes are raggedy and hanging off my bones. I am glad Jakob cannot see me like this.

With our hair gone, we had lost the very last of our femininity through the final humiliating act here in Ravensbrück. "Boy, are you pretty now," Binz said after they were through as we stood with tears in our eyes. Elisabeth does not look so terrible, as her blue eyes are that much bigger without her blonde curls. The guard that shaved Katja took her long red braid and pinned it to her SS hat, parading around, laughing. When my head was shaved, I was told what a nice blanket it would make for Hitler. So cruel! So terribly cruel!

Then it hit us—if they shaved our heads, we must surely be headed for the gas chambers and not the factories. We wait now in our bunks to see if we have received the death sentence.

Chapter Twenty-One

It is March 1945, and I have been here at the clinic in Sudenburg for about a week. I'm not working as a medic, but as a patient since I have double pneumonia. Maria, the Russian woman, a pediatrician, who helped me so much with Andrea, was at my bedside when I woke up. She was so nice, so comforting. She smiled at me, and I thought about when the SS beat her and knocked out her teeth. She has been here working at the factory for several months.

Yesterday Elisabeth had a mirror and held it up to me. I screamed. I look like death itself and said so. "I would scare the devil away, and probably the Russians!"

Elfriede said, "Well, start to look better. That begins with getting well!"

I still black out sometimes. All I am allowed is broth, no food yet. I am glad they found out about my disease here, instead of Ravensbrück. I would not be alive if they had. And if not for my dear comrades on the train, I would not have made it here. Elisabeth and Katja, both medics, knew just how to keep me alive. I am glad I was sent here. It was God's will. I just have to get better now.

Everyone works at a factory and comes back to the camp after work. We have fine women here. About four thousand prisoners live at the camp, but only seventy-five Germans, those of us who were sent from Ravensbrück. Not one unkind word is to be heard. It is the right place to enable a sick person to get well. No one is killed here because they are sick.

Maria visits me often. Also, Irma and Edith, both from Berlin, stop by. And of course, Elisabeth and Katja come every evening. They always tell me what happened during the day. Sometimes I am sleeping or unconscious and do not even know they are sitting on my bed. I hope my lungs will not fill with fluid again, as that would be like a death sentence, especially with inadequate care. I am still not sure of the date. There are no calendars, and everyone has lost track.

* * *

In Magdeburg today, the town near the camp, there was an attack, but we do not know by whom. There is no doubt Hitler's enemies are closing in, and I must get better so I can walk when the liberators arrive.

We found out it is April 1945. I felt better and worked at the depot four days in a huge hall where they make bullets. Mr. Neumann, our civilian foreman, had shown me over and over how to do it, but I still had problems understanding. Finally he got so mad, he reported me to the headman. He called me to the front. I told him I just got out of bed and was still dizzy at times. He said he could see I was not well, and he sent me to the plant doctor. I was terrified. But thank God, he was civilian, and nice. He checked me out and told my group leader I was to stay in camp the next day. "I do not want to see her until she is completely well," he said. He bade me farewell and said, "Take care of yourself." That had never happened before, the words of comfort from a white coat.

The SS did not like this very much, but complied with his orders. After all, I had to be well to make Hitler's weapons correctly.

Our women work day and night together with men who are POWs from France and Italy. They are fed well at the plant. Often the foreman will let the women have what is left over. He did not care where they came from. It was a different treatment after all these years.

I cry sometimes at night when I think of Andrea and Jakob. Edith, who is in the bunk above me, comforts me. I have told her about Andrea. Nobody knows what is happening at Ravensbrück. I worry and pray for all of those we left behind.

We had an air raid earlier today, and part of our camp was hit, but no one was hurt. The SS were upset while everyone else was glad. The battle sounds are coming closer and closer. Our SS guard is really nervous, but her assistant does not even blink. The comrades said that she was always kind to them. They even call her by her first name, Friedel. She said some of the SS had run off with stolen food. I was glad to hear that. Their running away could only mean the end of the war is close.

I only wish I was a little bit stronger. My legs feel as if they are made of rubber. It is good that no one cares here if I stay in bed, so different than Ravensbrück. I wonder if those mass murders are still going on there. I can only pray they are not. Maybe my friends have been rescued by now. Maria massages my legs every day, and while she does this I have to tell her about what happened at Ravensbrück after she left.

Katja, Elisabeth, Elfriede, and Edith all came back from work a little while ago. They were acting crazy, dancing around like schoolgirls. Elisabeth finally said to me, "Would you believe just one more week and we are free?" Then Katja exclaimed, "Hey, did you hear, one week? The Russians will be here in less than a week!"

"Yes, I hear," I yelled. I wanted to jump out of bed and dance with them, but of course I could not. For the first time in many years we were crying tears of happiness.

Friedel told us that her boss ran off with the commander. They broke into the kitchen last night and the cook chased after them with a meat cleaver. They jumped into a car and drove away. Now there are just six SS males and eight females here.

Friedel told us that the commander left instructions that all the Germans prisoners could leave the camp whenever they wanted to and go wherever they wanted to. Freedom is truly near.

Elisabeth sat on my bed for a while. She said they had been talking to Friedel and trying to decide what to do. It was exciting that we could leave, but it still meant going past the guard tower. There were still SS guards up there with weapons. No one wanted to be shot at the last minute. It was decided we would wait for the Russians. Wow, I never thought I would be happy to see Russian soldiers. But now they will be our salvation.

* * *

Without warning yesterday afternoon, every siren from the nearby town sounded, and then everyone began running in from the factory. They were all yelling, "They are here, they are here!" Elisabeth came and hugged my neck hard. "Oh, Vera, they are here. We are going to make it!"

"Oh, thank God," I cried. "The Russians are finally here!"

"The Russians?" she laughed. "No, the Americans."

"Americans?" I almost fell out of my bed. "The Americans? Why has all the talk been about Russians? I am sick, but not deaf yet."

Elizabeth was still laughing with joy. "The Americans and Russians have come together. Can you believe it? In a million years would you have believed that?"

Everyone was dancing around, still, but the decision had to be made as to what to do. There is a war going on all around us. I want to get up and dance with them, but I cannot. But I am alive and I will be able to walk out of here, God willing.

* * *

April is half-gone and we decided it was safe to go to a bomb shelter. We have been here for five days. We were brought here by Friedel, and told to wait. She was going to get us some civilian clothes. And here we are, waiting and waiting. We might as well forget her. She will not be back.

There were only seven of us Germans who left the camp—Elisabeth, Katja, Edith, Maria, Elfriede, me, and Friedel. The rest had moved into the vacated SS quarters to wait for rescue. We had just passed the gate when we hit the ground. The Americans must have thought the SS were still staying in their quarters. They threw grenades into and around the building, debris falling everywhere. We lay on the ground waiting for more to go off, knowing that many of our comrades must have been killed. When we finally had the courage to move on, we looked around for Maria and Katja. They were lying away from us in a pool of blood. Both of them were dead. This was the day we had looked forward to for so very long. Oh God, dear Maria and sweet Katja. We were all in such shock we could not move. We all lay sobbing, paralyzed with grief and fear. Beautiful Katja almost made it. And brave Maria. Oh God, it was so terrible. How could you have let that happen?

Friedel finally made us move. Our knees were wobbling as we moved along sobbing hysterically. We had learned that being free does not necessarily mean being alive. Friedel was just as scared as we were, but she was not in shock. Those were not her special friends we left back there. She was wearing her gray uniform, and she had to be thinking she was a target. When she got us to the bomb shelter, she immediately left.

And here we are, waiting and waiting. We have prayed and cried over Katja and Maria. They almost made it. And we have almost made it, but not yet. We are thirsty and hungry, but afraid to go outside. It is cold and dark down here. I have the beautiful scarf Lilo gave me so long ago wrapped around my stubbly head. At least in here we will not be hit with bombs.

* * *

Several young civilian women came down to help us while the bombing continued. They stared at us as if we had the plague. I cannot really blame them. We must be a sight. Ragged and skinny and nearly bald. We told them where we were from, and how long we had gone without food and water. One of them left and in a short while came back with the shelter commander and a little bread and cheese. How good that cheese tasted. It had been a long time.

Every time the door to the shelter opened, we had the eerie feeling the SS would come and get us, and it all had been a dream too good to be true. But yesterday in the early afternoon, we suddenly heard a loud rattling. Everyone who heard it was terribly scared. What could it be?

The shelter commander opened the door a crack then slammed it and said, "The Americans! The Americans are coming down the road! Jeeps, tanks, trucks!" A panic broke out. Everyone was terrified except us. They were German civilians, but we had been prisoners, enemies of Hitler for all these years. We were electrified. Americans were our saviors!

I jumped up, nearly well. For weeks my legs had been paralyzed, and now for the first time, they functioned like new. I went to the shelter door and struggled to open it. Then I stumbled out into the street, dragging my legs. Elisabeth was screaming at me to stop. Others were yelling, "Come back. Do not be crazy! They will shoot you!"

I went to the road in front of the first Jeep. I pulled my scarf off my head and waved to the Americans. They all looked alike with their olive uniforms and helmets, their faces dirty and sweaty. They grinned and laughed. Now I could see their beautiful white teeth sparkle out of their dark faces. All of them had those nice-looking teeth. I did not think for a moment that they might shoot.

The Jeep stopped, and I went to a soldier in the back and gave him a kiss. His face tasted sweaty and salty. I said in my broken English, “Thank you soldiers for coming. We have waited so long for you. But now you are here!” I began to cry. The soldier looked over to the place where I had stumbled from, and where my comrades stood. They were stiff and had their hands over their mouths just waiting for the soldiers to shoot me.

“Those are my friends!” I exclaimed. “We are all from the same camp. We have been Hitler’s prisoners for many years. They are so happy too!” The tears were flooding my bony face and I was rubbing them away with my scarf, crying, “Thank you, thank you!”

The soldiers were still grinning, and I suddenly realized how I looked in my shabby prison garb, so skinny and crippled, crying hysterically and speaking words they did not understand. Embarrassed I pulled my scarf back over my head and wished I had not been so emotionally out of control. I should have stayed in the shelter. I have heard of their country—their big cars, beautiful white houses, and their beautiful women. What must these men think of me? I hoped they would not judge our beautiful women by me.

But they had quit grinning. The soldier I had kissed said something to the man in the front seat. This man turned to me and spoke—German? Yes, German. He actually spoke my language! He introduced himself as Pierre. He said he had been a French officer and was a German POW for three years, where he learned to speak German. He was from Paris, and he also spoke English. The Americans had taken him along as a translator.

Pierre introduced the soldier that I had talked to as Captain Lewis James Happy, and said he wanted to know what kind of clothes I was wearing. He had not understood me. He also wanted to know what happened to my hair.

I began jabbering as fast as I could to Pierre, and he translated. I told him again that we had been prisoners of Hitler for many years. I apologized for the way we looked, and told them we had been at Ravensbrück, and that I had suffered many illnesses and beatings, that so many thousands had been gassed and shot and skinned and sterilized, and we had watched it all for such a long time. Then I was suddenly out of breath and began again to sob.

The captain I had kissed was now pale. He took his jacket off and put it around my shoulders. Then he took the scarf off my head and stroked the stubble. He had big tears rolling down his face and over and over he said, “You poor woman, I am so sorry.” I was shocked. These men looked like they had been in a terrible war for a long time, and here was this soldier crying for me.

I asked Pierre if they knew about Ravensbrück, but they did not. He asked if I was hungry. I was already so embarrassed; I did not want to appear needy, so I told them I was not. He spoke to the others in English, and then told me to go back to the shelter. He said they would come later. They all waved goodbye and drove away. Pierre turned around once more and hollered, “We will bring you something to eat.” I guessed he had not believed I was not hungry.

Did I ever have friends now back at the shelter. A big crowd had gathered to watch the scene between the Americans and me. Civilians who had before stared at us cross-eyed because of the way we looked now said nice things, probably motivated by Pierre calling out that he would bring food. They were probably hungry too. Elizabeth and I sat with our arms around each other sobbing with joy. Were we really about to be freed? God had heard me. Thank you, God!

Later, Pierre and his driver came back as promised. Oh what wonders they brought—blankets, pillows, and boxes of food. We were struck silent with their generosity. The driver was a man named Max from Brooklyn, New York. His grandparents were from Russia. He looked happy, but I felt really stupid and sat down on the floor.

"What is the matter?" Elfriede asked me. Elisabeth put her hand around me and asked if I was not happy to see all this food.

Of course I was, but the truth was that I did not want them to think I had run out and kissed a soldier just to get some food. I told Elisabeth, "I did not ask for anything."

Pierre must have guessed how I felt. He said, "Oh well, I know you did not ask, but I just thought we would bring something by anyway. You don't mind, do you?"

My comrades gave me a look that said, "You better not mind." I smiled at Pierre and told him thank you. He said, "Do me one favor girls. Eat very slowly at first. In France, we saw people die from eating after they were rescued." We knew what he meant.

I smiled when Pierre took out a bar of chocolate. The other people in the shelter came over and you could hear the "Oohs and ahhs." Pierre told them he was sorry, but this food was just for the girls who had been in prison.

Then the commanding officer came in. Elfriede spoke with him since she spoke pretty good English. It was easy to guess what she was saying by knowing a few words and watching her face. She told him there were many comrades living at the camp, mostly foreign. They were living off of what the SS had not taken. They had stayed there because they did not have any place to go, and most of them did not speak German. Then she told him about our escape here, and about Katja and Maria. Her eyes filled with tears, and then we all wept a bit. The men patted us all on the shoulders and said they were sorry. "You are free," one of them said, "Free forever."

Chapter Twenty-Two

When Pierre visited again, we were so glad to hear that his commander had given orders to send all the prisoners to their countries by special train and not in boxcars. He reported that the Gypsies had killed all of the SS left at the camp. They had broken glass out of the windows and were cutting up their slave drivers with it. I could understand their anger since I could remember when I was ready to kill. But still, it was shocking to hear what the Gypsies had done. Pierre talked about the POW camp he had been in. He said the Nazi's were evil and could do evil things to one's head.

I told them about the good deeds of two SS officers, Jakob and Reinhardt and how they had saved little Andrea. He promised he would relate this to his officers. He understood that sometimes there are good thrown in with the bad. He was also going to put in a good word for an SS guard he had known.

April is almost over. There are hundreds of people at the shelter where we have been living. Today I went into the toilets to pray. It was not the perfect place, but I wanted privacy to get down on my hands and knees. I took a long while and thanked God for all the help he had given me in the past eight years. I know I would not be alive today if not for him.

The firing has ceased, and the Allies let us out for two hours today. Pierre said that very soon we could go out whenever we wanted to. Freedom, yes, precious freedom was now ours for the first time in a long time.

* * *

It is now two months later, and I am sitting in a comfortable apartment where I have been allowed to stay. I still suffer nightmares, but when I wake up and look around and see my clean, warm bed, I thank God that I was only dreaming. So often in camp I had wished I would wake up and realize it had only been a nightmare.

Each night I read the Good Book, which asks me to forgive, but it is not easy. How is it possible to wipe these terrible images from my mind? I wake sometimes in the night because I smell flesh burning. I cannot look at a smokestack. Sometimes I hear a truck on the street and jump up to look out the window. I cannot look at a child without seeing the children at Auschwitz pulling those wagons loaded with ashes. I cannot see a dog without remembering women being ripped to death. I cannot undress and look at my own body without feeling the pain of lashings and beatings. And when I look at my crippled feet and legs, I know how lucky I am to still have them.

I cannot comb my hair without thinking of blankets. I cannot brush my teeth without thinking of the piles of bodies ghoulishly robbed of the gold in their teeth. I cannot look at a tattoo without thinking of lampshades. I cannot see a pregnant mother without remembering the screams of the young girls being sterilized without anesthetic. I am tormented with memories of eight years of hell.

I have met several comrades who had been at Ravensbrück to the end. The chaos worsened after I left, which seems impossible. In the morning hours of April 24, the SS stormed into what was left of every Block and chased everyone out on the road and made them stand in formation. They told them they were to be evacuated. A long line of people began to march, followed by the SS with their whips, dogs, and pistols. Three thousand women too sick to move were left behind with a voluntary medical staff.

On April 30, the Soviets finally reached Ravensbrück. They found hundreds of women dead in their bunks. They caught up with the thousands who had marched out, following the trail of bodies shot through the head. The SS were still with them, still killing.

Some women returned to the camp to look for friends and relatives. They said it was a strange feeling walking through the gate. Instead of the Swastika, the Soviet flags hung there. It was a similar scenario at Auschwitz, except the camp was nearly destroyed before the Soviets arrived. I do not know what happened to Lilo and Yvette. I did learn that Gerda died at Uckermark; how sad, how sad. Every so often I see a woman who reminds me of Gerda, pretty with red hair, and I weep. Erika was there until they began marching everyone out. It was reported that she overcame SS guard Binz, took her gun, and then shot several SS guards, including Binz and her lover Braeuning. In the end Erika was killed, but she got her revenge. I know God will forgive her. So many would have died if not for Erika.

I never want to forget about being freed by the Americans at Magdeburg. After the foreign comrades were shipped home to their countries, the Germans were temporarily housed at the Kirstall Palace, the best hotel there. Elisabeth and I were put in an ex-SS villa next to the American headquarters. She frets about her mother, and I about my brothers and father, and about Jakob and Andrea. Would we be able to find them? Were they still alive? Where did we, two displaced women, go from here? It seemed the whole world was in turbulence, and all we had were bits and pieces of information.

One day Elisabeth and I were taking a walk, talking, trying to devise a plan for finding family. We came upon a bunch of high-ranking American officers standing in a huddle on the street. Captain Happy was standing near their Jeep with Pierre. They called us over. We hesitated, shy I suppose. But they came over and took our hands. Elisabeth was blushing, and I am sure I was too. We talked, and Pierre translated to Captain Happy.

Then, all at once high-ranking officers joined us. Now Elisabeth and I were really nervous, both of us stammering as we were introduced, with Pierre apparently telling how he knew us. One of the men was introduced to us as a general, General Eisenhower. I did not know how important he is, but I thought him very friendly for a general. He did not shake our hands but hugged us both. He was all smiles and talked to us like we were part of his staff, hardly giving Pierre time to translate. He was talking about being with another general named Patton. He said they had visited one of the camps, Gotha, I think, and it was the shock of their lives. Then he cursed and shook his head sadly, telling us that it had been the same day that President Roosevelt had died. Elisabeth and I had heard about his passing while in the shelter, but we did not know how long ago. We both told the general we were sorry, and he nodded and kicked the dirt with his boot.

Then the general began talking to the other officers about all the treasure they had found stolen by the SS. This led to conversation among all of us about all sorts of horrors, with Pierre translating as fast as he could. Finally General Eisenhower said, "Damn those Germans!" I was very embarrassed, and Pierre was embarrassed to have heard it. Elisabeth was looking at her feet and tugged on my hand.

The general saw the shame we felt. He looked at us and said he was sorry, adding, "But you know what I mean?"

I answered, "Yes, sir, we do, but there were good Germans, even SS guards like Jakob and Reinhardt. They saved many people, including me."

The general then asked where we lived, and when we told him, he said he was sorry again. I told him that we had no idea what had happened to our families, but somehow we were going to try and find them, and others.

Rubbing his chin, the general tipped his hat back, as though he were thinking. Everyone was looking at him curiously. Finally he looked at me, and then at Elisabeth, and then at Pierre, indicating he should translate his question. "If we could find out about our families, then where would we like to live?"

Elisabeth told him that we had both talked about settling in Bavaria, as it looked so much like our homeland, except for the Alps. She had barely finished talking, when the general clapped his hands as though he had made a decision. He began rattling something to Captain Happy, while Pierre and the others looked back and forth at him and at Elisabeth and I as though we were the subject. Finally he asked Pierre to translate.

There were people being hired to work with the Americans, the Germans, and the Red Cross, to help find missing people, families like ours who had been separated or killed, and most importantly to track the Nazis who had escaped. The general wanted to know if Elisabeth and I would be willing to live in Bavaria and work at this job. There we would have assistance in finding out about our families, and also do a great service in bringing the Nazis to trial for war crimes. Elisabeth and I surely looked stunned, as we were, but eagerly accepted.

That night as we gathered ourselves, our thoughts, and our emotions for the train ride the next day, we wondered if it was true. Would we really have assistance in finding those we loved, and could we actually be a part in bringing those devils torturing us to their just end? We could hardly believe it was going to happen.

But it did, and it all went so smoothly, so easily. Captain Happy met us in Bavaria where we were given nice apartments and salaries and everything to be made comfortable. Life at Ravensbrück quickly became a hideous memory.

Elisabeth found her mother and brought her to live with her. It was a great and joyous reunion. Her mother was ill, mostly from worrying about Elisabeth, but very soon improved. Sadly, I found out that the Russians took our property and ran my father off with just what he could put in a wheelbarrow. He died shortly after, shot for trying to steal one of his own horses. I learned a few days ago that my oldest brother was forced to fight in the German army and was badly wounded. He is in a hospital in Berlin. My youngest brother completely vanished, but there are a few clues that he may be in Prussia hiding out. When everything settles down and my health is good, I will go search for him. I pray each night for my father's soul, and the health of my brothers. One day we will all be united. Of this I am certain.

* * *

In the two months I have been working at my new job, chasing records and pictures and clues, I have felt good about the reunions I have brought about, angry about the deaths I have had to report to families, and vengeful each time an SS is found and thrown into prison. Several times I have testified to the activities I witnessed. But vengeance is not sweet. I suppose that is why God says it is not our job, but his. I justify what I do by telling myself that I am only assisting God. Elisabeth gave it up about a month ago. She said the grief that it kept alive in her was not worth it. She is now working as a nurse in a nearby hospital. She feels she is doing more good there. I think she is right. Elisabeth has a way of healing that is like her sculpting—which she has taken up again—a sort of hands-on nurturing.

Shortly after Elisabeth began working at the hospital, she stopped by for a little dinner and conversation, as is our frequent routine. We always try to talk about current things and not bring up the past. That evening she looked happier than usual, and so pretty, as she always is. She asked me to come to the hospital the next day. There was someone there who she wanted me to meet, someone important who could help with my work. I asked her who, but she would not tell me.

The next day I met Elisabeth in the hospital cafeteria. She took me straight away to a ward on the third floor where a lot of women wore bandages. Most of them were war casualties, many children. When we stopped in front of a bed, I heard my name whispered by the patient. I could barely see her under the bandages and blankets. Then she whispered again, only this time, she said, “Mama.” Oh my Lord, my heart stopped. There she was, my little Andrea! God had given me another miracle.

She had been injured in a horse-drawn carriage accident. Elisabeth said that she had several broken bones, but she would mend. I stayed all day to talk with her. We cried and laughed and cried some more. She told me about her last day at the pig farm. She had been taken by Reinhardt to a place where they met Jakob. Bullets were flying through the air, but the two men carried her to a truck, and then buried her under straw until they could take her to another place. They could see the Soviets coming, and the men left her there. She did not know what happened to them after that. She was rescued and taken to a shelter, and then later moved to another shelter by a carriage that turned over on a steep hill and rolled down a bank. Then she was brought here. Yesterday she saw Elisabeth and recognized her. “No one has eyes like that except her,” she said.

I went to see Andrea every day after that. In my police work, I continued to search diligently for records on Jakob and Reinhardt. With Andrea’s description of where they had taken her, and what happened, I was finally able to locate them. They were both in prison near Berlin.

Andrea is now nearly mended, although she walks with a limp almost exactly like mine. She lives with me and calls me “Mama.” I know she will move on one day and have a family of her own, but for now, I am her family, and she is mine.

Chapter Twenty-Three

Tomorrow Andrea and I leave for Hamburg, where many of those Nazis who served at Ravensbrück will be tried for war crimes. With tons of help from my American friend, Captain Happy, in two days Jakob and Reinhardt will be given a review for leniency before a war crimes tribunal. Andrea and I will testify on their behalf. I try not to worry. After everything we have been through, I believe God will be with us. Captain Happy has told me this review will be held in a courtroom, but will not be a big trial, like for the high-ranking SS.

Jakob and Reinhardt will be among about a dozen being reviewed on the same day for leniency before sentencing. He said many reviews like this had already taken place. Sometimes sentences were reduced because of circumstances—apparently there were other SS guards who had also been kind. But Jakob and Reinhardt had not just been kind. They had risked their own lives to save Andrea. We vowed not to leave that courtroom without everyone knowing of their bravery.

* * *

Captain Happy met our train in Hamburg accompanied by a very young soldier, his translator Ben, whom I had met several times in Munich. We were given a room in a hotel a block from the courthouse where the next day we would testify. The captain and Ben had dinner with us, preparing us for what would happen. We once again went over our statements. He said we needed to be prepared to defend our answers against the prosecution team, who would be drawing a hard line against the two men. Andrea was nervous, afraid she would not be understood and afraid they would not believe a fourteen-year-old. The captain kept reassuring her that it would all be fine.

Andrea surely does not look fourteen. She has changed very little since I first saw her that day in the clinic, the orphan from Russia. I suppose her growth was somewhat stunted by diet, lack of food for so long, and possibly trauma. She has a beautiful face—those lovely soft blue eyes and wispy blonde hair, but her body is still quite frail. I am confident she will mature faster than I would like. On the other hand, I have gained back nearly all of my weight through too much pie and dumplings. I also have some traits that would annoy others. I cannot throw food away, and I certainly cannot leave it on the table at a restaurant. I carry all the leftovers around with me, looking for someone in need.

In our hotel room, Andrea and I talked again about her days at the pig farm. She wonders what happened to the man she called Godfather. He protected her many times and kept giving her little piglets. By the time she left the farm, Champ number six had been born.

Through my work, I have tried to find Godfather, and also Mavis. Captain Happy had physically followed some of my leads, leaving notices wherever possible. We had hoped if they could be found, they could add weight to our testimony, but we had heard nothing from them.

After Andrea was asleep, I paced the hotel room. Little by little I had become increasingly eager, anxious really, about seeing Jakob again. I tried not to think of it in a personal way. More than anything I wanted to help him for his kindness and bravery. I remember the time when he put his hand over my mouth, surely keeping Brauening from beating me. And I remember what he had said, calling Brauening and the SS swine. And I remember so well that dark night when Gerda and I met him and he snatched up Andrea and disappeared, risking his life, which he would do again and again for her. But mostly I remembered how I felt when he touched me, when he kissed me those two times, and how his light brown eyes looked when he watched me. I was so ugly, so skinny, and yet, he made me feel beautiful. How would I feel when I saw him in court? Would I still love him? Would he still care about me? I did not know the answer, but my knees become weak thinking about it. What a strange circumstance it will be.

The next morning Andrea and I stared at our beautiful breakfast and wondered why we were not hungry. She looked pretty in a pink dress about the same color as her cheeks. I had changed clothes three times, trying to decide whether to wear a blue suit or a gray one. Andrea finally insisted I wear the blue, as she liked the peplum on the jacket. I liked it too, but it reminded me of the suit I wore to my trial those years ago, and then wore on that long cattle car ride with Elisabeth.

Captain Happy and Ben escorted us to the courthouse. The captain was bright and cheery, obviously helping us prepare for what might be a long and difficult day. The review would not take long, he said, but there was no way to know where Jakob and Reinhardt fit on the schedule. He said sentencing would not happen until the next day. The judge would take the testimonies into submission and sentence each prisoner privately without audience. Emotions would be running high for a public sentencing of twelve prisoners. Limping up the steps of the courthouse, Andrea and I leaned on either side of the captain. When we reached the top, we all put our hands together and gave an affirmative nod. This was a very big day.

The courtroom had already filled up with people, but the tables and chairs beyond the wood railing were still vacant. Captain Happy had two American soldiers sitting in front row seats, making sure they were held for us. As we sat down, they left the courtroom and in came several German soldiers and two men in suits, all carrying boxes. They went through the gate at the rail and sat down at the tables, taking folders out of the boxes and passing them around to each other. Then came more German, American, and Russian officers, also with boxes, taking another table. It seemed to take forever for them to get themselves prepared for what was about to transpire. I glanced around at the people, wondering if there was a chance of seeing a familiar face, but they all ran together in a blur. I wished I had eaten more breakfast. Andrea fidgeted with her gloved hands until I took one of them and held it. Then she fidgeted with her feet.

Then, without any warning, there they were—twelve men in prison uniforms, all handcuffed, led into the courtroom through a side door by American soldiers. In a second my eyes had found Jakob, and he was looking right at me. A slight smile passed over his face when he saw that I was holding a bright yellow dandelion picked fresh in the grass by our hotel. In that instant, when he smiled, I knew I would always love my Jakob.

But oh, how desperately terrible he looked. So thin—gaunt really. His dirty prison garb, his hair too long, his beautiful hands locked together in iron cuffs. I wanted to run to him and comfort him. Andrea was staring at me, probably because I had become stiff and tense, squeezing her hand too hard, trying to stay in my chair. Reinhardt did not look any better. These poor dear men who had been so kind and had saved Andrea, now cuffed and humbled. I had lots to say and was ready.

The morning dragged on. One after another the prisoners were called to the front, sworn to tell the truth, and then interrogated by six different men, two German officers, one Russian, one American, and two civilians from the Red Cross. All of them had witnesses to testify of their good deeds, but sometimes there were also witnesses who swore they had been tyrants. It was difficult to ascertain the truth. The facts all swirled around like the horror of the camps. There were frequent gasps from the good Germans in the court who had stayed home during the war, and there were tears from family. I watched the faces of the witnesses, listened to their words, and promised I would do much better for Jakob and Reinhardt. Andrea, too, seemed to be preparing to put herself up there, leaning forward in her seat to hear all those German words she still did not know.

I was sweating at the thought of talking to the court, but then my eye caught sight of one prisoner who was staring at me. I looked away several times, but he kept staring, then looked away himself. He had on a bright black Nazi uniform with several medals and was holding his cap as his fingers twirled. When he looked back, I looked into his eyes and then I knew who it was—Otto, my dearly beloved Otto from the underground days. I sighed out loud and Andrea grabbed my hand, but I kept staring at Otto. Many thoughts went through my mind, but suddenly I realized something I had wondered about since my arrest—who had turned me in? Yes, I knew, it must have been Otto. How could he do that to one he said he loved?

When the name Otto Reising was called, I was in shock. He nodded to me and then was led up to the bench. Time was quick and despite words of favor from several people, I heard the word "death" mentioned and then he was led away. I cried a tear but my heart sank to know Otto had betrayed me.

The rest of the morning seemed like it took fifty hours. It was almost noon when Jakob Gottfried's name was called. He stood and walked to the place where those before him had stood and turned around to face the courtroom full of people. He looked straight at me, and then Andrea, and back at me, not hearing the instructions to state his full name and rank in the SS. He seemed to be in a fog of memory, and I knew how he felt. All those stories before him, all those hard questions he knew he would be asked, and death in the shape of a gavel waiting for him. My poor Jakob, my hero, my love.

He got through the questions, his voice weak and tired. He swore he had always hated the SS. He had a choice to serve with the SS or become a prisoner himself, and he thought he could do more good for those in the camps if he wore the uniform. He also said he feared for his family if he did not serve since his mother had been threatened with death. He was plummeted with hideous questions, but he just kept answering, "No."

Then the judge asked if there were any witnesses present who wished to testify in Jakob Gottfried's defense. Andrea and I both stood up, and I was called first. When I turned around to look at that courtroom full of people, something came alive in me, something I did not expect. I suddenly could see all their faces so clearly. It was easy to see that some were family of the prisoners, some were families of victims seeking revenge, some were witnesses waiting to testify, and it was clear which were which. It gave me an advantage. I looked only at the faces that had been in the camps, who knew the horror, and who would believe what I said. I was calm, determined, and ready for the questions, ready with God leading the way.

At first it was a lot of yes and no answers, and about the work I was doing now, until the Red Cross official started asking me for details of how, when, and where I had been involved with Mr. Jakob. I was very clear, specific, and emphatic. I told them every wonderful thing Jakob had done and how he hated the Nazi swine, and most importantly how he had risked his life to save Andrea, how he had showed so much courage in the face of evil. I also brought Reinhardt into the picture several times. When they stopped asking, I kept talking, loud and clear. I did not, of course, mention any personal feelings, and I tried hard not to look at Jakob, for fear I would lose my momentum. I was up there a very long time. When I was excused, I felt confident that I had never been stronger in my life. As I stepped down and walked past him, I caught his eyes a moment. They were filled with tears.

Then it was Andrea's turn. She was very nervous and so very precious, capturing the heart of everyone in the courtroom, no matter whose side they were on. In her sweet accent she told her whole story and a translator helped clarify. It began with her cattle car ride to Ravensbrück, how she had met me, the hole she had to stay in to keep from being sent to the gas chambers, and how hungry she always was. And then she talked about how Jakob and Reinhardt had taken her to the pig farm and kept her safe and brought her food, and finally how it all came to an end with bullets flying and her saviors making sure she was in the hands of the Russians. Every time she mentioned the two men, her eyes filled with tears, and she looked at them and smiled lovingly. Several times I noticed the judge blowing his nose, and others throughout the court had handkerchiefs to their faces. Mine was already wet, no use to keep dabbing my eyes.

Finally Andrea was excused, and came back to sit with me, grabbing my hand. I whispered how wonderful she had been, and she whispered, "Could they understand me?" I assured her that she had been very easy to understand, which would have been true if she had not said a word.

While we were whispering, the judge asked again if there were any more witnesses for this prisoner. Surprisingly he motioned for someone to come down. I turned around to see who it was, and there was Captain Happy escorting Mavis down the aisle and to the railed gate. Instinctively, I jumped up, so excited to see her, and then sat down quickly, remembering my place.

I had only thought that Andrea and I did a great job. Mavis, who now used a crutch, was incredible up there, a strong personality and a force for the prosecutors to reckon with. She had grown to know Jakob and Reinhardt very well, and had been a participant in their schemes of rescue. She did not have just Andrea's story to tell, there were many others. She told of a pregnant woman Jakob had taken out of camp in the night and hid until her husband, who had been contacted by Mavis, came to rescue her. And there were a number of times when he was told to march people into the woods and shoot them, and instead, he marched them to the pig farm and put them in hay wagons leaving for the hay fields. Reinhardt always rode part way with the wagons before returning. And Mavis told of the time Jakob had spent in the bunker for physically stopping an SS guard from shooting several children. This was the first I knew of why Jakob had been sent to that bunker.

I stared at Mavis and then Jakob and Reinhardt, tears streaming down my face. So much I had never known. It was clear to me that God, Christ the Savior, and the Holy Spirit had sent Jakob and Reinhardt as angels in disguise as SS guards to Ravensbrück. Mavis very clearly said almost those same words to the court, but she was not finished. Her last story was how Jakob had rescued her. During an argument with an SS guard accusing her of stealing, he had taken Mavis' side. The SS guard became so angry, he drew his gun, and pushed it into Mavis' face. But Jakob grabbed the arm of the guard, pushing it down, so that when it fired it hit Mavis in the foot. Jakob then knocked the guard unconscious, dragged Mavis into one of the pig stalls. He then went to her Block-eldest for help.

When Mavis was finally through with her testimony and stepped down, limping her way back to the gate, she stopped there, then very deliberately looked at Jakob and then Reinhardt, smiled, nodded her head, and said "Thank you!" I almost passed out, I was so touched by her love.

Then it was Reinhardt's turn, and we did it all again, only this time it went much faster, and there was very little argument from the prosecution. When Mavis had finished on behalf of Reinhardt, we left the courtroom. But not until I could give Jakob the thumbs up like he used to do to tell me my little angel was okay.

In the hall, Mavis picked Andrea up and squeezed her tight, whirling her around in a circle. Captain Happy and Ben came out and shook all of our hands. He was talking so fast to Mavis that Ben could barely keep up. And Mavis, too, was jabbering away, so excited that she had gotten there on time. One of the many notices the captain and I had sent out finally found her two days ago in Hamburg.

We all had lunch together and talked about the chances for Jakob and Reinhardt. Captain Happy said that in some of the previous leniency trials sentences had been reduced to as little as two to three years. He said that he thought much of it was determined by how strongly the judge felt about the SS. This judge had a reputation of being very anti-Hitler and the SS and usually passed out very stiff sentences. Oh God, I thought, this was going to be a very long twenty-four hours with a whole lot of praying.

That night Andrea and I got down on our knees and prayed with all our might, together and out loud. We asked over and over for as much leniency as possible for our two heroes. They were good men, God's men, and they should be rewarded, not punished.

The next day was to be a waiting game, but Captain Happy and Ben came while we were still having breakfast. Captain Happy left but Ben told us all about what had happened to the Americans while fighting their way to Berlin and our rescue, and how thousands had died. A couple of times his eyes filled with tears. What a sacrifice his country had made for Europe, I thought. What brave people.

Andrea kept him busy with questions about America and Americans, a country she had not heard about until she was at Ravensbrück. After lunch, she asked me privately if she would learn more about this country when she started school. I told her that we probably all were going to learn a lot about America.

At about two, we returned to the hotel. It had been a wonderful outing, tempered with the anxiety of Jakob's and Reinhardt's sentencing. Ben assured us that he and Captain Happy would return with the news as soon as it was available. We went to our room to wait.

It was four when the phone in our room rang. The hotel operator said that we had guests waiting for us downstairs. If we could have run, we would have. There they were, Captain Happy and Ben, sitting in big chairs smiling. It just had to be good news.

Andrea and I were both asking at once. "How many years, how long, what happened?"

Captain Happy told us that we would have to sit down to hear this. My heart was beating in my ears. Maybe it was not such good news. But it was, oh how it was! It was just a little complicated. It was the first time Captain Happy had heard of SS guards getting off with two years of public service. I was not sure what this meant, but it sounded wonderful, and Andrea and I were on our feet again clapping our hands.

Again Captain Happy asked us to sit down in order to hear the rest of the sentence. Oh dear, I thought. What else? The captain went on patiently. "The judge sentenced both Reinhardt and Jakob to two years of parole doing public service approved by the court," he said. Captain Happy was now looking very pleased with himself. He had spoken to the judge after the sentencing, asking if he could use the services of both men to assist with the location of missing persons and escaped SS—my job! "The judge said yes," Captain Happy said.

Again Andrea and I were on our feet asking, "Are they here? Where are they? When?"

The Captain gave up on making us sit. He said that all of the paperwork would take a few days. He would bring them both to Munich as soon as possible, as he too was in a hurry for their services. He had been given an opportunity to speak to both men after the sentencing, and he believed they were going to be a big help finding some of the principal SS. They knew them, and knew about their families, with ideas about where they might be hiding.

Then Andrea and I did sit. In fact we plopped down together in one of the big chairs and held onto each other and cried for joy. Captain Happy got up to leave and then remembered he had a note for me from Jakob. I put it in the pocket of my jacket. I would not have to read it in the toilet, but I did want to read it alone.

I did read the note in the bathroom, just in case I might cry too much in front of Andrea. But then I had to read it to her, because it really was to both of us. He wrote

> How beautiful my two girls are, and how grateful Reinhardt and I are to have you both. We love you and appreciate your friendship and loyalty. Vera, you are the love of my life, a life I want to spend with only you if you will have me. Your Jakob Gottfried.

* * *

It is two weeks later, and they will all be here any minute. My legs are bothering me so Andrea went to the train station to meet the captain, Jakob and Reinhardt. I am so eager to feel Jakob's arms around me. I have flesh on my bones now, and the strength to hug him tight. And I have a roast and potatoes and carrots and dumplings in the oven, and I made a beautiful cake, a real one, and slices of bread cut like a heart and frosted with jam and margarine.

In the center of the table is a small porcelain vase painted with bright-colored flowers just like Jakob's mother used to make. I found it in a secondhand store and filled with yellow dandelions. We will all dine together like real people, like real family, but not before we give thanks to God for sparing us, and for this perfectly wonderful day. Then I will find a tune to play and dance with my Jakob as the dandelions shine in the moonlight and I hold him so tight and tell him I love him.

Acknowledgements

Publishing this remarkable story would not be possible without the love and cooperation of Nancy Evans, the daughter of Cecelia Rexin, upon whose diary this work of fiction is based. To be certain, more than 95 percent of the story is true since Cecelia was truly an angel of mercy, a German Christian woman wrongly "convicted" by the Nazis and sentenced to one of the worst hell-holes in history—Ravensbrück Concentration Camp, the construction of which happened in 1938, 80 years ago.

For several years, Cecelia never gave up hope and was instrumental in saving the lives of many, many people who would have died if not for her courage in the face of evil. Bless her for keeping a diary so that this story may be told.

Thanks to the wonderful people at Crosslink Publishing for believing in this book. Especially helpful have been Rick Bates and Ashley Casteel.

Thanks also go to my loving wife Wen-ying Lu, who is always so supportive of my writing adventures. Like Cecelia, she has a heart of gold, and I love Lu dearly.

Of course, none of my books, especially this one, would be possible if not for the Holy Spirit shining down on me each day. I am truly the most blessed man in the world and so proud to be able to share with the world how hate turned to love during the horrors of the Holocaust.

Mark Shaw

About the Author

A graduate of San Francisco Theological Seminary with a Masters Degree in Theological Studies, Mark Shaw, a former legal correspondent for *ABC*, *CNN*, and *USA Today*, is the author of 20+ books including *The Reporter Who Knew Too Much*, *The Poison Patriarch*, *Miscarriage of Justice*, *Beneath the Mask of Holiness*, *Stations Along the Way*, and *Road to the Miracle*. He has penned articles for the *New York Daily News*, *USA Today*, *Huffington Post* and the *Aspen Daily News*, which he cofounded. More about Mr. Shaw, a member of the American Christian Fiction Writers Association, may be learned at www.markshawbooks.com, and Wikipedia (Mark William Shaw).